ISAAC
NEWTON'S
21ST-CENTURY
ENTANGLEMENT

T0159845

NOEL HODSON

Lightning
Books ⚡

Published in 2020
by Lightning Books Ltd
Imprint of EyeStorm Media
312 Uxbridge Road
Rickmansworth
Hertfordshire
WD3 8YL

www.lightning-books.com

Copyright © Noel Hodson 2020
Cover by Ifan Bates

British Library Cataloguing in Publication Data
A catalogue record for this book is available from the British Library.

Printed by CPI Group (UK) Ltd, Croydon CR0 4YY

ISBN: 9781785631825

For Ian, Sarah, Hugh, Rebecca, Art, Maya and Ben
– who will all go far

1

THE HUNGRY BUMPKIN

THE MAN'S GAZE – cold, intelligent and utterly concentrated, despite his feverish and fearful state – scanned the boy's flesh for blemishes, for any lethal rashes or buboes, which must at all costs be avoided. He was hungry, and he was deeply chilled, but caution bade him stay concealed, stay hidden, and observe carefully. He needed to know that the boy was alone – and unmarked.

The boy, who was alone, would not have come to the river bank on this misty Fenland morning but for an error of timing beyond his control. Nor, synchronistically, would the man be lurking in the dense blackberry patch just ten feet from the boy if he too had not become entangled in an anachronistic accident. He desired to approach the boy but too many conflicting signals paralysed his will. The boy was strange; his hair cut short like a Roundhead. He wore strange clothes – clothes which were perfectly and exquisitely stitched and seamed, in rich and rare colours and textures; clothes which announced great wealth but of a cut and style the man had never before encountered. And there were unsettling rumbling and whining sounds which percolated through the mist that the man could not decipher. Were other villagers working nearby? Did the boy have friends close at hand?

Also, strangest of all, the trees, the endless forests of trees, which, yesterday, had stretched to the horizon, had all but disappeared.

The boy sat under a gnarled willow that showed the first signs of spring. He was watching the River Withan, with his back to a bramble-covered ruin. The man's fierce focus on his face, neck and hands – on all his exposed skin – permeated his consciousness and made his hair prickle. He paused from delving into his bag and listened hard. He heard nothing out of the ordinary, shrugged and shifted his attention back to the food in his bag. He pulled out a box and, from the box, a fat package wrapped in kitchen foil. As the boy unwrapped his peanut-butter sandwiches, the man sniffed the damp air. He could smell food, reminding him he was ravenous, and he could not smell death, reassuring him that it was safe. Though was 'safe' a term he could apply to his present confusion?

His intellect whirled faster and faster in an attempt to process and rationalise the feedback from his senses but could not find sufficiently familiar sensations to anchor the kaleidoscopic information. He was dizzy and disoriented but a sudden flash of light glinting off the kitchen foil, cast aside a few feet away, captured his mind and drove out all other considerations.

He could see beyond doubt that it was silver-foil. But it was of such quality, consistency and fineness, beaten and finished with such skill by some unimaginable silversmith that the sheet varied not a jot in thinness across its whole area. It shone like Quicksilver and, despite its extreme fineness, it had not broken when the boy had wrinkled and creased it carelessly. It must be worth a King's ransom, and yet not only had the boy crumpled the fabulous sheet in his hand, but he had unconcernedly tossed it aside like so much flotsam. Was the child deranged?

But as soon as these thoughts invaded his mind the boy started to eat – and the man could see and smell bread and fruit – fresh fruit, but how could that be, in early springtime? – which occluded all further thought. He had to risk the boy and he had to eat.

Sweeping off his wide-brimmed black hat to avoid damage from the thorns, the man, glad of his thick greatcoat, forced his way along the child-sized tunnel through the brambles and undergrowth to emerge immediately behind the boy – who swivelled his head, eyes wide with surprise.

"Ullo,' said the boy, twitching his shoulders defensively. '...I'm allowed here – it's common land you know.'

The man had but one thought in his mind. He spoke with a broad local accent, 'I'm hungry. I need food,' and his eyes burned into the sandwich the boy was raising to his mouth.

The boy considered this for a moment in silence. He was ten years old and understood the imperatives of sudden hunger. 'D'ya want a sandwich?' he asked, with careless generosity.

The man stepped forward and reached out a hand. Then he withdrew very slightly and again scanned the boy's flesh from close quarters for the deadly signs of plague. But he could see none. The boy's skin looked firm and healthy. He took the proffered sandwich and smelt it curiously.

'Is this...food?' he asked.

'It's peanut butter,' explained the boy. 'I've only got that – or maybe...' he offered with careful reserve, '...a ChocoRoll if you'd like...' Then, with sudden hope and inspiration: 'Or you could have an apple or the orange... They're dead nice – really nice. I'll bet you'd like one.'

The man stood in silence, a peanut-butter sandwich in one hand and his hat in the other. He was touched by the boy's immediate willingness to share his vittels and he felt it incumbent upon him to observe the niceties. He also had a thousand questions which needed immediate answers.

'My name...' he bowed slightly, '...is Isaac. And I live on the farm just over yonder hill, at Woolsthorpe,' he said, pointing westward. His local brogue was unusually strong.

The boy had reckoned him for a farmer on first sight.

'And I am indebted to you, Master ...? For these shared commons.'

'Master, er, Archie,' said Archie, correctly assuming he was being thanked but not grasping all the words. 'Archie Wilkins.'

Isaac was munching the wodge of thick-sliced long-life bread and its gooey filling, both of which had adhered to the top of his palate in an alarming manner and silenced him as he wrestled with the sticky concoction. The boy, long-experienced at consuming the mixture, waited patiently for Isaac to master the technique. He shifted slightly to one side of the willow tree, implicitly inviting the man to sit beside him. Isaac sat down, wholly absorbed in chewing and redistributing the alleged food with his tongue. The river flowed quietly northwards, and the mists swirled, thinning a little as the morning wore on.

'I missed the bus for the school trip,' said Archie, explaining how he came to be here and not at school.

Isaac at last cleared his palate and was examining the sandwich narrowly, preparing for a second bite. 'The...bus?' he asked.

'Yeah! You know; the bus.'

But Isaac shook his head.

'The chara'...' enunciated Archie, slowly and clearly, 'for the class outing.'

Isaac gave no sign of recognition.

Archie was a determined communicator. 'Er, well, you know, the coach. I missed the coach.'

Isaac was obviously a man who valued reflection and silences. He gulped some more bread while making signs that he would reply when possible. 'Ah! Yes! A coach. You were to take the coach with your schoolfriends. To where?' he asked politely.

'Day out,' answered Archie promptly. 'To Skegness – you know, the seaside. School trip to the seaside. They've got a seal sanctuary at Skegness.'

Isaac pondered this intelligence for some time. 'By coach? To Skegness? It's a long way to Skegness,' he observed.

"Bout an hour an' a half,' volunteered Archie. 'Not really very far.'

Isaac glanced critically at the boy. At twenty-three years old and at the height of his mathematical powers, he was unforgiving of loose talk and sloppy thinking. But the boy still had food to share, Isaac was hungry and he was off-balance. Something was very, very wrong. He decided to gather more intelligence.

'Where are you at school?' he asked, giving his intellect time to compute.

'Grantham Primary,' muttered Archie.

'I too attended school in Grantham. How many of you would take the coach to Skegness this morning?'

'…I dunno really. 'Bout forty I think.'

'Forty boys?' said Isaac sharply. He really couldn't abide such a degree of error. His irritation broke through. 'On how many coaches, young man?'

'No. No. Not forty boys.'

'Aha!' thought Isaac, pleased to be pinning down the facts of the matter.

'Girls an' boys. Most of Class Four and Class Five are goin',' said Archie. 'On one bus – coach, that is,' he added, confounding his companion.

Isaac looked hard at the boy, who looked straight back at him. There was a certainty in his face which gave Isaac a strange disembodied feeling. He shivered violently.

'Forty children? On one Coach? To Skegness? In one day? Fifty miles or more?'

Archie nodded at each question. Isaac was nonplussed. He gathered his thoughts again. He needed more information.

'Surely you mean a wagon, not a coach. A long wagon. How many horses would draw such a load?' He came at the matter tangentially, seeking to fault the boy.

It was Archie's turn for a silence. He looked at the man's face for signals. 'You're joking – ain't cha?' But he knew that this was a face and a mind that did not easily lend itself to making jokes.

Isaac swallowed another mouthful of strangely clinging wadded bread and pursued his search for facts. 'Don't you know how many horses? And where would they stop for hostelry and new horses along the way?'

'Horses?' echoed Archie.

'Yes. How many?' demanded Isaac pointedly, feeling he was getting the upper hand at last in this garbled exchange.

Archie hunkered down into the defensive posture he adopted when tackling unanswerable enquiries from unstoppable adults. He expertly and effortlessly tackled a mouthful of bread, e-numbers, plastic and crunchy peanut butter – with a nonchalant ease which drew Isaac's tacit admiration – and he thought hard.

He looked sideways and up at Isaac's insistent, expectant face. A thought occurred to him.

'Are you Care-in-the-Community?'

'I beg your pardon. I am not familiar with the phrase.'

Archie was not entirely happy at introducing the issue – but he pressed on.

'Care-in-the-Community. You know. When they shut the loony-bins and put everyone out on the street. Are you one of them?'

To be fair to Archie, Isaac, displaying long hair and a lugubrious, anxious expression on his long puritanical face, heavily overdressed in layer upon layer of clothes, looked just like the schizophrenics who wandered into Grantham Post Office carrying several plastic bags full of treasured possessions to queue for their weekly allowance. He had also, Archie assumed, been camping out in the crumbled old stable or whatever it was, which Archie and his friends used as den, and whose faint stone outline was now buried beneath fifteen-foot-high blackberry bushes. And he dressed so oddly, with a massively heavy overcoat, high leather boots and a wide-brimmed black hat. He certainly wasn't normal, thought Archie. Care-in-the-Community fitted the bill.

Isaac deciphered the child's prattle. 'Loony,' he understood to be a reference to people whose mental state was affected by the Moon – lunar vapours and forces unhinging their grasp on reality. 'Community,' and 'Care,' he had no difficulty with; and he managed to extract Archie's meaning. He was careful not to react. One of them was clearly off-beam – and, after his recent experience, he wasn't at all sure that it was the boy.

He still needed more intelligence.

'Master Archie,' he tried another tack. 'Where did you get that silver-foil?' and he reached behind Archie to collect the glittering prize.

'From me Mum,' Archie said. 'We're a single-parent family, me and me Mum.'

'Your father has been taken by the plague?'

'No! Worse than that. I think he's working in Manchester. But he's never lived with us.'

Isaac decided it was ill-mannered to pursue further intelligence of the father. He ran his fingers over the foil, smoothing out the creases.

'Your mother gave this to you?' he asked incredulously. Close to, it looked more than ever like Mercury. He had never seen silver so thin or so evenly polished. His mind raced with the possibilities for his Optiks.

'Well, she wrapped me sandwiches in it.'

'And you would throw it away?'

'I'm not a litter lout,' Archie protested. 'I'd have put it in me bag and taken it home.'

'Oh! So, you would have retrieved it? You appreciate its value?'

Archie couldn't find a response to the assumption Isaac was making; he again ran the phrase 'Care-in-the-Community,' through his mind then thought he ought to say something.

'We've lots of it at home – in the kitchen. We use it all the time.'

'To preserve food and other precious things?'

'Er, yeah. Yeah. I suppose so.' Archie lapsed into silence.

The silence lasted a few minutes. Archie could just hear the distant roar of the A1 motorway, about a mile distant, which had found its way through the thinning mist. The sky was growing brighter.

Isaac was examining the extraordinary craftsmanship in Archie's clothes and backpack and, with the silver, or could it be Quicksilver, as added evidence, he put two and two together. 'You must come from a truly princely family. Of fabulous wealth.'

'Not really,' said Archie, wondering how to extricate himself from the ever-deepening misunderstandings.

Nature came to his rescue. The mist cleared, drawn upwards by the sun, and the air grew warmer. They could now see the old bridge, a hundred yards or so upstream, and a stretch of the winding country road leading to it. Isaac narrowed his eyes, and was peering hard at the smooth surface of the road when the Grantham bus, an elderly red single-decker, came trundling into view on its way to the bridge. Isaac's eyes were, at that moment, like the eyes of a madman. 'Loony,' would have been appropriate. Archie saw him staring at the bus.

'See – that's a bus. A coach,' he said dismissively, as if no one could possibly be interested. 'See, it's got 'bout forty seats. Takes two classes easily.' He felt vindicated by this solid, undeniable evidence.

The bus ambled up the road, rumbling and snorting with effort. It slowed for a tight corner and then rose up to surmount the bridge, its top far higher than the bridge wall. They could clearly see the driver at the wheel and a handful of blank-faced passengers, staring ahead, urging it on to Grantham market.

Isaac's mouth fell open. He gripped his head tightly with both hands. His breathing became laboured.

'Oh God, help me,' he cried loudly. 'God help me!'

2

PARTICULAR PANIC

Isaac sat by the river, rocking and holding his head in confusion bordering on despair, closely observed by a very alarmed Archie.

The day before, in Isaac's old, stone, college laboratory at Trinity College – now linked via a very high-tech, precisely level, 5.05-kilometre-long cyclotron pipeline to the Cavendish Laboratory, next to The Isaac Newton Institute for Mathematical Sciences in Cambridge, eighty miles south-south-east of where Archie and Isaac met – two equally alarmed particle physicists were rapidly punching the keys of a very sophisticated computer. It translated signals bounced from atoms held in the focus of an extraordinary microscope into visual images and displayed them on a screen, for all the world as if they were real.

It wasn't the image that alarmed them; to their practised eyes it looked perfectly normal. They were bombarding the observed atoms – atoms of Caesium cooled to near absolute-zero – with very high-energy hydrogen nuclei fed in to the target zone from a cyclotron or atom-smasher. What evoked a sheen of pale-faced, controlled panic in both men was an uncountable swarm of the electrons 'liberated', or perhaps created, by the impacts. According to the instruments and automated mathematics, these electrons were either travelling backwards through time or – equally weird and potentially explosive – coming from the past in large numbers and with gigavolts of energy. If the computers were to be believed, the physicists were wrestling with a temporal anomaly, which in turn was playing around with split-second energy bursts sufficient to power the whole of London.

They knew that in the Standard Model, in Quantum Electromagnetic Dynamics and as illustrated in Feynman diagrams, time reversal at the level of the mathematics of quantum physics was (theoretically) permitted without distorting or disturbing the essential logic of the (theoretical) algorithms. With a cheery 'Hey-Nonny-Nonny-Hey!' particles could travel backwards or forwards through time without (theoretically) having the least effect on the integrity of the experiment in the present. That was the theory.

But when the theory suddenly manifested streams of real rogue electrons – torrents of rogue electrons – racing through time, in the wrong direction, or pouring in from the past in a seemingly unstoppable stream, the physicists had to consider two things. First, that they may be the first experimenters on Earth to inarguably witness time-reversal – which would mean at least one Nobel Prize and possibly a whole slew of awards, celebrity and wealth. Second, that they, their laboratory and most of Cambridge might be blown – or sucked – to smithereens in a quantum instant; perhaps into a single minuscule unit of Planck-Time, with the whole shebang collapsing into a pinhead-sized black hole. The black hole would exist inside an inescapable event horizon, in which – they had no evidence to counter the theory – there would be little or nothing to enjoy spending the prize money on, even if they could take it with them.

As both were in their early thirties, in the prime of life, their sense of urgency was fired by the need to avoid this premature, implosive termination of their current existences. Along with those of tens of thousands of bright, hopeful, eager students, dozens of dedicated, brilliant tutors and a handful of patient domestic bursars. They bashed away at the computer terminal, desperately trying to shut down the power and disengage the cyclotron from the caesium target.

The two men, intent on saving their reputations, did not immediately call for assistance. They were supposed to know what they were doing. They were the experts whom lesser mortals called upon when their experiments went off track. Outside, the light faded from the sky. They sent a lowly lab technician for take-away food and hunkered down for a long battle. As the night wore on, the wave – or particle – front grew ever stronger, pouring itself into the supposedly switched-off cyclotron and bombarding the caesium target in its near-absolute-zero cloud chamber. Both machines were immovable. They dared not try to de-construct any part of the system while it played incoherently and inconceivably with energies which could fry the whole of Cambridgeshire. The men worked through the night. Dawn broke and the lab technician was deployed to raid other's fridges and food stores. Outside, the world awoke, birds sang and shift workers yawned, all blissfully unconscious of the threat of imminent oblivion.

'It's as if…,' conjectured a distinctly haggard-looking Professor Robert Hooke, Head of Research into Inertial and Field Energies, '…the effing machine has been programmed by Microsoft. I've unplugged the cyclotron, but it simply will not shut down.'

'We have got to disengage the damn thing,' hissed his white-coated, hollow-eyed companion. 'Do you think it could blow?'

Having fought determinedly, and relatively confidently – as world-class physicists and the top men in their field – through the darkest hours of the night, and having tried everything they knew to stop the experiment, they now panicked.

In the few moments since they had started to panic they had had no time to reflect on what might have been happening exactly three hundred and fifty-two years earlier (adjusting for leap years), in the exact spot where the magnificently complex electron-tunnelling-microscope and the self-energising cyclotron were now sucking in power. But on that spot in that minute, in Cambridge in 1665, before the second wave of bubonic plague returned to halve the population of London and most other urban centres over again, a young Isaac Newton had stood, with his complicated equipment dedicated to experiments on alchemy, light and gravity.

And in the course of these prismatic, chemical and mathematical adventures, he had, all unknowing, split paired photons and electrons and other even more obscure particles, which were then ever after entangled – whatever Einstein might have thought about action at a distance – and in relationship with each other, eternally and infinitely. And they remained related, according to quantum electromagnetic dynamics, regardless of the direction of the arrow of time. Furthermore, such particle entanglement had occurred with a direct impact on the atoms in the walls of this laboratory and in Isaac's body.

In the summer of the following year, to avoid the bubonic plague, he had gone back home to Woolsthorpe, near Grantham, Lincolnshire, to sit out the pestilence and the Fire of London before returning, complete with entangled particles, to Cambridge University. While at Woolsthorpe, Isaac had also, with more than a modicum of deep thought, watched an apple drop from a tree.

These very same entangled particles, oblivious of which geographic frame they were occupying, and transcending all limitations of time and space, were now, in their billions and trillions, streaming from Isaac to Cambridge (or vice-versa, depending on one's relative temporal frame of reference). And as they streamed they were pouring energy into the tiny focal field at the end of the electron-tunnelling-microscope where the super-cooled caesium atoms were under bombardment from the cyclotron.

The two particle physicists continued – with good reason – to panic, as bells, klaxons and red warning lights bellowed and flashed from every console.

Paralysed on the banks of the River Withan, Isaac felt a great flux of energy swirl around him as he peered in terror through his fingers. He was no longer terrified of the lumbering red bus, which he had quickly discerned as a horseless carriage – a concept proposed by Leonardo da Vinci hundreds of years earlier. But, on the evidence of the bus, the boy, his clothes and the magical silver-foil, he was terrified of the implications for Time and Space, and of his place, or displacement, in the Universe. His exchanges with the lad had, so far, occupied precisely twenty-two minutes and eight seconds.

Yesterday, before he had fainted, he was safely ensconced in his well-appointed study by the river, the ruins of which were now buried under the mountain of brambles behind him. In under twenty-four hours, the stone building had disintegrated, the forest had vanished, and he was engaged in conversation with an alien child.

As the Grantham bus receded into the distance and as Isaac perceived no threat to life or limb, his fear was edged out by curiosity. He recognised the river; he had often fished at this spot himself, but everything else – the fields, the trees, the road – had changed. He relaxed just a little, lifted his head and turned to Archie.

'What Time is this?' he asked.

Archie glanced at a coin-sized device strapped to his wrist. 'It's ten twenty-seven,' he announced.

Isaac's reputation as one of the greatest mathematicians and scientists ever was well-founded. He instantly realised what Archie was saying.

'You mean, er, that it is after ten o'clock in the morning?'

Archie nodded.

'And that your timepiece tells you it is precisely twenty-seven minutes…' – Archie nodded his agreement about the 'minutes' – '…minutes, then…after ten of the clock?'

'Yeah,' said Archie, flourishing his wrist and a black digital watch in Isaac's face. It's a Casio me mum bought at the market. And it's waterproof down to thirty metres,' he added proudly.

'Casio', 'metres', such a priceless device on a child's wrist all overwhelmed Isaac. He sat in silence, slowly shaking his head. Eventually his mind calmed a little.

'I meant to ask not what time of day it is; but what year is this?'

Archie gave the man another of his 'Care-in-the-community' looks, but he got the point and answered without side.

'It's two thousand and eighteen,' he said with assurance, then glancing again at his watch, 'and it's March the fourteenth.'

Another long pause followed.

'Then it is three hundred and fifty-two years after my time,' Isaac murmured, almost to himself. 'My time is the Year of Our Lord, sixteen hundred and sixty-six.'

So shocking were the implications that Isaac could barely breathe the words. But Archie got the drift.

'So you're a Time Traveller,' he said matter-of-factly and with relish. This could prove to be better than going to Skegness.

Isaac absorbed the implications and answered slowly with another question.

'Such, Time Travellers are known in these days?' he asked.

It was Archie's turn to consider carefully before answering. 'Well, in books and films and things. But I don't know of any real people. I've never heard of anything happening in real life like that.'

'Films?' queried Isaac.

Archie was a good teacher and he was getting the man's measure: 'Yeah! Stories in pictures. Moving pictures. Ya know?'

It was enough for Isaac to interpret that time travellers were only found in children's stories. The rest of the intriguing information, of moving pictures, he would leave to another time. He considered all that he had learned since dawn – and thought long and hard.

🍎

In Cambridge, Robert Hooke and the now large number of his desperately self-controlled colleagues, all about to be annihilated by an explosion of the electron-tunnelling-microscope and the rogue cyclotron, had an idea.

'This anomalous energy is coming in from one direction,' Professor Hooke shouted above the hubbub. 'We should be able to track it back to source. Shouldn't we?'

There was a desperate rush of desperately self-controlled, possibly doomed physicists to find compasses, antennae, radar dishes, radios, Geiger counters, maps and all manner of equipment that might help to track the relentless particles. The red lights flashed and the alarm bells rang as forces built to dangerous levels in the laboratory equipment. People yelling into mobile phones rushed to different parts of the building, clambered onto the roof and ran into the streets to get whatever triangulation they could.

'It's nor-nor-west. Definitely nor-nor-west,' jabbered a white-coated lab technician who sailed a dinghy in his spare time.

'How Far? How Far?' hollered his fellow condemned colleagues.

'Difficult to say – not far. Less than a hundred miles. Get a car. Get a car. Who's got a car? Quickly!'

A tall order when Cambridge City Council's constant war on motorists not only made it impossible to penetrate the heart of the city in a car in under five hours but also made it illegal to park within a three-mile radius of just about anywhere. Nonetheless, a privileged don's elderly, faded blue Volvo estate was discovered tucked discreetly behind the Climate Change Study Unit offices – and hot-wired in a trice by the combined intellects and anti-social criminal tendencies of the physicists. Within a few minutes, packed with seven assorted scientists, it was charging out of Cambridge, the wrong way up a one-way street, heading nor-nor-west.

With both courage and reluctance the remaining physicists returned to the overly energised laboratory and the self-propelling cyclotron to carry on panicking. Also to do what they could to stop it exploding, or imploding, in a cataclysmic, if academically fascinating event.

The faded blue Volvo was now racing straight towards Archie and his troubled and puzzled companion.

3

ARCHIE THE EXPERT

ARCHIE WAS beginning to enjoy himself. For the first time in his short life he was an expert on everything. In fact, he was THE expert, as Isaac had none other to explain the marvels of the modern world to him. Archie explained how a zip worked as Isaac ran the precise mechanism up and down, opening and closing a long pocket on Archie's nylon backpack.

'But the precision,' marvelled Isaac. 'All those small pieces of bone cut to such exact dimensions and fitting so wondrously together. 'It's simply not possible.'

"S not bone,' said Archie authoritatively, recalling a How it is Made, early-morning TV programme. 'It's plastic.'

Archie had already grown used to Isaac's thoughtful, long silences as he processed new information.

Isaac fingered the white zipper material and examined it closely. 'Plastic, you say?'

'Yep. Plastic.'

'And what is…plastic made from?'

Archie knew this too. 'It's made from oil – mostly. I think. Yeah – from oil.'

'Lamp oil? Whale oil? Walnut oil? Beeswax? Fish oil?'

Archie needed to interrupt while he could still hold the litany in mind. 'Nah! None of them. Engine oil.'

Isaac looked at him steadily, clearly not understanding, and waiting for amplification.

'You know. Oil for cars and lawn mowers and the like – engine oil.'

Isaac did not know, though he thought he understood 'engine'. He waited in silence while Archie searched for more information.

'Ya know,' he challenged Isaac, 'oil from an oil well. Oil you drill down into the ground for.'

Isaac showed some spark of understanding but said nothing. Archie pressed on.

'Ya know,' Archie insisted, 'oil they get from drilling down into the rocks – in foreign countries. I think – mostly.'

Isaac was following with unswerving concentration. 'Rock Oil?' he proposed. And without needing an answer. 'Petra-oil?'

'Yeah. That's it,' encouraged Archie, 'petrol. They get petrol from the oil as well. From underground. And it comes whooshing up in a great spout. A great black fountain – really messy – when they first find it. And it can catch on fire too. Huge fires that are really dangerous to put out.'

Isaac was a rewarding pupil as he listened, analysed, remembered and slotted new facts into some kind of logical order. Archie was finding that his tutoring skills improved with each sentence. Nevertheless, his pupil was a bit unreadable.

'D'ya get it?' he inquired solicitously.

'I think I understand. They dig into the ground…'

23

'Drill,' corrected Archie. 'Drill with drills as big as that tree.'

Isaac estimated the young black poplar at about thirty feet high – and looked at Archie for confirmation.

'Yeah!' said Archie. 'Easily as high as that tree. And then they keep adding more and more pieces. And it goes deeper and deeper and deeper…'

'Like digging a well?'

'Yep – like I said, it's an oil-well. Until they hit the oil – then whooosh! Up it comes. Black gold they call it.'

'And where does the oil come from? How does it get underground?'

'Old jungles. You know – forests; trees and ferns and things. All rotting away. For millions and millions of years. Since the dinosaurs.'

Isaac quizzed Archie and unravelled 'millions,' and eventually understood 'dinosaurs,' but this new data horrified him. 'Is this seemingly innocent child a Godless demon?' he wondered. For Isaac knew for a fact that learned and revered professors and philosophers had fathomed the age of the World from rigorous Bible studies, counting the ages of Kings, Prophets and Pharaohs to conclude that God made the Universe some six thousand years ago. The child was, as Isaac had thought earlier, either deranged – or perhaps he simply had trouble, as even the most advanced mathematicians had difficulty, with manipulating zeros. He was confusing his hundreds, thousands and millions… Or he was committing foul heresies for which he should be severely punished.

Isaac put it aside.

'And from this black oil this, er, plastic substance is drawn, or cooked, reduced, or, rendered?' asked Isaac, peering at the white zipper and running his fingers up and down it.

'Yeah! I think so. I saw it on the telly.'

'Telly?' mused Isaac. Archie, at first, felt on solid ground.

24

'It's a box – 'bout this big,' he explained, opening his arms. 'With a glass front. An' it shows moving pictures – and voices – and music and stuff. Its real name is television. And everyone's got one.'

'"Tele" – in Greek means "at a distance". "Vision" – means to see… It sees at a distance; things far away. Like my Optiks?'

'You mean like a tele-scope?' said Archie.

'Yes – of course. Tele-scope,' repeated Isaac, seizing triumphantly on the word – which he understood.

'Nah!' drawled Archie. 'No – not at all like a telescope.'

'Then why "at a distance"? Where do the pictures, these moving pictures, come from?'

Archie considered. This was a question to ponder. 'They come mostly from London, I guess. And there's a lot of American stuff shown; that might come from America,' he added uncertainly.

Isaac could make neither head nor tail of how the primitive American colony figured, so he fixed on London. 'London! That's two or three-days' travel. How do the pictures get to this machine – this tele-vision?' He was growing impatient with the gaps in the boy's knowledge and with his own inability to patch the information together into a construct which made any sense.

Archie quailed a little. Isaac Newton, in sternly critical mood, was very obviously not a person to upset further. But Archie thought he knew the answer.

'The pictures…,' he told the genius slowly – to ensure he would understand, '…come from a big aerial in London, through the air, to all the little aerials on people's roofs. Then down a wire from the aerial,' he paused until he was sure that Isaac was still with him – though he wasn't, 'through a hole in the windowsill. To a little plug on the wall.' Isaac's face was reflecting blank panic. 'And then you plug the telly in there – and it shows the pictures. Oh! And the sound, of course.' He wrapped up his explanation with a showman's flourish.

'This is madness,' groaned Isaac, burying his face in his hands again.

'It's right though!' protested Archie. 'It's how it works. Look! Look will ya?' Look over there at the cottage by the bridge.'

The familiar words 'cottage' and 'bridge' comforted Isaac, and he obliged Archie by lowering his hands and looking where he was told to.

'Look! On the roof. On the chimney.' Archie waited to check his companion was peering in the right direction. 'That little stick, gate-like thing? That's the aerial. That's where the pictures come in. See?'

Isaac saw not at all. But he was as dogged in his search for knowledge as Archie was in his determination to inform Isaac with explanations. His mind, hot and very bothered as it was, still managed to process what Archie had said – and the clearly visible aerial on the chimney stack. He fought for a rationalisation.

'Is it,' he ventured painfully, 'is it like a prism, a glass, which captures the invisible light, and converts it into colours – colours like those we observe in the rainbow?'

Archie wasn't at all sure about this. But he wanted to encourage such a brave attempt. 'Yeah – sort of. And it is in colour,' he assured Isaac. Then he became inspired. 'I think it's more like electricity than light – you know – like lightning. And it runs down that rod,' he pointed at the cottage, 'and down the wire.'

Isaac was sitting up again – he knew of lightning and of static electricity.

'Only you can't see it – like lightning. And there's no thunder. It's really radio waves that come.'

Isaac tried one more rationalisation before letting his jaw and mind go slack. 'Does this...tele-vision...only come during daylight?'

'No, no. It comes at any time. All the time. There's always something on.'

Archie, sensing they had encountered an event horizon in his knowledge and reached an impasse in mutual understanding, and seeing that Isaac needed to rest his intellect, gave him a plasticised, brightly printed, oblong, cardboard carton of Ribena to drink, complete with plastic straw. He also showed him how to pierce the little silver tab, insert the tube and suck the juice. This basic exercise in modern living enabled Isaac to focus only on what was immediately in his hands — deeply and mystifyingly alien though it was — to reel at the taste of sugars, packaging, preservatives and fruit, and to close his mind to everything beyond two-feet distant.

'That's plastic as well,' observed Archie, tapping lightly on the side of Isaac's carton, dislodging the straw and causing him to dribble purple juice from the corner of his mouth.

The great man remained slumped silently over his drink, in a profound state of shock.

4

PHYSICISTS IN THE FIELD

A DISPENSABLE junior researcher wearing antique motorcycle goggles stood up through the Volvo's sun roof pointing a large radar dish in the general direction of Woolsthorpe. In the front passenger seat Professor Hooke hunched over a screen wired to the dish and shouted instructions at the windswept observer, whose feet, fighting for balance, threatened to deny the opportunity for future offspring to driver and professor alike. He shouted at the harassed driver, who misheard and mixed the orders he received due to the rush of wind, visiting a myriad of near-death experiences on the whole enterprise. But the blue Volvo charged indestructibly on – on a west-north-westerly bearing.

It swept through Grantham, triggering every speed and traffic camera en route, and collecting a fistful of fines and penalties for the innocent, careful Volvo owner, which would guarantee him bankruptcy and several years in Grantham Gaol. It frightened the elderly, amused the young at heart, alarmed the daydreamers and even woke a police patrol-car driver – who thought he must have dreamt that an elderly Volvo estate was passing at sixty miles an hour, and so plunged back into sleep.

The driver flashed the headlights, blared the horn and bellowed scholarly imprecations in classical dead languages at any who dared to use the roads, crossings and pavements ahead of them, as the car hurtled and swayed through the town.

'The beam is very strong here!' shouted Hooke. 'And it's increasing exponentially. The source must be within a mile or two. Damn! Damn BT – there's no bloody signal! It's buggered my mobile phone. I can't raise the labs over the static.'

From one of the scrum of four scientists crammed into the back seat with all types of sensors and navigation aids came a warning shout: 'Take that B-road up on the left,' she urged. So preoccupied was she by the imminent destruction of Cambridge – and their collective scientific reputations – that she was not even aware, still less able to comment on the fact, that one of her many male admirers, a small unprepossessing Russian, was enjoying being pressed against her far more than he should, if his brilliant mind was ever to become engaged in contributing to the task of saving the planet.

The driver, obligingly and with a cavalier flourish, to the delight of the aroused Russian, swung the car to the left, then sharply to the right as the back road sneaked and snaked out of Grantham towards Woolsthorpe. A tractor pulling a muck-spreader dripping with interesting nutrients to be spattered generously on the nation's crops of cereals and vegetables, crept churlishly out of a farm gate. It showed no reaction to the squeal of brakes, horns, lights and educated insults hurled at it, and trundled sullenly – and very slowly – ahead of them.

The standing Volvo pilot was bent double by the inertial forces over the sill of the open roof as the car ground to a halt. Without pause the windows were wound down and a crop of white-coated scientists sprouted from every opening, urgently, helpfully and energetically advising the tractor driver as to how he might better direct his machine. The language deteriorated into distinctly non-classical phrases mixed with incomprehensible deep-throated Russian ejaculations as the small, dandruff-speckled man experienced an incontinent response to all the excitement.

Archie glimpsed the tractor, the trailer and a faded Cambridge-blue Volvo jigging from one side of the road to the other and rocking violently, with white-coated protestors hanging from its windows, crest a hill about half a mile from the bridge before the convoy disappeared in a dip in the road. It was getting on for twelve o'clock, the mist had all but cleared and the sun was just visible through the low cloud – warming them as they huddled on the river bank. Archie wasn't hungry or thirsty just yet, as they had brunched from his lunch box. But his autonomic systems were monitoring the falling energy levels and stored fats and sugars, and they directed his gaze towards the unpromising pub by the bridge – which did at least sport a tempting ice-cream sign by its front door. But before Archie could weigh the chances of talking Isaac into a bar snack, the Volvo juddered to a halt near the bridge and a gang of young men and women, carrying what Archie took to be metal detectors, forced a way through the hedge and tiptoed towards them, their eyes glued to their instruments.

Isaac still had his head in his hands, so Archie jogged his elbow. 'Don't know who this lot is,' he warned his friend.

Isaac watched warily as the seven assorted adults picked their way across the fields and started along the path by the river towards them. He straightened up and regarded the newcomers attentively; as the group drew nearer Isaac stood up and faced them quietly.

'We're very close. Very, very close,' called one of the scientists.

Exchanging data and measurements, and with the fate of the

world hanging in the balance, the group pressed on past Isaac and Archie, with no recognition that they were there at all.

'It's altered. The signal has shifted,' exclaimed one of them from ten yards or so up the path. 'It's behind us now. It's coming from that ruin in the brambles!'

They turned and hurried back, again shoving past Archie and Isaac, and started to fight their way into the blackberry pile, snagging their white coats and getting cut by the thorns. The blackberry tendrils won the battle and all the scientists stopped moving forward and struggled to back out of the bushes.

'I think ye will find,' said Isaac quietly, his deep country brogue carrying over the curses and imprecations, 'that it is to my person your instruments have brought you.'

Professor Robert Hooke, disentangled from the thorns, took a quick, fierce, impatient look at the heavy-coated, long-haired tramp and the small boy. If he was to save Cambridge, he really didn't have time for these quaint locals.

'We're busy. You'd better buzz off!' he said, and waved a hand at them dismissively.

Neither moved.

The other scientists had freed themselves from the brambles and had the pile surrounded with clicking and whistling counters and pointers, like hounds with a treed quarry.

'It's definitely in there, Professor,' called the weekend yachtsman. And all eyes turned to follow his finger, which was pointing at the faintly discernible stones inside the lethally barbed shrubs.

'That's our den!' said Archie loudly, with the surety of long-established squatters' rights.

'That,' said Isaac levelly, 'is…or was…my library.'

The authority of his still, even voice, the unquestionable authority of ownership, penetrated the consciousness of the Cambridge visitors, wrenching their concentration away from their problem to take in this eccentric young man.

Professor Hooke made another quick assessment. He turned to Archie in preference to getting embroiled with his abnormal-looking companion. 'Look. There's an emergency. A real emergency. Who are you and what are you doing here?' he snapped.

'I'm Archie Wilkins – and he's Isaac,' answered Archie promptly, nodding at Isaac. ''E might be Care-in-the-Community,' he confided in a stage whisper, confirming what they all had been silently assuming about Isaac.

Professor Hooke nodded fast, just on the civilised side of being furious. Time was very, very pressing. 'And what are you doing – just here – and right now?'

'I missed the school outing bus – and him…,' Archie nodded sideways at Isaac, '…'e was hiding in our den – in there,' he added, pointing into the bramble. 'He's a farmer – from over that hill.'

Isaac stood quietly, unperturbed by the slurs being cast upon him. His stillness, his low peripheral movements, signalled hierarchical authority. In spite of their intellectual assessment of him as a tramp or a deranged countryman, medicated by the local out-patients' department, the frantic boffins were unconsciously obliged to recognise that this oddball was somehow quite special. The professor reluctantly addressed him.

'What were you doing in that ruin?' he demanded.

Isaac reflected for some seconds. 'I would not in most circumstances answer such an impertinently posed question. But I, too, am as disturbed as you and can forgive your agitation and lack of manners.'

Hooke almost stamped his foot but contained himself.

'Last evening, I was in my library, as usual, recording my observations of the incidence of colours and angles of light entering and leaving prisms,' his voice quickened and rose as his attention was swept within, back to the challenging calculations he had been making.

Professor Hooke did stamp a foot; but said nothing – very loudly.

'And I took a glass of porter, and fell asleep, without having put away my notes, nor tidied my Optiks.' This lapse clearly puzzled him, but another sodden thud of Hooke's shoe closed the diversion. 'And when I woke – this morning – my room was a ruin, overgrown with bramble-thorn, and this lad was sitting on the river bank.' His voice trailed off.

Hooke pushed his face forward, consumed with the urgency of his task but unable to disengage from this screwball. 'Prisms? Light? Optiks? – Just who in God's name do you think you are? Isaac bloody Newton!'

There was the profound silence of the Universe taking a discreet step backwards.

'Er, indeed, sir. And whom do I have the privilege of addressing?' said Isaac, proffering his hand.

Hooke gave a little jump of rage, its sharp message muted by his landing on wet grass. He snapped his fingers at a colleague – a normally highly respected, esteemed and internationally renowned colleague – but at this moment, to Robert Hooke, he was just another fumbling dolt charged with navigating the local map. 'Where are we? Just where exactly, the hell, are we?' he snarled.

The esteemed physicist could only work at the speed dictated by a crumpled, large Ordnance Survey map and the vision his steamed spectacles afforded. Thanks to being one of the cleverest men on the planet he still managed to deliver a rapid reply that penetrated through the wall-to-wall panic.

'Just here – River Withan flows north. That pub and bridge over there are marked – Woolsthorpe Hall – just over the hill – behind us.'

The little crowd of highly educated persons fell deeply quiet.

None looked at Robert Hooke, or Isaac; most looked up into the innocent, grey, luminous sky. All knew that Isaac Newton, the real, original Isaac Newton, Lucasian Professor of Mathematics, Fellow of Cambridge University, possibly the world's greatest ever scientist, was, as a matter of fact, raised at Woolsthorpe Hall.

They waited with interest for Professor Hooke's response.

The tableau was frozen for a few seconds; the only movement being Professor Hooke's head trembling as he stared intently at Isaac, then at his team, then back at Isaac – in frantic indecision.

Suddenly his indecision vanished. He snatched out his mobile phone, thumbed a few buttons, waited for a connection, cupped the phone to his ear and spoke into it. 'Hello – Atomic Energy Commission?... Put me through to Peter Johnston, It's a disaster. An emergency. Yes – an atomic emergency. A real emergency!

'...Hello Peter – Robert Hooke here... Yes, yes – from Cambridge, yes! We met at the Queen Elizabeth Hall conference last year... Good, good! We have a runaway surge – a quantum particle surge of huge energies...on our cyclotron at the Clarendon in Cambridge. It could implode or explode at any time... Of course it is bloody dangerous. This is a crisis, man! A genuine, enormous crisis. Now I need your resources!... There is no time to explain...'

'It's a mobile phone,' Archie whispered loudly, responding to Isaac's fiercely questioning gaze. "E's talkin' to someone in a nuclear power station, I think.'

Isaac nodded his incomprehension and his eyes flashed from Hooke to his colleagues, to the phone and back to Archie. But he said nothing.

'Yes, yes, man. Now listen! I need one of your security squads out here... Just as fast as they can get here... Don't you have helicopters?... Bugger the cost, man. The whole county might blow any minute... Just do as I say. I need a man held. He may be a wandering imbecile, or he may have something to do with this crisis. But we need to test this whole area… No! We are NOT in Cambridge – follow the phone signal. We're out near Grantham, on the river bank. There's a pub by a bridge… I can't see the name. Wait a second…

'Christopher! What's that damn pub called? Oh…it's the Queen's Head…the B2039 I think. Yes, the B2039. We're a hundred metres west of the road on the river bank… How long?… Half an hour? Make it sooner if you can. And get some experienced nuclear scientists to my Cambridge lab – a.s.a.p.'

Professor Robert Hooke, pulses pounding but satisfied with his executive actions, turned to ponder the oddly compelling tramp he'd just arranged to have taken into custody.

But Isaac had gone. He had responded to urgent tugs at his sleeve from Archie and, following his new-found friend, had melted silently into the undergrowth.

Archie, hearing the phrase 'a man held', knew enough to anticipate the approach of officialdom when it was threatened – and was street-wise enough to take the precaution of not being around when it arrived. They slipped away on earthen paths winding under bruised hawthorn bushes that Archie and his friends used for bird-nesting, pirate ships and Cowboys and Indians. Within twenty quiet steps they were out of sight, and five minutes later were in a sunken farm lane overhung with dense foliage and heading to Grantham.

The trees made such a complete canopy that Archie and Isaac didn't even need to duck when the Atomic Energy Commission helicopter flew directly over their route.

5

ISAAC GOES ONLINE

EMERGING THROUGH a broken fence, which bounded acres of neglected allotments, Archie led Isaac into an aging 1950s council-house estate. They walked through quiet, neat streets lined with parked cars towards Archie's home. As they crossed three side roads, Isaac twice came perilously close to going under the wheels of passing cars as he froze in astonishment, unable to judge their speed or comprehend their means of locomotion.

'Green Cross Code,' muttered Archie, alarmed, as he dragged Isaac onto the pavement. 'Green Cross Code. Look right; look left, if it's clear, look right again – an' then cross the bloomin' road.'

But Isaac was too bewildered to hear Archie. He slumped onto a kitchen chair as Archie closed the door behind them, his eyes glazed, his skin pale and his breathing rapid and shallow. He was in shock – Future Shock.

Archie – single-parent-family Archie – confidently took charge.

His mum often had similar symptoms after unscheduled visits from the local money lender, an insidious, bullying journeyman who always threatened to 'be back tomorrow'.

What revived his mum, and what he now made for Isaac, was a nice cup of tea – laced with two teaspoons of sugar. Isaac only allowed himself a nervous glimpse as Archie filled the transparent plastic kettle from a tap, which presumably ran with drinking water, plonked it on a matching base and flicked a switch. Energy – noisy, fast, hot energy – surged into the water and started it bubbling. Isaac decided discretion was the better course…and yet again buried his head in his hands.

The darkness and warmth behind his cupped hands was blessed and comforting as the gentle pressure on his eyes eliminated sensory input, which he could not assimilate. His ears, however, wilfully tracked the noise of a kettle boiling fast and furiously – without a fire; noted a loud click which stopped the boiling; traced Archie's steps from sink to cupboard to fridge. He wondered at the sucking sound and draught of cold air as Archie opened the fridge and clinked a bottle of milk; recognised water splashing from a tap into a pot; wondered at the rumblings, clicks, whirrs, whines and sighs as the fridge motor cut in. And at last the sounds and refreshing miasma from hot tea cajoled his curiosity to open his eyes and peek through his fingers – as Archie triumphantly placed a steaming, dark brown brew at his elbow, still spinning from a vigorous stirring.

'W'd ya like a biscuit with your tea?'

Isaac took his customary pause. 'You are most civil. I would welcome a biscuit, with this…Tee?'

Archie, his encyclopaedic knowledge once again called upon, happily fielded the implicit question. He shook a half-empty box of teabags at Isaac. 'Yeah! It's tea. Y'know tea, don't'cha? I mean, everybody knows what TEA is? Even kiddies know what tea is.'

Isaac rose to the challenge from his small critic, removed his hands, set his face and gazed levelly at Archie. His eyes sparked with recall. He put a teabag to his nose.

'It is, I believe, a rare and valuable spice, or herb. Which comes from the east, with merchantmen, and is credited with beneficial, healthful properties.'

There was no hint of query – and something of a challenge in his voice. Archie, though very foggy on the origins of tea, bluffed his way through.

'Yeah, yeah, that's right,' he confirmed, to the world's greatest scientific genius – or to this deluded long-haired tramp who graced his kitchen. 'It's from hot places, and from bushes,' he added shrewdly, suddenly noting on the box, and interpreting for the first time, an illustration of dark-faced, exotically dressed women bending over hedges and tossing leaves into baskets strapped to their heads. 'It will do you good!' he added, with a medical certainty gleaned from his mother's folk wisdom.

Impassively, Isaac observed Archie's gaze and the coloured pictures on the box. An unreadable flicker crossed his solemn face.

'You have a wide knowledge, lad. I am indebted for your valuable intelligence.'

Archie knew better than to grin happily and give the game away. He turned and reached for the biscuits – and plonked two McVitie's Chocolate Digestives by Isaac's cup, and took two for himself.

In the warmth of the little room, lulled by the background hum of the fridge, they drank their tea and ate their biscuits in companionable silence.

'Master Archie. What did you understand of our white-coated visitors by the River Witham?' Isaac asked, after a minute or two.

'They was in a proper panic,' observed Archie carefully, 'and the boss called for helicopter back-up. So he must've been important?'

'He was the man who was shouting into his, er, tele…phone, who introduced himself as Robert Hooke?'

'Yeah!' said Archie. The others called him professor – so I guess he's from Cambridge. Ya know. From the university?'

'Yes, Master Archie. I do know of the university. And, strangely, I have a colleague, in my time, also called Robert Hooke. A solid natural philosopher, in my own field. Sound but uninspiring. And, if ye would be so kind, what is a "heli-copter", that he demanded?'

'It's a big machine that flies. It's got a big propeller on top that whizzes round an' round very fast, an' lifts off the ground.'

Isaac waited for more – intently.

Archie looked up at the ceiling for inspiration. It came.

'Hang on. Hang on. I've got pictures.'

Within seconds, he had bounded upstairs and back again flourishing *The Boys' Monster Book of Weapons*, which he leafed through rapidly.

'There it is. That's it. A military helicopter gunship. Carries, er, twenty-five troops.'

It took all of Isaac's mental discipline to ignore the other coloured pictures, to focus on the drawing that Archie stabbed at with his finger, and to resolve the lines, perspective and colours into a meaningful image. He slowly realised that it was an astonishing machine, flying through the air, packed with soldiers.

He paled as he took in the implication of what he was seeing. 'Professor Hooke was summoning such a machine to come to Woolsthorpe…'

'And arrest you!'

'Arrest me?'

'Yeah – lock you up. Put you in prison.'

Isaac paled some more, but gave a determinedly defiant look.

'I must thank you for my timely rescue.'

'Oh, it weren't nothing. Just our secret paths.'

'It was something. You thought and moved quickly. And you have my thanks and gratitude. What do you think they were panicking about?'

'Well the boss said something about a nuclear explosion. In Cambridge, I think.'

'Yes. Professor Hooke said that his "cyclo…tron" may "implode or explode" at any time. I do not recall the word "nuclear". Would such an explosion be large?'

It was Archie's turn for the colour to drain from his face – and it was a more eloquent answer than words could convey.

'He called the bloomin' nuclear power people. He called their police force. Would it be large…it'd be humungous. It'd wipe out the whole place!'

'The whole farm?' gasped Isaac, aghast.

Archie stared back at him – and extended his hands, slowly widening them.

'The whole of Grantham?'

Archie's hands wiggled further apart – with urgency.

'The whole of Cambridge?' asked Isaac – now disbelieving.

But Archie's pallor and obvious fright contradicted this assessment.

'A NUCLEAR explosion'd take out the whole bloomin' country. Everybody – and everything,' Archie whispered hoarsely.

He turned a few pages of the book lying on the table. 'Look… There's one. And it says it's an old-fashioned one, just a couple of megatons. A big one'd take out the whole of London, at least!'

Isaac could make neither head nor tail of the picture Archie pointed at. It looked like a badly drawn mushroom against a cloudy sky. He studied the unfamiliar, illegible text for clues. Suddenly his nervous system jumped.

'This is my name. Here. It is my name. Surely it is?'

Archie came around the table and read the words.

'Sir Isaac Newton. Are you a Sir?'

'No – no – but it must be me. It mentions my work. Please read on.'

'…*discovered the laws of gravity in 1666 while staying at his farm at Woolsthorpe in Lincolnshire, during the Black Death. Newton was considered to be the greatest scientist who ever lived – but his reputation was eventually surpassed by Albert Einstein who discovered the power of the atom, with his famous formula $E=MC^2$ – that's M C with a little number two at the end – without which mankind would not have made the atom bomb.*'

There was an Isaac-moment of contemplation.

'Remind me again of the year we now live in. It is most strange to hear of myself, my future self yet to come, spoken of as in the distant past. What year is this?'

Oh, it's two thousand and eighteen.'

'And this famous formula which Mr Einstein conceived – what does it refer to – what do the symbols represent?'

Archie considered blustering, but he reluctantly admitted that he didn't know.'But we could look it up on my PC – on the internet.'

Archie wondered at the wisdom of exposing his guest to computers, as Isaac slowly leafed through *The Boys' Monster Book of Weapons* shaking his head in wonderment and bewilderment at the book itself, at the pictures on its pages, and at how on God's Earth such a marvel could belong to a mere child like Archie.

'Your pee-see?'

'Well, me mum's really. She works at home some days and 'as it on broadband.'

Isaac didn't try to follow that lead.

'It's in the front room with the telly.'

Isaac took a deep, long breath and bravely rose from his chair. His greatcoat swept a spoon from the table, which they both ignored as Archie took the hint and led his frightened, reluctant but enraptured student into the next room.

'You could take your coat off – if you want,' said Archie, suddenly aware of the limited space around the computer console. Isaac stood stock-still, weighing up the large, blank TV screen that dominated the small room.

'Ah, yes. It is uncommonly hot and airless in here. I will remove it – thank you.'

Archie had never handled such a heavy coat. With difficulty, he wrestled it and Isaac's large hat back into the hall and onto a hook behind the front door, and returned.

'When I switch this on,' he warned, 'there'll be bright pictures – shining out of this screen.' He ran his hand across the screen. 'And,' he added, even more sternly, 'there'll be sounds, loud sounds – voices an' music and things. Are you ready?'

Isaac nodded gravely.

Archie slid out a desk panel with keyboard and mouse from under the TV set, picked up the remote and fired it at the TV. As the screen came alive with moving images and colours, and as music and commentary filled the room, Isaac sank slowly to his knees on the floor, gaping at the miracle.

His hand reached out tentatively – and his fingertips encountered a glass screen. Archie flicked the mouse around the desk top, opened Google, and with his hand hovering over the keyboard, he turned to Isaac, 'Now, what did you want to look up?'

'Is this… Is this a…tele…vision, of which ye told me earlier? Is this the machine that sees the pictures sent from London?'

'Yeah, it's a TV. And it's on the internet as well. It's a PC and a telly – all in one.'

Isaac gave Archie one of his expressionless stares. 'Inter…Net?'

Archie was on solid ground. 'It's the biggest library on Earth – ever,' he told Isaac confidently. 'And everyone's got it. Tell me that formula you wanted to know about – and I'll show you.'

If Isaac reacted more slowly than he was wont, he did so with good reason.

'Ah!... It was in your book. You read to me about an...Albert Einstein and his "famous" formula.

'Oh yeah! Here it is. It says E equals M C with a number two. I'll Google it and see what we get... I'll try this Young Scientist site... It says "...*Einstein's most famous mathematical equation, E equals M, C, Two...means that Energy, E, is equal to the Mass, M, multiplied by the speed of light, C...er...squared. For example...*"

He looked at Isaac's face in the hope of seeing dawning comprehension – but Isaac remained impassive and expectant. Archie struggled on, feeling this was an intellectual burden too far.

"*For example...the energy, E, (expressed in Joules) locked in a gram of iron...*" – Isaac nodded imperceptibly, and Archie soldiered on. "*...is equivalent to one gram...multiplied by the speed of light...*" – Archie groaned inwardly at the injustice and incomprehensibility of the universe, but the pressure from his new friend was unrelenting – "*...multiplied by itself...or squared.*"

Archie ground to a halt, setting down his Herculean task with a sigh and slumping back from the screen.

'And the next line in this most famous of equations, Master Archie...' He did not try to disguise the intense excitement in his quiet, level, insistent voice.

Archie heroically sat up to the screen and tried to read on.

'It's all long numbers,' he complained. 'Really, really long numbers. I don't know how to say them.'

'Put your finger on the line – and we'll read them together,' insisted Isaac.

Between them they mouthed the words and numbers, with Isaac bending ever closer to the glowing screen with mounting excitement.

"*The speed of light (or more correctly the rate of propagation of a light wave) in a vacuum…'"*

'A wave…not a mote. In a vacuum?' pondered Isaac. 'Yes – of course, it has to be in a vacuum.'

'…"*Is approximately 300,000 kilometres per second (186,000 miles per second)*."'

'One hundred and eighty-six THOUSAND MILES, in one second? What is the source of this supposed intelligence? It cannot be true.'

But there was deep doubt in his voice.

'There's other sites,' said Archie. 'We can check it on hundreds of other web pages, if you want. Actually, there's thousands of 'em.'

Isaac didn't try to unravel the suggestion. He doggedly pursued the equation, his finger now pressing hard against the screen.

'"…*which, squared, is 90,000,000,000 (90 billion) kilometres per second, (56.2 billion miles per second)… Multiplied by the weight of 1 gram is 90 billion grams/second.*

'"*If we use the precise 'speed' of light, 299,792.458 kilometres per second; one gram of matter (about the weight of a pound note) contains 89.9 terajoules of energy (89,875,517,873,681,764 joules).*"'

Even Isaac baulked at trying to say the immense number set in brackets.

'"*(A joule is the force of one Newton moving an object 1 metre along the direction of force – A Newton…)*" That is my name – again!'

'I think you were quite famous, in your day,' Archie added generously.

'"…*A Newton weighs 100 grams – which is about the weight of a small apple*".'

'A small apple? Why would a measure of force, given my name, be related to the weight of a small apple?'

Archie knew this.

'Because,' he enunciated slowly, with exaggerated patience, 'when you invented *gravity*, the big idea came to you when you saw an apple fall off a tree down to the ground. Bonk! You're dead famous for inventing gravity.'

Isaac looked at him, thought a while, almost smiled and replied, 'It might be, Master Archie, that the good Lord above "invented" gravity – and that I, at a later stage in my life than at this most strange time, merely investigated it.'

'It fell on yer 'ead. Bonk!'

'And mayhap knocked some good sense into me?'

'It might 'ave. But I think you were quite bright even before that. At least that's what our teacher said.'

Isaac lapsed into one of his thoughtful silences. Archie waited.

'I am analysing celestial forces of movement and motion – at my home – reading tables of the observed movements of planets through the sky. I am developing a mathematical engine I call Calculus, to measure their course. And, of course, of the moon. There are many unanswered questions.'

Archie got it immediately. 'We can look things up on the Internet. D'ya wanna do that? What do you want to know?'

Isaac looked at Archie, and at the glowing screen. His suppressed excitement, building up in his mind, charging his entire physique, filling the room, would have stopped an express train. He controlled his tremors and marshalled his thoughts. 'How far from our planet, Earth, how far is the sun?'

Archie summoned Google and tapped the question onto his keyboard. It found more than six million sites. The first entry on the screen included the answer with a picture of the fiery orb:

Sun
Star
The Sun is the star at the center of the Solar System. It is a nearly perfect sphere of hot plasma, with internal convective motion that generates a magnetic field via a dynamo process.

Radius: 695,700 km
Surface temperature: 5,778 K
Mass: 1.989 × 10^30 kg
Rotation speed: 1.997 km/s
Distance to Earth: 149.6 million km
Did you know: The Sun is the brightest star by apparent visual
magnitude (V = −26.74). (**wikipedia**)

Isaac gasped and leaned perilously close to the screen, as if trying to absorb the information through his open mouth. Archie put a restraining hand on his shoulder. Isaac eased back a little, with his eyes riveted on the top item, to cut out the bewildering array of other information. He concentrated fiercely on the short summary.

'Master Archie, if you please, what is this measure?' And he put his finger on the glass. Archie looked and politely shifted the big man's big finger.

'Er. Oh, that's 149.6 million kilometres. That's how far away the sun is,' he added confidently.

Isaac was frustrated, but his scientific rigour injected a large dose of patience. 'Do you perchance know what that means in my measure – in English miles?' he asked hoarsely.

'Sure. Archie flipped up a new search tab, looked for 'kilometres in miles,' typed in the number, counting the places to make sure he was doing millions – and the answer came up '92.95713 million miles'. Archie was at his best. 'So,' he announced importantly, I can shorten that long number, I can *round* it to 'ninety-three million miles. That's how far it is to the sun.'

'Hey,' he suddenly protested, 'I knew that. It's ninety-three million miles to the sun. Everyone knows that.'

'And if we can return to the question about the sun...' Isaac insisted, unstoppable in pursuit of future-perfect knowledge.

Archie flipped back to the previous tab.

'Radius 695,700 kilometres,' quoted Isaac.

'I can look that up,' offered Archie.

'Please do. And, to save you further trouble, ask how many kilometres in one mile.'

It came to 437.9 thousand miles.

'Rounded,' said Isaac, 'we could say 438 thousand miles for one radius. And one kilometre in miles?'

'Oh yeah,' said Archie, beginning to tire. 'That comes to 0.621371.' And he read out the long number.

Isaac took some paper from a pad and a pencil from by the phone and wrote it down. 'And if I could trouble you further,' he persisted relentlessly, 'the moon? Can we enquire about the moon?'

Archie was wilting under the crush of data. Data overload. He had a bright idea. 'Hold on! I've got all this stuff in a book me dad bought for me birthday.' Before Isaac could pin him down, Archie skipped from the room and bounded upstairs. Isaac could hear him scrambling around. 'Got it,' sang out Archie, and bounded back, clutching a small fat book with a vivid cover. 'You can have this. It's got all that stuff in. Planets and everything. And how long to fly there and all that.'

Isaac read the title: *The Junior Book of Wonders – Our Universe*. He opened it, found the index and carefully studied it. In silence he leafed through to the chapter on the solar system. It was his turn to suffer an attack of information-overload as he saw the highly coloured artwork of the planets circling the sun, in the void of deep space. The text did, as Archie had promised, have all the 'stuff,' that Isaac, at this stage, could think of asking. And it offered far, far more.

He closed the book and held it tight. 'I am deeply indebted to you, young sir. This is a most welcome and generous gift. It will greatly advance my work.'

Archie waved aside the thanks airily. 'I can always look it up on the Internet.'

Isaac felt that as a blow. Instinctively, he knew without any doubt that he could not take the internet back to 1666. But he so much wanted, craved and yearned for 'The Largest Library Ever'.

6

A STRICTLY IMPOSSIBLE GHOST

As ARCHIE AND ISAAC marvelled at the miraculous internet displayed on a homely television screen, Professor Hooke and his team wrestled with the mysterious temporal anomaly on the banks of the River Withan. Meanwhile a chattering helicopter circled above, looking for a landing site and for a prisoner to arrest and apprehend for serious crimes or civil offences yet to be defined.

In Trinity College, Cambridge, seemingly infinite streams of quarks, neutrinos and electrons – emanating from, or drawn to, an otherwise unexceptional bramble patch in Lincolnshire, or its displaced owner – arrived, or perhaps tried to leave, depending on the observer's temporal frame of reference. They rushed about in great profusion, in wave-particle surges of energy, impelled by memories of past, or prophecies of future, inertial patterns. They tried desperately to re-create and re-forge the material environment, indeed the entire universe, precisely as it had been 352 years ago.

This included the living form of a paranoid, lugubrious, long-headed genius, who, as Archie's school teacher had taught, was 'quite bright, in his day'.

These fundamental sub-atomic particles (or waves – depending on who was measuring what, where, how and when), finding on arrival that their appointed positions in the universe were already occupied by their 352-years-older identical twins, bounced around in great distress. They grew hotter and hotter with each random collision as they tried to re-install themselves and re-boot the universe as they intended it to be. The laboratory walls were becoming noticeably warmer, despite the damp, cool, spring air.

The few junior staff left on duty while the senior people rushed about the countryside in an old blue Volvo, at first enjoyed opening all the windows and casting aside their Harris-tweed jackets with leather elbow patches. Some hours later, they became anxious as the walls became warmer, and then descended into depressive states as their irresistible anxiety met an immovable wall of helplessness, and a nuclear or electro-magnetic explosion or implosion seemed ever more inevitable.

The junior scientists were greatly relieved when a bright red helicopter, whirring and bucking wildly, sporting intriguingly powerful black symbols and letters, landed in the back yard and eight figures in yellow plastic suits and helmets dashed authoritatively across the small lawn, flourishing an official reel of red and white plastic warning tape. Their heroic images were only slightly tarnished by needing to ask a gardener, caught in a rare moment of repose leaning on his spade, which door they should enter. Also by their consequent about-turn manoeuvre, complicated by having to mouth instructions from inside their helmets, to follow the gardener's pointing finger.

The nuclear authority security team arrived simultaneously with, and so was able to bear witness to, the first manifestation, on the ground floor, of a ghostly, transparent seventeenth-century figure. Although it was attempting to become corporeal, centuries of surface changes ensured that it remained only faintly visible, from time to time and in certain lights, and only from the thighs upwards. This fluxing, and obviously irritated apparition struggling to come into existence, added a psychic phenomenon which further discomfited the scientists, disconcerted the nuclear team and amazed the curious gardener who had followed them in. It completely buggered their belief systems, scared them witless and short-circuited their operating paradigms.

One lab assistant immediately texted an indignant note from her BlackBerry to Professor Richard Dawkins, who had failed or refused to address this kind of thing in *The God Delusion*, his credo of humanism, which unswervingly and religiously denied such arrantly nonsensical occurrences – at least in this universe, the one we all inhabit.

The particles collided. The walls grew warmer. The apparition fluxed and fumed. And the people panicked. A yellow-suited and hooded officer officiously erected little grey poles with black polyethylene bases, stringing reflective red and white tape from pole to pole. This displayed dire warnings and penalties to any who dared to cross the lines, which encouraged everyone to share the illusion, or indeed delusion, that matters were now being brought under control.

🍎

In a small, anonymous council house in Grantham, Isaac felt the subatomic tug-of-war being waged across the centuries – and in his alchemical soul he wondered at it, and in his logical, giant intellect he pondered over it.

7

THE DANGEROUS
NUCLEAR FUGITIVE

'YES! YES! I'VE GOT IT. He said his name was Archie. Archie
Wilkins, I think. Am I right, Godfrey? It was Wilkins, wasn't it?'
Robert Hooke appealed to his colleague.

'It was. Yes. The boy told us his name was Archie Wilkins. And
he introduced the outdoors-looking character with him as er…as
erm…as Isaac Newton.'

One of the nuclear security officers hid a smirk behind his hand.
Another wrote the names carefully in a pocket book.

'Oh! And he said something about Care-in-the-Community,'
added Godfrey reluctantly.

The smirking officer smirked some more. Four other officers
lurked on the edge of the group, fidgeting uncertainly. All six
security officers were armed with pistols.

Professor Hooke turned suddenly on the two nearest men.
'Well, get on your phones. They are on foot. They must be locals.

They must live near here. Find them, man! Find them! This is a crisis – and that lunatic may have some role in it. After all, the coordinates led us straight to him. Get onto it, man! Get onto it! And two of you get over that hill and search Woolsthorpe Manor. Quickly now!'

Grateful for direct orders demanding simple action, the six officers huddled like a rugby scrum for a few seconds. Two broke away and started up the hill and two tapped things into their mobile phones, cupping their hands over the instruments and walking away to quiet positions as they spoke. The other two went to the helicopter and found maps to study.

'Got it, sir! Wilkins lives at 17 Blueberry Avenue on the Clothfield Estate, just a mile or so over there.' He pointed to the south-east. 'The lad lives with his mother – there's no father in evidence. And goes to the local school in Grantham.'

'Drive over with us!' snapped Hooke, indicating the Volvo by the bridge.

'Police are already on their way, sir. I said to hold them and wait for orders.'

'Good. Well I need to see that man again – so let's get going.' He turned back to his colleagues. 'What are the detectors showing, Angela? Is it still transmitting?'

'Yes, Professor. There's still a strong signal coming or going, and it still seems to be linking this location with Cambridge. At least that's the best interpretation I can make for now. It's fluctuating wildly! And it may be growing in strength.'

'See what's happening at the labs. Phone Michael Barlow on his mobile. Come on then. Two officers and we three,' said Hooke, gathering his team with an imperious hand. And he marched off towards the road. The other four followed him, half-walking, half-running to keep up.

Isaac and Archie had switched off the TV, switched off the internet and put away the colourfully illustrated books of war machines – all in tacit deference to Isaac's over-excited nervous system. Isaac stowed Archie's priceless gift of knowledge in a pocket in his greatcoat, hanging in the hall. The sombre man needed a break from the reality of the brave new world he had woken to earlier that day. Archie had made them another cup of tea and found some Long-Life Teacakes, which he had wrestled from their plastic wrappers, toasted and buttered, and which they now silently ate in the lounge, as they drank their tea.

As the elixir of life, the restorative brew, did its magic, Isaac broke the silence. 'All the pictures and sounds have gone. Why, and to where? Where are they now?'

Archie finished a mouthful of teacake. 'They've gone, 'cos I switched it all off.' He paused and thought hard. 'Where they've gone? They don't go nowhere. If it's switched off it can't get any electricity. So it won't show any pictures.'

'The elec-tricity we spoke of before? The same stuff as lightning is made of? The airs that carry the pictures from London?'

'Yes,' nodded Archie. 'And it heats up the kettle to make our tea.'

'And can you, er, switch the elec-tricity on again? Can you control it?'

'Oh, sure I can. I just press this button.'

'Not now, please. And that calls the pictures from London – to this glass?'

'Yeah, probably,' obliged Archie. 'And we call it a screen. The glass. It's a screen.'

'So, the pictures and the sounds are all now in London?'

'I suppose so.'

'And where is the elec-tricity that you summon with that button?'

Archie was fading fast. His head was getting hot. He was stuck. But then inspiration struck, like lightning. 'Yeah! It's in the power station. They make the electricity in a power station and send it down all these wires. Here; look; it comes along these wires, from the power station, to this room. And to all the rooms. And to all the houses. All over the world...' He tailed off, overcome by the enormity of his vision.

His companion was silenced, again.

'But you have to be dead careful with the wires. The electricity is in the wires and if it gets out it can kill you. Stone dead.'

Isaac was alarmed by this. 'Does it leak out of the wires? Into the room? Is it leaking now?'

Archie was flummoxed and exhausted. He was saved by the bell – or rather, by the thunderous sound of a helicopter, its blades thrashing as it was trying but failing to land on the allotments at the back of the houses. Outside the front window, cars were bouncing up onto the pavements. Uniformed people leapt from the cars before they fully stopped. Blue lights flashed authoritatively up and down the street.

Archie raced into the hall, grabbed Isaac's large coat and hat, raced back and out of the kitchen's back door, grabbing his friend's hand on the way. Crouching low, he sneaked along the hedge, followed and copied by Isaac, who was surprisingly nimble for a big man. They then ducked through a child-sized gap into the next garden, under two dense laurel bushes, through another garden hedge, skirting that garden to a brick wall, threw over the coat and hat, scaled the wall, dropped behind a neighbour's garage, ran under an avenue of carefully wired apple trees, through a small gate – and emerged into a dark, concealed corner of allotment sheds and tarpaulins. Home free. It was, after all, Archie's territory.

They slowed their pace and made towards the Norman church and grounds which the town planners had left at the centre of the

Clothfield Estate. Professor Hooke, three nuclear security officers and several lab technicians were bell-ringing at Archie's front-door, uncertain whether the emergency warranted being so impolite and un-English as to break the flimsy door down. The helicopter roared and bucked in the background, its noise blocking all conversation and confusing everyone, before it clawed frantically back up into the sky, unable to land on the allotments. Baffled and frightened by the urban jungle of sheds, barrels, pea-sticks and bamboo tripods, it veered off like an angry gnat and landed on the open field beyond the allotments.

The officials hesitated, wondering what terrible crimes their quarry was accused of. They paused to consider their manners, upbringing and the correct etiquette, appropriate for dealing with suburban subatomic emergencies that might destroy Cambridgeshire. Isaac and Archie escaped into the churchyard, under dense, dark-green yew trees, followed narrow lanes eastwards behind rows of Fifties houses and then strolled out into the wide surrounding countryside.

8

ENTANGLED IN NON-THEORETICAL PHYSICS

The north-facing interior wall of one of the smaller and more ancient research laboratories in Cambridge was getting ever warmer. Alarmingly warm. Dr John Beamish had been summoned from The Rutherford Appleton Laboratories, Oxford, to take charge of the ragged, tired technicians left to wrestle with the disconnected but still mysteriously functioning microscope, computer and particle accelerator. And to explain or to dismiss the (intellectually denied) ephemeral, transparent, fluctuating spectral figure and the terrifyingly active target chambers.

Beamish, with a mobile phone bouncing in his top pocket, was running both hands over the wall and shouting into the phone. 'No, no – it's not the entire wall. It's definitely a patchy effect. Hotter in the centre. Cooler towards the edges of this shape... My guess is, it's about six feet high and three feet or so wide. Yes, yes! We're getting an infrared camera. It's on its way. I'll send the pictures as soon as we have them. What's happening your end? What are those nuclear guys doing?'

On the other end of the phone, his colleague, one of four scientists prowling the streets of Grantham in the old blue Volvo, who was standing up through the sunshine roof to get the maximum signal, needed urgently to pass on the facts with all possible speed, but he hesitated, embarrassed by what he had to say.

'Well, well, Professor Hooke is focused on finding a boy and a man who ran from the spot to where we traced the transmissions… Er, no – no. We found no equipment. Just this, er, tall farmer type and a young boy… Well, Hooke seems to think he might be central to the phenomenon.

'And the transmissions might be thought, by some' – he distanced himself from the scientifically suspect and indeed risible observations – 'to somehow follow or be affected by the presence of this odd fellow… Er, odd?… Well he's dressed like a tramp. Great thick overcoat. Old-fashioned, large hat. Leather boots. Frilly shirt collar. And, er, well, he says his name is, er…ahem…is Isaac Newton.'

There was then what they both perceived as a long, long silence, which was in fact only five seconds. The Volvo crawled on another twenty-five yards and the patch on the laboratory wall warmed by another quarter of a degree centigrade.

'Newton! You said 'Isaac Newton?' repeated Beamish.

The Volvo scientist felt compelled to justify himself. 'And where we found them is just over the hill from Woolsthorpe Manor.' An intake of breath while, at the other end, Beamish made the impossible historical connection. 'In the grounds, in fact… Oh, just an ordinary schoolboy. A lad. A primary school boy. A kid. Hooke dismissed them immediately and they crept away – but now Hooke seems to think they are the key to the whole emergency. He's got a helicopter, police and nuclear security guards – and us –

all hunting for them and… It doesn't make any bloody sense at all. No sense! Nonsense!'

Dr Beamish took in this bizarre information, and paused a moment. 'But then, this whole anomaly doesn't make any sense. It is also nonsensical. I've unplugged everything here. Cut the power to the building. Switched off every damn thing, but these particles keep coming – or going – thick and fast. It's as if Feynman's Time-Independent virtual-particle theories and the ideas of entangled photons, and faster-than-light action-at-a-distance, have suddenly become real. But they can't. They are only illustrative concepts. Scribbles on paper. Not reality. Not real at all!'

Both became silent again.

From inside the car came a shout. 'Look – there they are. Across the field. East of us. Just across the field. Call Hooke. Call Hooke!'

The standing man cut off Beamish and dialled Hooke, as across a huge, ploughed field that was just showing the first blush of the tiny green shoots of spring, the distant figures of Archie and Isaac straddled a fence and melted into a copse where the trees ran along a shallow defile.

Half an hour later, the Atomic Energy Unit's helicopter was directing the rush of highly intelligent, highly motivated and highly equipped personnel across the east field. They were stomping rapidly over deep plough furrows, but they failed to find and intercept the two fugitives.

The shapes on the Cambridge walls were a little warmer, as Beamish and his team pored over astonishing infrared camera images, the stuff of legends that the ambitious physicists would never put their names to. Dr Beamish had a sudden Nobel Prize-worthy, if completely and utterly illogical, insight.

He abruptly commandeered the nearest blackboard, scattering less determined academics like skittles. He reached for his scientific calculator that could juggle formulae with twenty variables and values up to the power of fifty, took out his notebook and pen, and scribbled and scrawled symbols with feverish concentration and energy. It was a process that only a hero or a fool would dare to interrupt.

As Beamish worked frantically, the monitors on the computers and cyclotron beeped and glowed and (impossibly, as they were switched off) displayed steadily increasing dangerous levels of energetic particles spiralling through the system.

'Get Hooke on the phone. Get Hooke NOW!' hollered Dr Beamish. A few moments later, one of his colleagues thrust a phone into his face – between his perspiring brow, his staring eyes, and the chalk, ink, calculator and paper.

'Hooke? Can you hear me? Hooke? – yes – you are right, man. You must get that tramp – that Newton fellow, AND the boy. Both of them. Yes, both of them. And bring them here. You must fly them here as quickly as possible… Why? My theory? Is now the time for explanations? I think I've got it – but it's beyond the pale. We'll be blackballed worldwide. Can't tell the scientific community. Mustn't tell the scientific community.'

But Professor Robert Hooke, steeped in scientific and academic caution couldn't let himself be the instigator of an even more intensive search, which was bound to create a media storm, without understanding why. He would rather die and take the whole of Cambridgeshire with him than be exposed to the slings, arrow-shots, cannonballs, poisoned darts, scorn and derision of his peers. He would not lose his international reputation over a Care-in-the-Community deranged hobo and a commonplace ten-year-old lad – whatever the threat to mankind.

He answered Beamish calmly, firmly and quietly. 'I need the

theory, Beamish. I can't mobilise more forces unless I know the reason behind it. Those two have disappeared again. Quickly, man – what's your theory?'

Beamish, sweating freely in the glow of the flashing red lights, saw the logic of Hooke's position. He took a deep breath and threw caution to the winds.

'Your Isaac Newton fella is Schrödinger's cat. He is in a state of superposition. He is both here and not here. He is transcending several Space-Time frames. Schrödinger was wrong – his cat can be both dead and alive in the box. Einstein was wrong to reject entanglement. Feynman was right about time reversal. The Copenhagen conclusions are right. Quantum particles do exist outside time, in all possible waveforms, until an intelligent observer collapses the waveform, and the object manifests in our reality.'

Hooke responded even more slowly as he juggled Beamish's ideas. And the atomic-particle energies crept nearer to a critical explosion – or implosion. 'Why the boy, Beamish? Why should I bring the boy?'

Beamish was also close to exploding, imploding or just weeping with frustration. He was, at this moment, the only person on Earth who could see the pieces of the puzzle and intuit how they probably fitted together. And, if he was right, time – Cambridge and Grantham Present Time – was fast running out. He had to stick his precious academic neck even further out, on the basis of a few minutes of unverified, untested, wild ideas and calculations.

'I think the boy is the intelligent observer. I think he channels the waveform. The Isaac Newton waveforms. I think he is the television aerial that captures the coherent waves and he is the TV set that displays them as images in our world. The boy has no disbelief to suspend. He believes in the spectre, the manifestation, and acts as the catalyst. I… I…can't speculate more without evidence. This is madness.'

Hooke was silent for what seemed like minutes. He tacitly agreed it was madness – and he'd rather Beamish, not he, was pronounced insane by the scientific community. But time truly was pressing. So he pressed on.

'So,' he proceeded cautiously, dropping his tone to a conspiratorial whisper, 'if we, er, eliminated the boy, would the problem vanish up its own time anomaly?'

'No! No! I don't think so. I don't know. But we can't take the chance. If the boy went…' Beamish didn't want to explore where the boy might go, '…and took Newton with him…'

Both men winced at the crazy assumption they had to allow into their discourse.

'…Then how would we switch the particle stream off?'

Hooke didn't get this. Beamish had made a logical leap, deeper into scientific heresy and insanity, that Hooke hadn't followed. 'What! What are you talking about? Spit it out, man! Spit it out! Why can't you switch it all off?'

Beamish took another deep breath and swallowed his pride, before spitting out this part of his theory. Any hesitation he would certainly have had in disseminating his theory in, say, the Senior Common Room in normal times, was smashed aside by the fear induced by the instrument readings. The instrument panels on the unplugged, switched-off machines were approaching critical atomic-energy thresholds.

'I think,' he said, with deep conviction, 'I think that Newton, our laboratory, where Newton worked, and that ruined library where he appeared are all out of our present time frame. We can't switch them off because they are in a different space-time frame. They are cycling through all possible waveforms – as is your tramp – and, I think, that only he can match the space-time region and switch the bloody things off!'

This last sentence he spat out, as demanded of him, warning

Hooke to back off and pay heed.

But Hooke wasn't easily cowed. He insisted on pondering one more vital piece of the puzzle. 'One more moment, Beamish. I just need one more explanation, before I call up the Royal Air Force and the Royal Marines and the whole damned Household Cavalry to track a tramp and a child. Where from and how are these energetic particles or waves being generated? Backwards or forwards in time – whichever bloody way they are flowing; what the hell are they?'

Beamish clamped his hands to his forehead, gave a despairing gasp, and abandoned all past investment and future hope in his reputation as a man of science. 'I think,' he muttered bravely, 'based on what I'm seeing on these infrared images of the wall, that Newton worked here, in this room, for some time. The infrared shows the image of a man in the wall.'

'And...?' demanded Hooke.

'And I guess that he worked in that ruin you found, on the same experiments, on his Optiks and Gravity, for many months or even years,' Beamish carried on with no further prompting. 'And Newton travelled back and forth to Woolsthorpe regularly, over a couple of years.'

Hooke's total silence demanded more. Beamish obliged. 'I think these transmissions are of entangled photons and other particles, not just from one moment of entanglement but of split-second after split-second, over maybe years of contact, organised by or coalescing around Newton's concentration, which became part of the structures – of the walls, of the wainscoting, of the glazing, of the floors; trillions of trillions of subatomic particles in relationship and harmony. And something, some event, I don't know what, yet, possibly connected in a type of Bose-Einstein-Condensate – I haven't had time to think about it – triggered them to flow, like an electric current or telephone signal, from magnetic field, to current, to field, to current...'

'Yes, yes, Beamish! I get the picture,' Hooke interrupted harshly, reminding them both by his tone that they were about to be annihilated in a black hole, atomic fusion or atomic fission – and it didn't really matter which one it was. 'And I assume that you think that these flows are also circumventing our exact space-time frame – so we cannot intercept them?'

'Precisely,' breathed Beamish. 'Or something along those lines. Only the phantom of Isaac – Schrödinger's cat – who inhabits both here and there, past and present, then and now – can intervene in the process.'

'And he, or it, needs the boy, Archie Wilkins, to manifest in our world?' added Hooke.

'Yes – we need this cat to be kept very much alive.'

'I'll call out the troops,' said Hooke.

9

ELECTRICALLY CURIOUS

As the warm afternoon wore on, reminding both Isaac and
Archie that it was fast approaching teatime, Isaac's nervous system,
battered by future-shock, became sufficiently restored for his
scientific curiosity to re-emerge.

Even here, on one of the local children's unmarked, elusive,
efficient rural pathways that paid no heed to *Private Keep Out* or
No Trespassing signs – this one leading to a City banker's weekend,
exclusive, peaceful and well-stocked *No Fishing* pond, set in
woodland in a delightful managed estate – even here, the modern
world made its presence known. In the hazy blue sky, visible
between the green-tipped branches, was a five-mile-high con-trail
from a four-engine passenger jet ploughing silently eastwards
towards the North Sea and the continent of Europe. Isaac stopped
and stared in astonishment at the sight. To his left, beyond the
wood, also glimpsed through the unfolding spring buds, marched

a line of seventy-foot-high metal pylons, carrying eight electrical high-tension wires; looped cables as thick as a man's wrist, transporting lethal charges of energy to or from the south. Was the power coming, or going? And how? And why? In the distance, traffic thrummed and throbbed along minor and trunk roads.

They arrived at a small clearing by the pond and sat on tree roots at the edge. Isaac contained his dozens of questions. Some would answer themselves. Some he could eventually answer himself. And the rest he would put to the lad, employing their shared, developing language, and tease out the meanings and logic from Archie's obliging, if sometimes fanciful replies.

The wash of the jet-airliner's booming engines startled Isaac into voicing one of his pressing questions.

Archie was very sure of his ground. 'Oh, the noise,' he replied. 'That's the plane, up there, breaking the sound barrier. First, we see it – like that,' he said, pointing upwards, 'then after comes the sound – 'cos the plane's going faster than sound.'

'And what speed is that? How fast does sound travel – today?'

Archie paused for thought. ''Bout five hundred miles an hour, I think.' Then inspiration struck him. 'It's like lightning, you see. You get the big flash of light, then after, you hear the thunder. And if you count the seconds, it says how far off the lightning is.'

'Lightning in a thunderstorm?' Isaac ventured. He, too, had counted such seconds.

'Yeah. Just like that. You can see the plane before you hear it.'

The world's greatest genius considered the information, correlating it with the unbelievable speed of light he'd read on the internet at Archie's home. 'How far away is that, er, plane?'

'Five miles high. Just as high as Everest.'

Isaac ignored the tempting diversion into 'Everest'. 'And I'll warrant, many miles away from here,' he murmured. He blinked at his mental calculation of the probable size of the distant speck;

blinked at the scale of this mechanical bird. Talking more to himself than to Archie, he continued, 'If light does move that fast, the plane in the sky need not be travelling faster than sound to account for the gap. Though, also, it may be.' He turned to Archie and spoke slowly, 'The…plane need not be travelling faster than sound to account for the time gap between us seeing and hearing it. The gap can be caused by the difference between sound-speed and light-speed'.

Archie nodded amiably. But he had more pressing issues to discuss. 'I'm hungry,' he said.

Isaac was also aware of his need to eat, but he had no clear course to help them find food. He was a stranger lost in a familiar land.

'There's a Post Office Stores in the village, over there.' Archie pointed east. 'With a tea shop. But I've only got this money. Not really enough for two of us.' Archie took a purse out of his back pack and displayed the three pounds fifty his mum had spared for him to spend in Skegness.

Isaac rummaged in the pockets of his greatcoat and pulled out a small leather pouch and a larger wooden box. 'I have my purse with several gold guineas and silver shillings. And I have my tinder-box with matches. And I'm sure I have a line in here.' He delved deeper into inside coat pockets and came out with a neatly coiled, fine string with a hook nestled in the middle. 'We could take a fish – and cook it.'

Archie did a swift calculation of his own and set aside the entertaining and enticing thought of a campfire, and of poaching with such simple tools. 'It'd take a long time – and I'm hungry now. But if you've got some money as well, we'd get to the shop in about ten minutes. Or we could go home. About half an hour to get home.'

'In this Time,' queried Isaac, 'do you use shillings and guineas for payment?'

'I've heard of shillings; they're old coins – but don't know any guineas,' said Archie. 'What do they look like?'

Isaac dipped into his purse and showed Archie a golden guinea alongside a silver shilling. Archie eyed them dubiously. 'Nope – they're too foreign. Shops would spot them, and won't take them,' he said decisively.

Isaac sighed, and Archie's shoulders slumped. 'So, we'd better go home,' he said.

'Professor Hooke and his officers will be waiting for us. But perhaps they can help me return to my own time and place,' mused Isaac. 'Or I could catch some fish?'

Archie and Isaac chewed over this thought in silence. From Archie's view the options were either to starve to death in the woods, wait an eternity for Isaac to catch and cook a fish – or go home for tea, and be arrested.

Isaac's choices were far more complex. He was hungry – but that could wait. He was time-shifted, into this fascinating if alarming future, and at root he did want to go home; he was aware of homesickness and did not want to be stranded far from his familiar haunts and habits. He had been transported against all reason and without his permission; a transport which might affect him physically. Would time-travel make him ill? He was aware, at a subconscious, dream-like level that he was in two, perhaps three places simultaneously; with tremendous energies linking and flowing between the locations – all focused on his body and mind. His intellect was aware that these energies, these forces, were growing exponentially, to dangerous levels. Professor Hooke had not been exaggerating his fear of the consequences if the energies were not contained. And Archie's face had confirmed the fear of, of...what? Of some sort of explosion. A 'nuclear' blast – which Isaac had connected to the Greeks' 'atoms', the smallest indivisible particles, the building blocks of all things. And he had connected the atoms to lightning bolts of elec-tricity; immense bursts of fire from the sky, which modern people had somehow tamed for myriad uses. He felt a responsibility to assist Hooke's team to tame the invisible powers, which he could feel coursing through…no, not just through his body, but through his being, his very essence. Might he disintegrate, be torn apart by these mysterious powers?

Most of all, however, overmastering all else – he was curious. He wanted to know. In this future-scape of miraculous technologies, he was greedy for knowledge. Greedy for scientific miracles and explanations that he could take back three hundred years to his college and colleagues. But at what cost? And at what risk?

And so, sitting by the banker's fishpond, he pondered.

10

MILITARY ABDUCTION

ROBERT HOOKE HAD used his credentials with the Nuclear Authority to contact the Royal Marines Fleet Protection Group with responsibility for nuclear submarines. The Naval Nuclear Propulsion Programme provided training for all such personnel, including this special Royal Marines commando force which was tasked with protecting Britain's nuclear weapons. Commodore Bruce MacDonald heard Hooke's strange story, quickly got the picture and mobilised men, women, machines and vehicles to take over the search for a tall man, answering to the name 'Isaac Newton' and a wee lad, aged ten, known as Archie Wilkins.

Commodore MacDonald sent experts by helicopter to Woolsthorpe, to Cambridge and to the Wilkins' home – where they set up a search centre. Surely, the two absconding 'persons of interest' could not elude capture much longer. The nuclear scientists conferred with Professor Hooke and his team, who took up positions outside 17 Blueberry Avenue on the Clothfield Estate, effectively surrounding the house, front and back. Signal-tracking devices showed the main stream of energetic particles circulating between Cambridge and Grantham – and a diverted lesser stream pointing at the local woods – which dissipated and faded out under the dense trees. But it gave a clear direction.

'That's him. It's them. I'm sure of it,' said Hooke, pointing at the screen.

Archie's mother, Marjorie Wilkins, returned home early from her job-share as receptionist at the local yoga and alternative therapy centre, carrying a plastic bag of groceries. She was both worried and thrilled by all the attention, particularly so when TV crews turned up and tried to park large vans with large dishes and aerials between the military and police vehicles. The security squads shooed them and the rest of the media away, behind a red-and-white banded plastic tape barrier.

Nobody tried to stop her entering the house. She was clearly the owner or occupier and could freely exercise her natural rights. But, equally, no one tried to reassure her about her son – whom she quickly learned was being urgently sought by all these uniformed and lab-coated and plain-clothed officers.

'Where is my Archie?' she asked. 'He's supposed to be on the school trip to Skegness,' she added.

And it suddenly occurred to the searchers that she might know, or guess, the lad's location.

Robert Hooke wound down a long call to his publishers. 'Yes – that's the heart of my theory. You've got it. It's all on tape, is it? I want you to contact my I.P. lawyers, Hardwick and Sedgemore, and get them working on establishing my exclusive rights immediately. Right away. It's an important new and unique contribution to quantum physics – which others might try to claim to credit for... Yes... Yes, it's certainly Nobel Prize stuff. Absolute cutting edge...

71

Title?... Yes, I have got a working title for it. It's 'The Phenomena of Feynman Temporal and Anachronistic Radiation Cycling, Transmitted between Locations, of Entangled Sub-Atomic High-Energy Particles, Manifesting Prior-Established Identity Patterns and Increasing Exponentially in Power – by Professor Robert Hooke, Head of Research into Inertial and Field Energies, Cavendish Laboratories, University of Cambridge'... What? Oh, collaborators... No... No, it's entirely my own work. And strictly confidential. But I'll probably allow a credit line to an Oxford chap – a Doctor Beamish, who I asked to check some of the mathematics for me.

OK? Good. Ask Hardwick's to call me on this number as soon as they start on the filing.'

Satisfied with his fleet-footed piracy and plagiarism for the moment, Hooke turned his attention to Archie's mother, a trim thirty-year-old, who was in the kitchen waiting for the kettle to boil, with her expression cycling rapidly between looking extremely worried and highly excited. Hooke entered the room and wedged himself at the small table.

'Aha. Now, Mrs Wilkins,' he began.

'What have you done with my Archie?' she snapped at him, as he tried and failed to switch from portentous departmental head and celebrated TV science don into an empathetic, caring investigator.

'I? I haven't done anything with your Archie. He's quite safe, I think. He's over in the woods beyond the church,' said Hooke, gesturing vaguely through the glass in the back door.

'Then what's all these police and soldiers doing here? And the TV vans? And you! What are you doing here? In my house?'

Professor Hooke changed tack and decided to be authoritative, but calm. 'Madam,' he said, rising from his chair. Unfortunately, his thighs jerked the table as he stood, spilling the milk jug and sugar bowl onto the floor. Archie's mum reacted with a tea-towel and dishcloth, and an admonishing glare. As she knelt down, he spluttered, 'I'm so sorry. Excuse me. So clumsy of me. But, but, there is a national emergency. A nuclear emergency. A major event. And I'm in charge of fixing it – of making the country safe.'

The shock on Mrs Wilkins' face told him he'd said too much. He may have rescued his dignity and communicated his elevated position – but he had blown the gaff.

The sincerity of Hooke's tone and expression left no room for doubt.

'Oh! Oh my God!' she whispered. 'Then, then, what's my Archie got to do with it all? Where is he? What have you done with him?' Marjorie Wilkins' voice began to rise. Hysteria was a few seconds away.

'He is safe. He is not at fault. He is over in the woods. He is with a man we want to talk with. A man who we think can help us. A safe man. A nice man. A clever man.' Hooke extended his hands in a placatory, reassuring manner.

Then, more calmly, Hooke added, 'Your son, er, Archie, is not in danger. But I do have an emergency. Time is short, Mrs Wilkins. Very short. I need to know precisely, exactly, where Archie might have taken this man, this friend. We assume, our instruments indicate, that they were here, in this house. Does he have a favourite place – a den – a playground – over there? They are on foot. Walking.'

Again, Hooke pointed out of the window, across the little back garden, and he watched her intently, insisting on her attention and an immediate answer.

Marjorie was frightened but a little calmer. Her brain shifted from on-the-verge-of-hysteria mode to how-can-I-help-Archie?

'He…he likes to go to the Post Office Stores in the old village to buy crisps and things. About a mile beyond the church. That way.' She pointed north-east, as had Hooke. 'But, but, he hasn't much money. Only what I gave him for the school trip. Some pocket money to spend in Skegness. But that's where he might have gone.'

Hooke was at the back door before she finished her sentence. He summoned two uniformed men, Royal Marine Commandos, and in a few words, had them consulting GPS screens and sent them running in the direction of the Post Office Stores to find and hold Isaac Newton and the boy Archie Wilkins.

Archie's mum was equally quick. Before Hooke could close the door, Marjorie was out in the small garden, through the first hedge, and moving at high speed – just a few yards behind the heavily equipped commandos. They were battle-ready, super-fit, fully trained, fighting men, the best-of-the-best, on an urgent, top-secret mission. She was a mature, ferocious mother, a tigress, instinctively protecting her cub, in her own territory. The soldiers had little chance against such imperatives of nature. The odds were stacked against them. Marjorie passed them in the fast lane, and they hurried along behind her, under the yew trees in the churchyard – all three making for the old village. Marjorie reached into her jacket pocket and took out a mobile phone.

Outside the front door of Archie's house, at the same moment, a senior policewoman, also a mother, had a sudden inspiration. 'The lad. Archie. The boy. He'll likely have a mobile phone. They all have phones, now.'

Overheard by a gaggle of scientists, detectives, journalists and Royal Marine commandos, she unwittingly triggered a frantic flurry of calls – enquiries to various central licit and illicit telephone directories, contacted in a few seconds. 'Yes – Wilkins W I L K I N S, Blueberry Avenue, Clothfield… Grantham… Yes, Grantham.'

Commodore MacDonald had landed by helicopter in Clothfield ten minutes earlier. Now, displaying the effortless superiority of military telecoms, he was already on a direct line to GCHQ, Government Communications Head Quarters, in Cheltenham –

who, though they never, ever, ever spied on any UK citizens without a Court Order signed by a High Court Judge and countersigned by the Secretary of State, on this one single nuclear emergency occasion, gave the commodore Archie's phone number, which initially had been his mum's number. They disclosed his exact Ordnance Survey, real-time map reference and offered immediate satellite surveillance of the elusive boy. 'But only this once. Under the threat of a nuclear incident'. They also offered a complete record of all the conversations, internet searches and journeys for the phone, since its manufacture.

MacDonald opted for satellite surveillance and sent the search coordinates to the two commandos, who, burdened with full field kit, were trailing in the wake of the unencumbered, rapidly advancing Marjorie Wilkins – who was speaking to her son on her mobile phone.

'Archie! Archie! Where are you? Everybody is looking for you. What have you done? What are you up to? Are you all right?' she panted, still moving fast.

Two hundred miles above the blue sky, in the black vacuum of space, barely imagined by Isaac, a government communications satellite slowly adjusted its cameras and made minute course adjustments as GCHQ directed it to survey Grantham.

'I'm OK,' grumbled Archie, disgruntled at being checked-up on by his mum – like a small child. 'I'm all right, Mum. They're not after me. It's Isaac they want. I'm just helping him.' Then, thinking she might have some view or advice if he shared his concerns, he cupped his hand over the phone, turned away from Isaac and added in a low voice, 'He's a sort of time-traveller, and a bit lost, and, he's probably, ya know, Care-in-the-Community or something.'

The news that her only son was in the company of a mental patient being hunted by the police, the army and assorted boffins did nothing to reassure Marjorie, but she had little breath to spare, so she confined herself to the main priority. 'Are you at the shop? At the post office? I'm nearly there. And there are two soldiers following behind, with guns!'

'No – we're not in the village,' said Archie. 'We're in the woods; near that new place, Cherry Copse.' He carefully glossed over the fact that they were trespassing in the middle of the banker's exclusive weekend grounds. ''Bout a mile, I think, from the shop.'

'Meet me at the post office, Archie. Meet me in the village.' Marjorie cut the call and hurried on. Twenty yards behind and unseen by Marjorie, the two commandos veered left off the path, scaled a stout new fence and dropped into a charming cultivated woodland.

They made straight through the trees towards Archie's location. A large military helicopter appeared and chattered overhead. High, high above, the satellite's cameras manoeuvred with clicks and whirs as a previously bored spy, at a desk in Cheltenham, excitedly zoomed in on the spot where Archie's phone, though switched off, was silently broadcasting its coordinates – just as its Californian designers and Chinese manufacturers had intended. To be fair, the design engineers were simply following orders – secret and confidential orders – from the Pentagon, via Homeland Security, that all mobile-phone circuits must include tracking signals.

Isaac, sitting next to Archie, was too astounded by the phone to take in the meaning of the one-sided conversation. But as Archie folded it and slipped it back into a pocket, Isaac shook himself and stood. He had come to a decision.

'I believe we should meet Professor Hooke. I am of the opinion that he and I can be of help to one another. Let us go into the village.'

Archie struggled to his feet – tired and hungry, but re-energised by the excitement, by his mother's anxieties, by the helicopter overhead and by the indefinable possibilities of the rapidly unfolding events. Not least, he was excited by the scientists' fear of a nuclear explosion – which, Archie knew, might wipe out the whole country. Now that would really be worth seeing. This was definitely better than the school trip to Skegness.

Isaac brushed his coat, straightened his hat and they made their way across the gardens to the eastern boundary. They climbed the fence with some difficulty and dropped down into a flat twenty-acre field, still in its drab winter colours and old stubble.

They took a few steps into the open. Two Royal Marine commandos jumped from the fence behind them and a large Royal Navy twin-rotor helicopter dropped noisily down from the sky to land just fifty yards ahead of them. Commodore MacDonald and Professor Hooke leapt from the aircraft, followed by two WRENs and three more male commandos – who ducked under the whirling blades and marched towards Archie and Isaac.

Again, overcome by future-shock, Isaac Newton sank to the ground and sat heavily, pulling his greatcoat around him. Archie took in the whole scene with huge pleasure. Wait till he told his pals about this.

Robert Hooke looked even more tense than he had been at lunchtime, as he peered fiercely at an electronically hardened military-scanner and screen in his hand. It told him that the dangerous energies were indeed growing exponentially, with unpredictable peaks and troughs in transmission. The main stream still swarmed to and from Woolsthorpe and Cambridge, with a side swirl that swept in a wide curling band to…exactly where they were standing.

The commodore leaned over and shouted in Hooke's ear; pointing at Isaac. The noise, turmoil and dust from the helicopter blades made conversation difficult.

'We need them both – both the man and the boy. Don't split them up. Keep them together,' shouted Hooke, reinforcing his message with hand signals.

MacDonald leaned over again and said something about Archie's age and his mother. 'We haven't time,' shouted Hooke. 'No time – we must get them to Cambridge now! Immediately!' The commodore used hand signals to have the marines bundle the two captives into the helicopter, part-hauling Isaac, as his legs seemed to have given way, and he was on the edge of fainting.

Then he waved a WREN aside, away from the noise. 'Listen, sergeant – his mother's name is Marjorie Wilkins. She'll be at the post office – just across these fields. Down that lane. Stay with her and keep in touch with me.'

'Yes, sir! What can we tell her about the emergency? Is it a secret operation?' asked Sergeant Mary Bullock RN.

MacDonald frowned, and sighed, 'I wish I knew sergeant. I wish I knew. I'd like to know what the hell is happening. Keep off the science. But the press is here already – so there has to be a story. Just stick to the basics. Taking her boy to Cambridge. Perfectly safe. He's helping us communicate with...with...Isaac Newton – so-called. A bit strange in the head, but clever. Whom he's befriended. All perfectly safe and hunky dory. Take his mum home. Keep the press off her.'

'Yes, sir.'

'I'll phone as soon as we have a coherent tale to tell. I'll get the PR guys on to it. Must go.'

He ran to the aircraft and within minutes it was airborne; full of soldiers, sailors, bewildered scientists, a beaming Archie and an ashen-faced Isaac, who was kindly squashed between two huge and supportive marines, with his face buried in his hands – and his ears muffled with a scarf and earphones.

The marines instantly recognised battlefield traumatic stress syndrome when they saw it and they silently administered comradely Care-in-the-Community.

11

EXPLOSIVE LESSONS

'I CAN SEE THE CHURCH. And there's our house and our school. I can see everything!'

Archie's excited commentary, obviously fearless, the reassuring relaxed bulk of the Marines and, most insistent, Isaac's burning curiosity, provided the courage and strength, despite the nerve-jangling noise and vibrations, for him to peek through his fingers. He wisely looked first at his fellow passengers, familiars in this bewildering future-time and terrifying place. They all looked unafraid, unconcerned and preoccupied with normal life. Isaac risked glancing out of a window.

'Aaaaaaaghhh!' he screamed silently. His mind raced – for the zillionth time that day; his first day out of time – as he computed the distance to the ground, calculated the helicopter's speed compared to fluffy white clouds in the blue of the sky and, against all logic, he tried to haul his feet, legs and torso UP by sheer willpower. Vertigo threatened. Panic threatened. Madness threatened.

'You hungry, lad?' asked one of the nuclear submariners.

'Yeah – I'm dead hungry. We missed lunch and tea,' said Archie, including Isaac with a nod.

The sailor took a box from his pack. He hauled the lid off and passed a fat ham sandwich to Archie. He nudged Isaac, who despite his alarmed, near-insane, staring eyes, recognised what he was being offered – and accepted a large sandwich of ham and cheese with tomatoes.

'I am indebted to you, kind sir,' Isaac managed to gasp.

The sailor looked confused.

''E means thanks,' interpreted Archie. 'He talks a bit old-fashioned. A bit funny. Care-in-the-Community, I think,' added Archie in his stage whisper. 'But this is good. We've not really eaten all day.'

'We were told to look after you. And I've got a boy myself. So we thought to grab some from the canteen. There's plenty more. What's goin' on? What's the panic all about? Who are you two?'

Isaac was mid-bite, so Archie fielded the question. 'I'm Archie Wilkins and this is my friend, Isaac Newton. He's a time-traveller'.

The sailor would have laughed; except that half of Her Majesty's Armed Forces had been put on full alert to find these two. This was a serious matter. He nodded dumbly.

Archie ploughed on. 'And he invented gravity – before – when he was younger – back then.'

Isaac was too occupied by munching his sandwich to correct matters.

'And we're going to stop a nuclear explosion – in Cambridge, I think. I think it's Cambridge.'

'Ah! So that's why we're here. We are nuclear weapons specialists.'

Isaac had swallowed his mouthful and was fiercely focused on what the sailor said. 'Please explain to me – if you would – what is a nuclear weapon and what is a nuclear explosion.'

The sailor took in Isaac's greatcoat, his long hair, long face and high boots, and gave a quiet sigh. But he also noted the strange man's steady, intelligent gaze – and Archie, nodding reassuringly at his side. He sighed again, willing to explain but – where on earth to start?

'He's all right,' Archie encouraged him. 'He's quite bright, really.'

'But he doesn't know much about atoms,' Archie said with conviction.

Isaac took another bite of his sandwich. The sailor, with sudden determination, plunged into tuition mode.

'Well. What's the biggest explosion you know of?'

Isaac chewed thoughtfully. 'I recall a small keg of gunpowder, for the cannons celebrating the King's birthday with a salute, in London, near The Tower.'

The sailor nodded.

'I was fifty yards away – and a spark must have fallen into it. It exploded with a tremendous noise. And a flash. It killed several soldiers. And knocked many people off their feet. Even shielded by the crowd and half a field away – I felt the blast – and was deafened for some minutes.'

The sailor looked at him curiously, but he knew that Isaac was reliving a real – at least, real to him – and powerful experience.

'Well, we've developed far more powerful explosives since then. Dynamite, TNT, plastic explosives, and liquid explosives like nitro-glycerine. Far more powerful than gunpowder.'

Isaac raised his eyebrows enquiringly.

'Yes – many times more powerful. The biggest bombs we used in the last war.'

Isaac shook his head – but meaning he wanted the man to continue.

'Well, in the last war, we made huge bombs and measured

them in tons of TNT. Its chemical name is trinitrotoluene – and it's about one and a half times stronger than gunpowder. Your powder keg would weigh no more than, say, ten kilograms – twenty pounds. We dropped a bomb in the war that weighed ten thousand kilograms – it was called Grand-slam.'

Isaac had done the maths. 'So, your big bomb was one thousand five hundred times more powerful than the gunpowder keg?'

'Yes.'

'My God! And a nuclear bomb?'

'Phew! The first nuclear bomb used in war, dropped on a city called Hiroshima – was equivalent to twenty thousand tons of TNT – about thirty thousand tons of your gunpowder. And that was a small one by today's standards. Killed more than a hundred and fifty thousand people.'

Isaac was aghast. 'Thirty thousand TONS of gunpowder? One hundred and fifty thousand people killed?'

'Yep! The whole city was wiped out – "Not a stone standing on a stone", as the Bible says. And that was a small bomb. Today's bombs are many times more destructive. But the nuclear explosives, the plutonium and so on, weigh only about one hundred kilos.'

'Kilos? Remind me.'

'Ah, Yes. Do you work in pounds? About two hundred pounds.'

Isaac was silent, his face grave. Archie had watched the exchange as if at a tennis match. He, too, was silenced by the enormity of it all. The thunder of the helicopter engine and blades encompassed them and the other passengers. Isaac was lost in thought, looking out and down but no longer afraid of falling out of the sky. His emotions were suspended under the assault of imagining a nuclear explosion and its terrible death toll. His curiosity restored his voice, as if speaking from the depths. He didn't need to ask how the bomb was delivered – from his vantage point in the flying helicopter he had figured out that it would be dropped from the sky.

'How can anything – so little of anything – not much more than a well-fed man, have that much explosive power?'

The submariner hauled himself back from the gravesides of thousands of innocent but damned souls and tackled the explanation, guessing at Isaac's level of knowledge. 'Do you know how gunpowder explodes?'

'Hmmm. I think so. I apply a flame and the powder burns very quickly. If it's spread out in a line, the fire runs from speck to speck. If it's tightly contained, it bursts from the container. It explodes. It is the speed of combustion that governs its explosive power; I would warrant.'

'Yeah. That's it. And the more powerful the material, the faster it combusts. Burns,' he added for Archie's benefit. 'Well, the plutonium and…well, never mind…other heavy metals that are radioactive,' – Isaac blinked but did not interrupt – 'they burn very, very, very fast – and so they explode very, very, very violently. We call it nuclear fission. It's a chain reaction.' Isaac, and Archie, learning from Isaac, stayed silent, demanding more information.

'Do you know of atoms?'

Isaac and Archie nodded. 'Greek,' said Isaac. 'The smallest pebbles that form all matter.'

'OK. But atoms are not the smallest. They're made from dozens of all sorts of smaller particles, pebbles, all packed together in the middle of them. In the nucleus.'

'Ahhha,' breathed Isaac.

'…And all tied in by nuclear-forces – immensely strong forces – glue, that keeps them together. Tiny, tiny forces. The strongest glue on earth, in the universe, that makes them stick together.' He looked to Isaac to check he was following. 'Your gunpowder – the burning gunpowder – breaks chemical forces – chemical bonds.'

Isaac, an alchemist, nodded cautiously, knitting this information to what his experiments had taught him.

'It's just a fire, really. A very fast fire – but still just a fire – that breaks down the chemicals and releases what's gone into them – what's made them. In a flash of light. The fire lets the sunshine out.'

'Don't be daft,' protested Archie. 'Locked up sunshine?'

'Yep – whenever you burn some twigs, you release the energy that's gone into them. Water and sunshine mostly – and a few trace elements like carbon.' The sailor smiled mischievously, as Archie wrestled with the idea of burning water.

Isaac flicked his fingers, indicating the narrative should move on.

The sailor took a deep breath and soldiered – or sailed – on. 'When fire breaks down, say, wood, or gunpowder, it releases the energy that held it all together, but it leaves smoke, steam and ash. Fire doesn't break up all the elements things are made of.' Archie and Isaac listened intently 'But! But! – when you break up the elements themselves – at the nuclear level – at the smallest, very, very, very tiny level inside those atoms – you release ALL the energy that's been holding it together – that's formed it. And that stuff turns out to be light. Photons. Electrons. And other bits – which explode in a great flash of light and electricity – that heats the air – that makes a thunderclap. And – if you look at the light – it'll burn out your eyes.' He paused for his two students to catch up. And he took another deep breath.

Isaac did his impatient hand flick. Archie stared.

'It's the thunderclap – the air expanding – that flattens buildings and trees and people. The light burns everything. And it all comes from the energy locked up inside the atoms. It's E equals MC squared. Einstein.'

'Aha! That man again,' mused Isaac. 'The speed of light, multiplied by itself – isn't that what your Inter-Net on your Tele-Vision told us, Master Archie?'

'Oh yeah,' said Archie confidently. 'We know all about that. Me and Isaac.'

The nuclear specialist blinked in surprise. 'You've learned a lot in a short time...Professor Newton.'

Isaac acknowledged the courtesy of his title, inclining his head. 'I have an excellent tutor.'

Archie grinned.

'But,' pressed Isaac, 'how does the energy get into the atoms?'

Everyone in the cabin, including the Marines flanking Isaac, leaned in to hear the answer.

'We don't know. Nobody knows that. We can explode it out, but we can't put it back in again.'

'Humpty-Dumpty had a great fall,' murmured Isaac thoughtfully.

'We are about to land,' announced the cabin speaker.

12

ISAAC MEETS HIS GHOST

AS THEY STARTED to leave the helicopter, the thrashing noise of the blades invaded the cabin, and Isaac grabbed the sailor's arm. 'Pray, do excuse me, sir,' he shouted, 'but, how can we be involved in a nuclear event? I take it that there is no bomb? Yet Professor Hooke, who has arrested us, is terrified that such an event is about to happen. Indeed, that it is already occurring. And I am central to it?'

'I really don't know. I don't get it. Don't understand it. You'll have to ask Hooke!'

Isaac nodded. The group, instinctively ducking under the swirling blades, yards above their heads, crossed a wide lawn and made for a set of steps, leading to an ancient door, into an ancient, distinguished and revered college building.

Isaac stopped on the steps. The escort piled up behind him. His mouth hung open. He gawped up at the stonework.

'This,' he gasped, 'this is my college. Much changed, but it is my college. This is Trinity. It is Trinity College.'

Behind old diamond-paned glass windows, in shadowy corridors, peering round doorjambs, lurked dusty, suspicious, cynical dons, tutors and college officers. They were well-concealed; to avoid any slightest chance, any possible slur on their intellects, logic and international reputations suggesting that they for one moment believed this peculiar man, this theatrical figure, to be who or what he claimed to be. 'And yet,' whispered one whimsically inclined professor of ancient languages to a contemptuous, crusty mathematician, 'He does look remarkably like his, I mean like the, portrait in the dining hall, does he not?'

The mathematician responded with a dismissive snort. 'What do you expect? Of course, they'll have picked a look-alike.'

The ancient languages don was struck dumb; mute. Discretion was certainly the better part of valour in this risible new field of alleged time-travel. They both melted back into the darkness as the helicopter party strode after Professor Hooke, through ancient stone quadrangles – towards the laboratory that housed the rogue cyclotron.

Dr Beamish was bent, sweating over the benches, notes, computers, wires, tubes and boxes. They had silenced the alarms but the thoroughly switched-off warning lights still flashed urgently in several colours from several parts of the room. Computer screens, also determinedly switched off, glowed balefully with data from the cyclotron. Hooke marched to stand by Beamish, saying nothing, taking in everything and scanning the lab team and the walls and the windows and the skies for inspiration.

Isaac came into the room and side-stepped to stand with his back to a wall, a stone wall he knew well, by the arched doorway. As Archie hurried in with the nuclear team, Isaac grabbed his jacket and hauled him to a halt beside him – holding a finger to his lips to silence the lad; and he pointed at the huddle of frantic experts across the room. He also directed Archie's gaze with even more authority at the far wall – and looked at Archie with great solemnity, and greatly suppressed, stilled, tense excitement.

The wall was built of Ketton limestone from Rutland, plastered over many, many times in centuries of use, with varieties of lime, sand, gypsum, crystalline selenium and animal hair. Hundreds of natural philosophers and alchemists, later known as scientists, some elevated as professors, and their innumerable assistants, students, pupils and rivals had worked in this room. Their brains would have been working at near maximum concentration and output, broadcasting coherent and incoherent thoughts, often logical thoughts, at twenty to eighty watts – the power equivalent of fifteen or sixteen AA batteries. Emitting brain waves for hours, sometimes days at a time. At rest, these great minds ticked over at ten watts, munching platters of meat, fish, eggs, bread and fruits (in season), accompanied by tankards of beer and mead, all made from sunshine. They needed to consume the food to provide the basic energy to supply the brain, to broadcast – or narrow-cast – more great thoughts on their return to work after lunch.

Isaac had been, for a time, one, perhaps the greatest, of those unconsciously broadcasting professors. The stone, the plaster, the ancient glass, the metal frames, the old oak benches absorbed – willy-nilly – absorbed the electromagnetic waves emanating from the scientists' skulls and nervous systems. In the walls, in the atoms within the walls, subatomic particles paired-up with the professors' transmitted waves of particles, and were entangled with them.

Two hundred and fifty years later – after Isaac's most intensive work in Cambridge – in about 1920, a new science, Quantum Mechanics, probed the private innards of the atom and discovered particles – subatomic particles. Studying these tiny, minuscule motes of energy, the building blocks of atoms, led to theories that when some freed particles – electrons, photons and others – buzzed around the universe, they made friends with other particles of the same class, paired up, and became 'entangled'.

This and dozens of other discoveries about particles were woven into The Standard Model, which had since been tested and proved thousands of times in hundreds of ways. 'Entangled' particles become friends for life, and no matter how far apart they may roam, over light years and immense eons of time, they stay in touch and communicate instantaneously – how, nobody knows. When one of the particles changes, its paired twin also changes to match. Strange but true.

Isaac's successor, Albert Einstein, didn't like it, dubbing it 'spooky action at a distance'. But he reluctantly accepted it as true. Paired, entangled particles talk to each other, forever, over vast distances instantaneously, and throughout time. They are eternal, instant penpals. A few decades later, Richard Feynman demonstrated with Quantum Electrodynamics, QED, that the dancing entangled particles move backwards and forwards in time. From future to past – or from past to future – presumably pausing in the present. *Quod Erat Demonstrandum.*

The earnest, hardworking professors, including Isaac, who had occupied that room across two centuries or more, had, unknowingly, broadcast waves of particles, which had paired with other particles in and through the crystals that formed the walls. Forever. The walls and the furniture absorbed and recorded their presence and thoughts.

Then Isaac went back to Woolsthorpe Manor, while the last vestiges of the Great Plague ran its course. His associate paired, entangled particles hitched a lift, for a change of scenery and a few years of vacation.

Staring hard at the wall now, with Archie, Isaac Newton could discern an outline that was obviously not of the fixed materials of the wall. It was shadowy and it wavered; it moved. It was clearly annoyed and frustrated; not knowing whether it was coming or going – or even knowing what time it was. Isaac felt related to the shadow. The shadow felt related to Isaac; a man who was displaced in Time and Space. They were both right; they were definitely related. They were entangled.

A technician left the central benches, went to the shadowy wall with instruments, and ran his hand over the vague image. He focused on one of the instruments. 'Getting warmer. Without doubt it's warmer. Still absorbing energy,' he called over his shoulder.

Hooke and Beamish grunted their acknowledgement, but added nothing to fill the void of consternation, ignorance and fear which was palpable in the room.

Commodore Bruce MacDonald, carrying a black box with sensors attached, elbowed his way through the scrum of white coats to stand beside the two doctors of physics.

'Is this the focus of the radio waves?' he asked, keeping his voice below panic level and choosing his words to be as bland as possible.

'Yes. Yes, indeed,' said Beamish levelly. 'It's also heating up. But it is switched off and unplugged.'

'Unruly behaviour for a cyclotron,' MacDonald made an attempt at humour. May as well die laughing.

'Aha! Yes. Not typical. Not usual at all. That large stainless-steel piece over there contains a collision chamber; you'd call it a cloud chamber. To where we steer particles from the cyclotron into impact collisions,' explained Beamish.

'This is just a plain old-fashioned Geiger counter, souped-up a bit. I'll just take its pulse and see how the patient is doing.' Macdonald leaned over the machines with sensors in hand – like a medical doctor deploying a stethoscope.

'We've done that. We've done that. We're constantly monitoring for radioactivity,' said Hooke impatiently. 'We must move on, man.

Move on.'

MacDonald was unmoved and unimpressed. 'I'd like to check for myself, sir; before I alert London to expect a nuclear event – sir.' He ran the sensors over the nearest machines and then moved on to the collision chamber rig. His Geiger counter stayed silent.

'No bleeps, Commodore? No detection?' asked Beamish.

'Hmm. No Professor. No. We don't bleep any more. It might frighten the horses. Your equipment seems rather small, and Jerry-rigged. Three pieces of kit, is it?'

Hooke answered him, bursting with impatience and not a little panic, as he, above all others in the team, knew the instruments. He knew that they were acting as receivers of heaven-only-knows what energies – microwave, infrared, ultraviolet, nuclear radiation, across the whole damned electromagnetic spectrum and, he suspected, across the entire nuclear spectrum. Energies of ever-increasing intensity and, at subatomic levels, were heating up and re-radiating the energies at ever more dangerous wavelengths. 'Yes, Commodore. Yes, yes. This…,' he pointed sharply at a shining complex of metals and wires attached to several computer keyboards, 'is an electron-scanning microscope.'

'And this is a cyclotron…'

'Shouldn't it be round?' murmured MacDonald, taking in the two-inch-thick steel, perfectly aligned bolts and hardened computer screens depicting the collision chamber. He could feel the general panic in the room and hoped to calm nerves with his quiet voice.

Hooke ignored him and pressed on hastily, not at all calmed. 'And this,' he snapped through clenched teeth, pointing to the end of the benches – 'is a highly specialised laser, which emits a beam of protons; which are split here…,' he tapped a large square box with a pointer he had just picked off the bench, 'and the two beams diverge; are steered by these powerful magnets,' he tapped several anonymous looking clamps around what looked like an alloy tube, 'in opposite directions, out of this lab round the perimeter of the campus out to The Cavendish Lab; about five kilometres – our "Jerry-built" cyclotron.'

MacDonald hardly winced at the reprimand. 'The beams are fed into the cyclotron and boosted by those red-painted electric kickers. There are in fact two channels in there, and when they reach ninety per cent of the speed of light, held and guided by the magnets, they are directed into the collision chamber, where we hope they will collide. And they often do.'

'These other instruments are the usual detectors, and cameras and so on – to capture the events. And they are all switched off and unplugged. But, as you see, they are all active. Which is alarming.'

Professor Hooke stopped abruptly, looking hard at MacDonald and challenging him to make an intelligent response to indicate that Hooke was not wasting his time, casting pearls of wisdom before this all-too-solid officer. Was his head as solid as his physique? Hooke asked silently, but aggressively.

'It's a miniature CERN,' MacDonald said, marvelling at it. 'I thought the protons reached 99.9 per cent of the speed of light before collision; in a bubble, not a cloud, chamber?'

Hooke relented slightly, mollified by his knowledge. 'Yes – of course. At CERN they do. But this, as you say, is a miniature model. Yet it works very well and yields excellent research material.'

'And it is all powered down. All switched off. All unplugged,' MacDonald stated. 'But alive! And you've checked at the Cavendish end? All switched off?'

'Yes, man, yes.' Hooke stayed just on the civilised side of yelling into MacDonald's face. 'That's the conundrum. The emergency. That's why I called you. That's the danger. The bloody particles are pouring in – or out. We don't know which. Or from where. And they're building up. Just like a nuclear pile going critical, without any nuclear-fissionable material anywhere in the vicinity!'

While the scientists panicked, with good reason, Isaac stood back by the door with Archie, his face grave, watchful and composed, keeping one eye on the wavering pattern on the wall, and another on the complex of instruments and scrum of people at the benches. He bent slightly; his mouth close to Archie's ear. 'That shining, riveted iron box they call a Collision Chamber seems to me to be at the heart of this emergency. What do you understand of it?' he asked quietly.

Archie was not completely ignorant of the issues. He had watched a Young Scientists TV documentary on CERN. He too kept his voice low. 'It's where the bits of atoms they're shooting round the tunnel meet. Bang! And they fly apart. All over the place.'

'What tunnel? I don't see a tunnel.'

Archie had been listening to Beamish and Hooke. 'This is only a little one. The big ones have a huge tunnel. This one's only got a pipe. Look!' He pointed to the left-hand end of the benches at a heavily armoured pipe, burdened every few centimetres with what neither of them knew were powerful electromagnets, which went from the bench across to the back wall and out through a chiselled channel. 'The bits are flying around in that pipe; and they come around to the box – there! – very, very fast!'

'At the speed of light,' murmured Isaac. 'At three hundred thousand kilo-metres per second?' he uttered experimentally.

'Yeah! That's right,' said Archie admiringly. 'You got that from our internet-TV, didn't cha?'

Isaac almost smiled…but didn't. 'Indeed – while we ate buttered crumpets. And a kilo-metre is…how far?'

Archie faltered, stuck for a definition or measure. Isaac stepped up. 'Kilo means thousand,' he pondered. 'And a metre?'

'Oh, yeah! A metre's about this long'. Archie demonstrated with his hands apart. ''Bout this long – a bit less than a yard,' he suddenly recalled from an arithmetic lesson. Isaac nodded, inverting his attention as his mind grappled with the calculations. He lifted his eyes and gazed unseeingly at the ceiling. 'That is as far as the Moon. In one second!' he gasped with awe. Then he snapped his fingers – fast, in great wonderment.

'And the, er, particles are fired in opposite directions? And then made to collide; in that iron…'

'Steel. It's steel not iron,' corrected Archie. But Isaac wasn't to be diverted.

'…Box. And they split apart.'

'Yeah! In a big shower of bits. They've got photos of it.'

Isaac avoided 'photos,' as he had 'steel'. The latter he surely knew – and the former he could interpret with Archie's help later. 'So, they collide at six hundred thousand kilometres per second,' he speculated.

Across the room, over by the benches, Hooke, Beamish and MacDonald were in a huddle, fiercely debating, pointing fingers and consulting laptops. Isaac and Archie stopped their exchange when they heard their names as Beamish haltingly outlined his outlandish, unevidenced, heretical, frankly stark-raving potty, Schrödinger's cat theory of how they might stop the runaway nuclear reaction.

'It's urgent,' he was saying. 'No time for pussyfooting around our professional reputations.'

The other two nodded conservatively and silently; as if not speaking the words might immure them from being tainted by the bizarreness of the concepts being tossed around. Beamish pressed on.

'We must assume that he IS Newton?' And he peered challengingly into their defended faces.

'Yes, yes,' said Hooke testily. 'Improbable but not absolutely impossible. And we've no other hypothesis to work with.' He stared into MacDonald's non-committal face, demanding collusion. If he was to be branded a scientific lunatic, they would all be branded. All for One and One for All. *Morituri te salutant*, 'We who are about to die salute you,' as doomed Roman gladiators declaimed.

'OK – aye,' MacDonald agreed reluctantly. 'Let's get on with it!'

'He's Newton. Newton time-shifted. Newton entangled at a quantum level,' insisted Beamish. 'And he has to be entangled in his Time and in our Time. He IS Schrödinger's cat. Both here and not here. A quantum bridge from past to present and back to the past again. Which is channelling the radiation!'

'And young Archie?' queried MacDonald.

'He is The Observer,' cut in Hooke drily. 'Archie has somehow opened the box and observed that Newton is alive and present. Newton's presence here requires Archie's intelligent observation.'

'…And, I conjecture, needs his belief in what he is seeing, observing,' added Beamish.

They all three turned their heads to examine the young boy. Who looked frankly back at them from his place by the door.

MacDonald returned to their anxious, conspiratorial huddle. 'So, if the boy were…removed?'

It passed Archie by but was not lost on Isaac, who tensed to catch the reply. 'No, no,' said Hooke. 'We've been there. We cannot risk Newton vanishing, until he's switched off these machines and the radiation. We must keep them together, and here, and' – he dropped his voice – 'under guard.' The three heads lowered inwards, backs to Archie and Isaac.

But Isaac was on familiar territory. He had negotiated these stone rooms and outwitted jealous academic cartels of rivals, with great success. He had eavesdropped on whispering, scheming conspirators from places out of sight but in the focus of echoes both faint and strong. He had not failed to catch the drift of 'under guard'. He had no wish to be under guard. He nudged Archie's arm – finger to lips; and they slipped around the door post, into the corridor, down three steps, along another narrower corridor – and vanished into the interior of the great, revered and ancient stone pile of his college. It was Isaac's turn to lead them through little used passages and pathways, familiar to him, to avoid arrest. He needed time and quiet to absorb all that had happened so far that day – and to think.

'Professor! Sir!' called one of the WRENs. 'Professor! They just left. Out of the door.'

MacDonald instantly strode to the doorway. 'Get after them, men! Find them. And quickly!'

But Isaac and Archie had already crossed two courtyards and were climbing one of the many internal narrow stairways, with doors at each half-landing. Isaac pushed one open and led Archie into a small study; closing the stout door behind them.

He sat heavily on an upholstered chair at a desk in the window, pushed aside and determinedly ignored two piles of books and an open, glowing MacBook screen, put his head in his hands – and plunged into deep thought. Archie flopped gratefully onto a small bed on the opposite wall. It had been a long, eventful day; which was about to become even more eventful.

13

MARJORIE AND THE MEDIA

BACK IN BLUEBERRY Avenue, Clothfield Estate, Grantham, with the Navy helicopters gone, with most of the police, troops, Royal Marine Nuclear Protection Group, scientists, neighbours and passers-by dispersed, and the KEEP OUT tapes removed, the media swarm swooped on Archie's mother, intent on finding or fabricating a fabulous story.

A group of fifteen or so hollow-eyed, feverish hacks with cameras, microphones, mobile phones and notepads shouldered each other as they pressed towards the small front door of Mrs Wilkins' home – and knocked loudly.

Nothing happened. They knocked again – louder. Nothing continued to happen. The journalists knocked even more loudly, certain that their quarry was cornered in the house. They started to call and flap the letter-box.

'Marjorie. Mrs Wilkins. Mrs Wilkins. We need to talk with you.'

The door was opened by a small, tank-like, middle-aged, utterly unflappable, uniformed WREN, who calmly announced, 'It's all over. They have all gone. Nothing is happening here. Nothing to see here. And there is nothing more to say.'

The Press listened politely for about a full half-minute. Then a tall man from the *Times* broke in, speaking in authoritative public-school tones, his cultured voice penetrating the empty hall over the WREN's shoulder,

'Mrs Wilkins. Do please listen to me. It is most important that we protect your son, Archie. My newspaper, the *Times* of London, can do that. We have much high-level influence. We can give him full protection and rescue Archie from the danger he is exposed to.'

His bluff worked. An uncertain, worried mother – Archie's mum – appeared from the kitchen at the end of the small hallway, taking a few steps towards them.

'What danger? What do you mean? What danger?'

An incoherent babble of answers arose from the media scrum; which the *Times* flapped a backward wave at, ordering them to silence. The crowd got the drift of his tactic and, surprisingly, shut up.

'There is a nuclear "incident" occurring. We think, in Cambridge. Archie has been flown there by The Marine Commando Nuclear Fleet Protection Group. Your child needs responsible legal representation and care. He needs his parents, Mrs Wilkins. May I call you Marjorie? Archie needs his mother.'

The *Times* knew when to stop and let his message sink in. His large foot prevented Sergeant Bullock RN's attempts to close the door as Marjorie wavered and fretted. The crowd of media persons all adopted their most seriously concerned and child-caring faces and aimed their joint expressions of emotional support at Mrs Wilkins – a mother separated by faceless bureaucrats and military forces from her vulnerable son. Only the media had the power and empathy to intervene and reunite mother and son in these most perilous circumstances.

Professor Hooke's clumsy, undiplomatic words earlier in the day, as he had literally and metaphorically spilt the milk, rang in her head: *'There is a national emergency. A nuclear emergency. A major event.'* And now, ranged before her were the nation's most trusty journalists, flaunting their credentials and logos, many of which she recognised – the BBC, the *Sun*, ITV, Radio Grantham, the *Daily Mail*, the *Telegraph*, the *Daily Express*, The *New York Times* – and one she half-knew but couldn't place – Reuters – all clamouring for her attention and nodding in earnest agreement at the earnest warnings from the *Times*. The nagging worry she had suppressed after speaking with Hooke blossomed into full-blown paranoia and fed into her raw, animal, maternal instincts. She again, for the second time, transformed into a tigress defending her cub – she grew into a very dangerous beast – and pushed past Sergeant Bullock…and took charge.

'Take me to my son!' she commanded.

A babble erupted: 'Our helicopter is on its way'; 'Our Limousine is just around the corner'; 'We have a light plane about to land at the school'; 'I'll give you two hundred and fifty thousand pounds for an exclusive; come with me Mrs Wilkins', they clamoured.

'She goes nowhere without me,' stated Mary Bullock quietly, stepping in front of Marjorie.

'We'll go in the helicopter,' commanded Mrs Wilkins in a steely, adamantine voice. The BBC reporters, whose 'copter it was, smirked and gabbled into their mobile phones. 'It's nearly here. Two minutes. Landing in the ploughed field over there. Behind the allotments.'

'Marjorie – get your coat and things. And keys,' said Mary Bullock. Marjorie ran up the stairs.

'Who's the tramp? Who's the tall tramp, Marjorie? Mrs Wilkins.

Who is he?' shouted the woman from the *Sun*. And continued calling out until Marjorie reappeared, wearing a coat and carrying a handbag.

'Better to not say anything,' cautioned her bodyguard. But Marjorie was in charge and wanted the Press's reaction to the baffling things she had heard, which now threatened her boy.

'Archie called him Isaac, er, Newton,' she obliged. 'He's not a tramp. But Professor Hooke doesn't believe he *is* him. I think he's very important. Central to all this stuff.' Then, as some stifled nervous giggles, she had them all frantically racing for their cars, motor bikes and summoning fast planes as she told them, 'The Navy nuclear people are taking them to Cambridge. To Trinity College, Cambridge, I think. Yes. To Trinity College.'

Within minutes, the BBC helicopter landed in the field beyond the allotments behind her home. Mrs Wilkins, Mary Bullock RN and several BBC journalists embarked, and it took off in the direction of Cambridge.

And Blueberry Avenue was emptied as the Press took to the roads at highly illegal speeds – also in the direction of Cambridge. Calm and peace descended once more, and birds returned to sing in Archie's modest garden.

Within the hour, the BBC helicopter landed on Trinity College playing fields.

14

MR SCHRODINGER'S
REAL CAT

THE DAY WAS FADING, dimming the light admitted by the diamond window panes in the rooms sequestered – pirated – by Isaac and Archie. Isaac was tired, his head still in his hands, elbows on the desk, making no movement and breathing deeply and regularly. It had been a long, confusing, physically exhausting and demanding day. But, while he rested his body, Isaac's mind was ordering, re-ordering, evaluating and assimilating information. He could not recall any time before this when his intellect had been so absorbed and so extraordinarily excited. As never before, he applied rigorous discipline and fierce concentration to collate all the new experiences since he had woken in his ruined study and encountered Archie.

Though a man of logic and science, with one of the finest minds ever known, though every fact had to slot into place and be linked to his prior knowledge, Isaac was not driven to need to make everything fit. He could cope with 'fuzzy logic'.

He had been trained from birth in Christianity, and had Faith that The Lord Would Provide – in this case, provide direction and answers – as decided by The Lord that Isaac needed them. Even though he rejected most of what had been drummed into him by Christian tutors, teachers, priests, dons, nuns, pastors, bishops, confessors and professors (professors of the faith), the training was deeply embedded – and he could rest in God's grace. He had no need to 'know now'. Answers would come in time. He had a vestigial, unconscious faith in miracles.

And Isaac was an alchemist. He experimented zealously and with intense focus on The Elements; reducing solid minerals, fluids and gases to their constituent parts – and recording their characteristics and behaviours in great detail. He delved into the secrets of ancient manuscripts, which linked to the work of medieval magicians and witches. He had pursued the Philosopher's Stone that could bestow Eternal Life and all knowledge – and he had tried time and again to learn spells or processes that would reduce lead in Fire, Air, Earth and Water in the hope of seeing it turn into gold.

Dimly understanding that he possibly was, in his person, what Hooke and the others referred to as Schrödinger's cat – both here, in this time, and not-here, perhaps in his own time, this was no more magical in principle than what he had explored in the most extreme fringes of Christianity and Alchemy.

What Isaac, in his meditation and contemplation of the miracles of this fantastic day, did not notice, as darkness slowly filled the room, was that he was fading. Archie, the necessary and vital Conscious Observer – was falling asleep.

In the laboratory, mayhem and panic were taking over.

'The signals! The flux! It's just doubled in strength. Most of the bandwidth has switched from long-wave to short-wave, and from fifty gigahertz to more than one hundred gigahertz…,' yelled a physicist. 'The collision chamber casing is very hot. We've got to switch off.'

Hooke bit his lip. But he wasn't paralysed. 'Find Newton! And the boy!' shouted Hooke. 'Find them and bring them here. The lad's got a phone. Track it. Track it now!'

Commodore MacDonald was ahead of him. 'My men have already got the trace, via GCHQ. They are going straight to it.'

The stout oak door protecting Archie and Isaac in their peaceful retreat burst open and two large commandos lumbered into the study. Others stood outside on the stairs. The soldiers fixed on the two occupants, then shook their heads and rubbed their eyes, peering at a phantom in the gloom at the desk. Archie jerked awake. However tired he was, this was too good to miss. Isaac solidified. The soldiers dismissed what their eyes had told them. No need to report strange goings-on, for which they had no explanation or even an adequate description. They escorted Archie and Isaac back to the laboratory. The skies darkened, and all light was lost.

The guards took Isaac and Archie into the heart of the room, into the middle of the team gathered around the rogue equipment. Two soldiers stood in the doorway to head off any more attempted escapes, or innocent meanderings.

Professor Hooke seemed slightly war-weary, looking the worse for wear after a night and a day without sleep – a day crammed with urgent journeys and acute decisions. He took a deep breath, set aside his critical faculties, and addressed Isaac.

'We need your help, we believe, to switch off these machines. When the machines are switched off we hope that the radio signals...' – Isaac blinked at 'radio,' but did not interrupt – 'will also switch off. And that this crisis will be averted.'

Hooke paused. His shoulders drooped with tiredness. His executive aggression was spent. He was at last seeing Isaac as a man, not an obstacle or a tool for his use.

Isaac took his customary pause before speaking. 'I will help you,

Professor Hooke. What will happen to me if I am able to "switch off" your machines?'

Archie looked first at Hooke then at Isaac, his features reflecting in turn excitement and concern, trying to read their minds. His view was eclipsed by several tall, white-coated figures crowding around the two professors, anxious to hear the logical answer, if any logic could be applied to this unique discourse.

It was Hooke's turn to pause. He shook renewed energy back into his face and shoulders. Dark shadows crossed his face as he looked Isaac up and down, as a person, for the first time. He saw him as a person who was about to embark on a perilous, possibly fatal course of action. 'We...we don't know, Professor Newton. We don't know what will happen when the radiation stops flowing. We can conjecture of course. But we do not know' – he took a deep breath – 'because this event, these circumstances, have never been known before. By anyone. Ever.'

'What about Mr Schrödinger's cat?'

Hooke smiled, a weary, embarrassed half-smile. 'The cat is only a metaphor, Professor. A construct to illustrate that certain theories – subatomic theories, that is, theories concerning minuscule particles that make extremely small atoms, that make all things – cannot be true. It is a cat in a box that, if the theory were true, would be both dead and alive at the same time. Which is of course impossible.'

'And yet. It might possibly be so. We simply don't know.'

'I would hope,' said Isaac, 'to be returned safely to my own time and place when this phenomenon ends. Is that a possibility?'

Another long pause ensued, while the group crowded closer around the two professors. Archie was edged out to the back of the group. Hooke felt obliged to apply his mind to this utterly impossible and insane happening. A man's life – a most important and prestigious life – was at stake. It was a life that had to be balanced against an atomic implosion which might obliterate

Cambridge and kill millions of folk. But it was only one life.

Hooke looked round the room, at each face in turn, tacitly requesting support and inspiration from his esteemed colleagues.

John Beamish accepted the reputation-sabotaging baton. He spoke carefully. 'I imagine, sir, without any evidence or time to construct any working theory, that your presence here, clearly connected to the immense flow of waves and particles – to the radiation, which, as far as we have tracked the flow, is between here and your home near Grantham – has not diminished or replaced your presence back in your own time.'

He paused. 'There is nothing in your life story, nothing in history, that indicates a period – even a day or so – when you, ahem, dematerialised or went missing from Grantham. And there is a strong, irrefutable record that you lived, in your own time, to a good age – a far greater age than you are today – with a most successful, remarkable and celebrated career. In fact, some regard you, Professor Newton, as the greatest scientist who ever lived.'

'I told you, our teacher said you were quite bright,' Archie chipped in from a gap in the circle of adults.

Isaac nodded at Archie, but his concentration was at peak intensity, fixed on Doctor Beamish, urging him to continue his monologue.

'So, thus, therefore, I deem it probable that you do still exist in your own time, and in your own place, with your family and colleagues. You are, Professor Newton...' – the academic group flinched at the unsupported brazen implications underlying Beamish's logic – 'You are – in all probability – both Here. And There. Simultaneously! You are, indeed, Schrödinger's cat.'

'So, if, as we hope, and when you interrupt or switch off the flow... My guess – it can be no better than an educated guess – is that your presence here will disintegrate, as it were, will evaporate, and your real self in Grantham will quite simply continue.'

Isaac lowered his eyes and took his customary pause. 'And the boy? Why do you need Master Archie here?'

John Beamish sagged slightly and shook his head. How could he explain the Conscious Observer to a scientist who was three hundred years behind the times? Hooke took back the baton.

'That, Professor Newton, is a rather esoteric and complicated theory. To do with the very smallest parts of the atom.'

Isaac nodded his understanding.

'And to do with what we now call The Standard Model. How the atom works. It's known as Quantum Theory. Quantum Electro Dynamics. Decades ago, a group of theoretical physicists – top world scientists – met in Copenhagen.' Isaac nodded at 'Copenhagen'. 'They concluded that certain constituents of the atom, parts that are so…ahem…light, weightless, but nevertheless vital and real building blocks or parts of the atom, when freed from the atom, only manifest their characteristics, their identity, their actions, when observed. Observed by a conscious human being.'

Isaac shook his head.

'Photons; particles and waves of light can be such energies. That require a conscious observer.'

Hooke was getting breathless. He was exhausted and needed to end this lecture quickly.

'We surmise. We have a theory. Doctor Beamish has formed the theory. That Archie is your conscious observer. That without Archie, you might not be here – or be seen here. Archie believes in you. His attention completes your existence – in our time. It is a quite respectable and attested phenomenon.'

Hooke felt obliged to add the weight of a hundred years of quantum-theory and the gravitas of Nobel Prize winners to his pronouncement. 'The double-slit experiment is strong evidence for both the conscious observer – and for spooky action-at-a-distance. It is believed.

'I cannot explain it further.'

Isaac felt Hooke's cornered, weary embarrassment. He spoke to relieve the social tension.

'I, too, have colleagues who believe in phantoms, conjured by and reliant on our minds. Others ascribe happenings to angels of God – or to the magic behind Alchemy; which I myself have studied deeply.'

In normal circumstances Hooke would have leapt to fiercely defend his reputation against this slanderous assumption that he, a world authority, a pragmatist and rigorous scientist, believed in angels, phantoms, and in gods and demons. But these were not normal circumstances and he was tired.

'The flow of particles is growing, is more energetic. It is pouring energy into this room; into our equipment. We fear an explosion or implosion of atomic-bomb proportions. That is many kilotons of, er, gunpowder. Many, many thousands of tons. Our main hope, now, is that your Schrödinger's cat state can intervene. We'd be obliged if you would turn on all the equipment – then turn it off. Beamish has a theory that your hand might connect with the time-frame of the equipment. We conjecture that these energies and you might be out of synchronisation with our real-time – by perhaps a few seconds. Or even parts of a second. But that puts the phenomenon into a different time-frame, which we cannot access, but you can. We can but hope.'

Isaac followed the fingers pointing at a dozen or so switches and buttons on the machines, and he followed the imperative indications to push switches up or down and to press buttons in or out.

He finished the ON sequence just as Archie's mother came into the totally silent room. The silence was deep and menacing. She froze. Nothing happened.

'And if you'll now switch them off again,' said Beamish, gesturing to the others to again guide Isaac through the sequence. 'My theory is that your subatomic particles are "entangled" with the wavicles, which I imagine are blocking the present functions of the machines.'

In an even deeper silence, as the world held its breath and darkness pressed in through the old windows, Isaac, prompted by the men and women in white coats, dutifully followed the sequence – in reverse order.

He disappeared.

There was no movement, no sound, the air did not stir, but the tall, substantial Professor Isaac Newton, complete with eccentric hat, greatcoat and boots, blinked out of existence. He hadn't gone, in the way a person might leave a room, or drop through a stage-magician's trapdoor. He simply was no longer there. It was as if he had never been there. As the room froze in shock and awe – MacDonald, Beamish and Hooke were reading the dials.

'It's gone,' said Beamish. 'The radiation has gone. The heat has gone. It's vanished along with Newton…into another time-frame, I guess.'

'Did we get him on film?' Hooke asked urgently. 'Have we any evidence of him? Did we record him at all?' He swung round and parted the group with his arms. 'Archie. Archie Wilkins. Did you take any photographs on your phone?'

But of Archie there was no sign. He too had blinked out of existence.

The looks on the faces of the academics, armed forces and massed scientists told Marjorie all she needed to know. Their astonished fearful expressions, as their gaze swept the room, confirmed what her mother's intuition knew at the instant the man and boy, her son with whom she was deeply, deeply entangled, had vanished.

'Where's my Archie?' she whispered in horror. A whisper that filled the entire room and occupied all the empty space in that room. Then she wailed in great distress, 'What have you done with my Archie?'

15

ARCHIE IN ANOTHER AGE

ARCHIE, HAVING needed the long sleep that all ten-year-olds require to refuel and to dream, to re-order the experiences of the previous day, woke and stretched and yawned. He woke refreshed, to a bright morning. The rising sun shone through the small diamond panes in the old window, illuminating a stone room, lined with bookshelves, furnished with tables, desks, two upright chairs, a large rocking chair and a weather-beaten rug on the stone floor. Isaac was hunched asleep in the rocking chair, his coat pulled round him.

Archie threw back a cover and stood up by his narrow truckle bed, tucked into an alcove by a large stone chimney hosting an open fire, now smouldering with the last of a couple of nearly spent charred logs in a bed of hot ashes. Despite the warm fireplace the room was cold and felt damp.

The stone, the window and the books and papers persuaded

Archie that they were once again in somebody's study in Trinity College. He didn't recall leaving the laboratory and walking to this room, but he did remember the breathless frozen excitement as Isaac manipulated the controls – and he remembered his mum entering the room at that moment. Then he must have fallen asleep.

Isaac was clearly in a deep sleep. Archie needed food. His mum would surely provide, as mums do. He made for the door and opened it quietly, slipped out, and carefully pulled it shut.

He was surprised by the river flowing nearby. He hadn't realised a river flowed through the college. He was more surprised when he partly recognised a particular, familiar configuration of the riverbank with a young willow tree weeping over the water. He was astonished when he looked along the river and saw a bridge and a new stone house with outbuildings that looked not unlike a forerunner of the old pub he knew by the river, back at Grantham. The ice-cream advert was missing.

He was hungry. He needed breakfast. He turned around to figure out the lie of the buildings and he sniffed the air, hoping to catch the exquisite, unique perfume of bacon and eggs, frying in a college canteen. He was very, very surprised that there was only one small building. It was stone, a tall single storey, about the size of a double garage – and it was eerily familiar.

Archie backed away a few feet to get it into perspective. He knew that shape. He knew where its foundations lay. If he covered it in a mound of brambles, a few hundred years of brambles, he would swear that it was their den; a low pile of mildewed stones, lying back from the river bank, concealed beneath scraggy hawthorn trees, shrubs and piles of blackberry.

Suddenly alarmed, Archie ran back to the door, burst in and assailed the somnolent figure in the rocking chair. 'Wake up! Wake up! Something's happened. Something is wrong. I'm not home. Wake up!'

Isaac turned away from the insistent hand. But the insistent hand kept on being insistent; Archie kept shaking him until finally Isaac was roused – opened his eyes and looked around him.

'My good Lord. My library at Woolsthorpe. We are home. Archie...we have come home.'

Then he saw Archie's pale and anxious face. Archie's eyes were fixed on Isaac in a state of shock. Isaac knew that feeling only too well. He sat up then stood. He took Archie's shoulder in a friendly firm hand. And then he paused.

'I am indeed home, young master Archie. Back in my own time. In my century. In my year. You should have stayed in Cambridge, at Trinity College, in your era. There is indubitably something amiss. We must analyse the predicament. Mark the present discrepancies. Investigate and form a theory – and find your way home.'

Archie stayed stock-still and mute, frozen in an irresolvable dilemma which he felt no power to explore, let alone to answer.

Isaac acted decisively; 'I am hungry. You must be hungry. We will go to the farm and have food... What time is it on your Casio device?'

Archie slowly moved his arm and head a fraction to look at his watch. 'It's seven twenty-two,' he whispered hoarsely. 'AM. That's morning time.'

'Aha! Then it's break-fast for you, my lad. A good hearty break-fast.' Isaac steered Archie through the door, and still holding his shoulder, he led the bewildered boy through the trees, uphill along a narrow track.

'What,' he inquired solicitously, 'what would you usually have to break-fast?'

This broke through the numbing fear to Archie's practical and demanding instincts. 'Uh Huh! We have a cup of tea. Some cereal – Sugar Puffs – and maybe some toast. That's bread – toasted brown. With butter – and marmalade,' he added hastily, lest the sweet confection be overlooked.

'Hmmm. Tea could be difficult. It is an expensive rarity out here in the countryside. Fresh milk might suffice? Cereal we surely have. With plenty of sugar for you. And there is always bread in the kitchen. Fresh-baked or no more than two days old. Now, marm-a-lade…?' He toyed with the thought as Archie kept pace alongside, gazing upwards.

'Is that, I suppose, a compote, made with oranges? Oranges from Spain or Italy? A sweet preserve with an orange tang?'

'Yeah,' muttered Archie. 'That sounds about right.'

'At this time of the year,' mused Isaac, 'it will more likely be plums, preserved from last year, from the last harvest. Preserved in sugar. I recall we have some jars in the pantry.'

'Plum jam can be just as good,' said Archie politely.

'And I'll warrant we have a platter of cold meats. With pickle. And certainly cheese,' Isaac anticipated eagerly, his own appetites whetted for home produce. 'And for you…,' it occurred to him triumphantly, 'perhaps a tankard of small-beer.'

Archie managed not to exclaim, Yuk! 'Oh – no. Not for me, thanks. Thanks all the same.'

Isaac chanced a grave solicitous glance at young Archie. 'You are a most courageous time-traveller, Master Archie. I salute you!'

Archie wasn't entirely sure of the compliment, but it put a spring in his step, and his back straightened a tad.

They crested a hill looking over a gentle green valley. 'There's the farm,' announced Isaac. 'There is Woolsthorpe Manor. Onward to break-fast.'

'Breakfast,' Archie corrected him. 'It's one word now.'

Isaac let it go, and slightly relaxed his reassuring guiding hand on Archie's shoulder, as they made down the open fields.

'You and I, Master Archie, we are, according to Professor Hooke and Doctor Beamish, "entangled" at what they called a "subatomic" level and you are, or were, our "conscious observer"; necessary to manifest us, to conjure us into beings, in our different times. I suspect this complicated and extra-ordinary theory is more due to the work and thoughts of Beamish. But Hooke does endorse it. And none of the company assembled at Trinity contradicted it. They will be searching for you!'

Archie stayed quiet. Keeping up their steady pace towards the house that promised food.

'I will contemplate and focus on the concept that we must be still connected to the energetic waves they spoke of and which they greatly feared. And I will put my mind to the logic of finding a way to return you to your own time. In the meantime, it is pleasant and safe here. And well-found. You might learn of our time and customs.' He paused. His voice dropped a decibel or so – 'What a mischief it would be to bring you to my esteemed colleagues and show them your Casio machine. I would so much enjoy their consternation… But perhaps not. You are my friend. You generously shared your vittels with me. I'll not expose you to their curiosity and intrusions.'

In another time and another place, sixty miles as the helicopter flies and a few hundred years away from Woolsthorpe, physicists were gathering, conferring and suspending their critical faculties. The cyclotron was switched ON, behaving normally. The sensors were pointing, blinking and winking quietly, within their expected ranges and parameters. God was in his Heaven and All was Right with the World.

Aside from the small matter of a lost – a dematerialised – child, Cambridge University might conveniently have brushed over the past two days, rationalising the runaway energies coursing through the cyclotron, the conjuring of a man purporting to be Isaac

Newton (how utterly ridiculous!) and the evaporation of a man and a boy from the midst of a crowd of highly observant world-class scientists (which was clearly a staged illusion. It quite simply had to be).

Unfortunately for the university, the Fleet Air Arm helicopter on the lawn and the boy's mother were not illusions. She was very clearly physically here, very distressed, and increasingly loudly demanding to know what 'they' had done with her only son. How long before the college was accused of kidnap? Marjorie had seen Archie, here one moment, gone the next, without moving a muscle. She knew, absolutely knew, that he had not walked, skipped or slipped out of the room. He had vanished before their very eyes.

The panic and opinions of Marjorie Wilkins could have been defused, over a few days, and ascribed to the fantasies of a neurotic mother who had lost her son – who had clearly wandered away into Cambridge and would doubtless turn up, somewhere, at some time. The scientists could then have got on with their science, ignoring the inconvenient truth of the evidence of their own eyes. She could have been side-lined, muted and dismissed, were it not for the testimony of several Royal Marines, WRENs and Commodore MacDonald from the fleet atomic protection unit, not given to flights of fancy, illusions or delusions. They, like Marjorie, had seen the figures vanish, and they were not about to be persuaded otherwise.

So the scientists reluctantly conferred and discussed the unreal but real event and concocted theories as to what had happened. Prodded relentlessly by Mrs Wilkins, they even started to consider how Archie might be reached, recovered, repatriated, reassembled, restored. Which required them to acknowledge that he (and awkward Isaac – Best Forgotten) were once HERE, now NOT HERE, and so, not dissimilar to the fictional state – the paradox posed to disprove a theory as nonsense – of the simultaneously alive and dead Schrödinger's cat.

Once the physicists and the witnesses from the armed forces got on the case, their curiosity overcame their professional embarrassment, supplanted their over-full commitments to vital projects, and their deep cynicism, and they tackled the mystery with intense vigour. Archie's mum could stop pushing. But she might have a very long wait.

She puzzled over the time implications – assuming Archie had gone back with Isaac. If, say, Marjorie was frozen into suspended cryogenic animation, a science not yet remotely possible or likely, to await her son growing up from, say, 1666; it would be 350 years before he could come and wake her. But, no, no. That was the wrong way round. It would have to be Archie frozen in 1666 – to be discovered and wakened in 2018 or so – by his mum. But would she then be 350 years older? No, no again. Archie would be coming back to her in the present day. All she had to do was wait – and of course find the cold room (a cave, perhaps) packed with ice, and see it thawed out to release him from his long, long sleep. As she imagined the unimaginable scene, she wept for her lost darling boy.

Having slept, eaten, showered and changed, Doctor Beamish and Professor Hooke were refreshed, and leading the scientific team. They decided that first they needed to understand how Isaac had materialised in the present – that was probably the conundrum with the most tangible facts and Beamish's theory to build on. Three physicists were briefed and started on the problem.

Secondly, they needed to understand how Isaac, with Archie in tow, had dematerialised, as the rogue electronic waves were switched off by Isaac – and to speculate on where their dematerialised bodies and souls had gone to – and whether the pair would have re-materialised in Isaac's time-frame, and if so, at which location. Three more physicists were tasked with wrestling with this great, impossible mystery.

And, if the second team could get any handle at all on how and where Isaac and Archie had gone, the third team then had the utterly, completely impossible task of conceiving a way to locate and bring Archie back to his own time. Hopefully without Isaac.

That night, Marjorie fell into an exhausted sleep – and dreamt vividly and repeatedly of her son.

Could her dreams transcend Time?

16

A SERIOUSLY LONG WAY FROM HOME

THE GRASS WHICH they crushed underfoot smelt sweeter to Archie, and energised him more, than the diesel-fume-saturated grass of home. The air he breathed brought him a thousand new signals. The deep, deep, traffic- and factory-free silence soothed his soul and washed him with sighing breezes, birdsong and the beating of butterflies' wings. They passed a pigsty, which was rank to Archie's nose, but not offensive. Hens, white Aylesbury ducks and common geese pecked at the ground by their feet. A collie dog ran out and barked in greeting – which Isaac silenced with a wave of his hand. Wood smoke drifted down from the tall chimneys, carrying forest perfumes that Archie almost knew. Before they entered the kitchen door, he checked his phone. It had some power but there was no signal. He was not altogether unhappy about it and he had certainly expected it. He looked at his Casio digital watch, which continued to precisely blink away the seconds and display the time of day, which didn't seem vitally important; it was enough to know that it was breakfast time.

The large square kitchen was breezily open to the outside, the door and two windows were wide open, the door into the hall was also open – and it seemed to Archie that at the other end the front door was open too. He caught glimpses of several people bustling about the house. A hot fire burned low in the fireplace, heating large and small blackened pots suspended at different heights above the logs.

'Mrs Cartwright, Mrs Cartwright, may I introduce my young friend Archie?

Archie, this is our redoubtable housekeeper – and cook – Mrs Cartwright. And this is Master Archie Wilkins. He has been most kind to me, and has travelled exceedingly, extraordinarily far to get here. He will stay as our honoured guest for some days. And right now, Mrs Cartwright, he needs a thundering good breakfast. Before he is famished and fades away,' added Isaac, with a tiny conspiratorial smile at Archie.

It was not Mrs Cartwright's place to comment on the strange costume of their guest, nor on his bewildered appearance. But she noted his incredibly neatly stitched garments, his cleverly cropped hair, his soft fair hands and slender arms, and his perfectly fitting, very strange and obviously very expensive shoes – and took him for a pampered princeling from a foreign, merchant family. She paused. But then saw he was a boy, a lad, and he needed feeding up.

'I've just cut ten rashers of bacon, Professor Newton. And young David collected at least a dozen eggs this morning. And there's fresh bread from yesterday. More than enough, I'll warrant, to cook you up a good platter of break-fast for the both of you.'

'That will be most welcome, Mrs Cartwright. And do you perhaps have a jar of fruit preserve; and some butter to put on the bread, to accompany it?'

'I'm sure we do, Professor. I'm sure we do.' And she bustled away to the pantry to gather the ingredients.

'And to drink, Master Archie? Milk, water, ginger beer?'

Archie was busy taking in all the new impressions from this old, this very old, kitchen. 'Uh? Oh! Yeah. Thanks.' He recalled he was not about to be offered a nice cup of tea. 'A glass of milk would be nice. Thanks.'

Isaac went to a sideboard and poured himself a tankard of ale from a large covered jug. He drank deeply, with relish, glad to be home.

'Mrs Cartwright,' he called through the kitchen door, 'could you bring a glass of milk for our guest? Oh…and do we have a strong, warm jacket or coat that will fit him?'

'Yes, yes,' came her reply from inside the pantry and store-room. 'Presently, sir. Presently.'

The breakfast, cooked on an iron stove set in the fireplace, and served on wooden platters, was every bit as good as Archie had hoped for when he awoke, imagining he was still in Trinity College. The milk tasted odd and was far creamier than he was used to, but good manners prevailed, and he sipped it down. The bread was brown, chewy and wholesome – ladled with plum jam, a meal in itself. Mrs Cartwright presided over the table with proprietorial pride and authority, as both child and man ate everything she had put before them. Two men – farm workers, it seemed to Archie – came in from the yard, blinked with surprise at Archie, but forbore to pass comment. Mrs Cartwright set about making the men's breakfast while Isaac made introductions and Archie nodded politely at them.

A thick tweed boy's jacket was unearthed from an attic chest, which Isaac insisted Archie wear. 'You are not used to our outdoor life, young fellow – and I want to return you in the best of health to your friends and family.' A remark that bolstered Archie's spirits.

But Isaac had not the faintest idea how Archie could be sent back to the future; sent home to his time.

♠

'He has got his mobile phone with him. Let's at least try to get a track on that,' urged Commodore MacDonald, taking a commanding position at the front of the almost intellectually paralysed laboratory team.

Hooke remained silent. Not about to be drawn into baseless optimistic activities until he could see a logical way forward.

Beamish was more bullish. 'Can we trace the signals through variable space-time?' he murmured. 'Theoretically it's possible. Feynman showed that, at the quantum level, the arrow of time is equally valid whether it is pointing forwards or backwards. We should at least try... Unless anyone has a better idea?'

No one had a better idea.

'Then let's get our heads around this,' Beamish urged. 'How can we prepare, to give it the best chance of success? We want to trace a mobile phone tracking signal – probably no further away than Grantham...'

'But in a different century,' chipped in Commodore MacDonald. 'In fact, we can get the right year if we think about it. Newton gave us clues. When was he born? Anybody? What was his birthdate?'

Professor Hooke felt it was safe to contribute. 'It was 1642,' he pronounced authoritatively. 'Yes, he was born in 1642. And died in, I believe, 1727. I think I'm right,' he added with faux modesty.

'So, when did he leave Cambridge and go back to his farm?' asked MacDonald. 'During the plague years, wasn't it?'

Hooke cleared his throat and ventured in again. 'It was possibly in 1665, when, I understand, Cambridge was vacated due to fear of Bubonic Plague. Yes, I'm reasonably sure it was 1665 – but I don't know the month. And…,' he paused, thought better of it and closed his mouth, not wanting in any way to lead this insane thought process.

MacDonald had no such qualms. 'Born 1642?' Several nods affirmed this. 'Back to Woolsthorpe in 1665?' More nodding backed him up. 'So, he was, or is, twenty-two or twenty-three when he was here yesterday. Depending on getting the months right.'

Hooke and a few other academics shifted uneasily at being reminded they had witnessed the absolutely, utterly impossible. A fact they wanted to bury as deep and as fast as possible. After all, how would it look on their CVs? 'Recently met and conversed with Sir Isaac Newton, at Trinity College, Cambridge.' Best forgotten. Least said, soonest mended. Nothing in writing.

Mary Bullock had been busily consulting her iPad. 'Closed on 7 August 1665 – Reopened November 1666,' she read out. And she followed up the logic. 'It's now early spring – 23rd March – and he appeared yesterday by the river, on the 22nd. So, let's assume he travelled in the same time-zone. No quick leaps to other months or days; he would have come from 22nd March 1666, wouldn't he?'

'Yes,' said MacDonald slowly, counting on his fingers. 'You are right, Sergeant. March 1666 is where he came from. And the most likely assumption is that he and Archie have gone back whence he came' – MacDonald thought the olde English 'whence,' was fitting – 'to March 1666.'

Beamish picked up the theme. 'So, we think we know Where. And we perhaps know When. So, what next?' He swept his eyes across the group of world-class scientists, who avoided meeting his challenging gaze.

'Einstein…,' started a timid voice from the back of the group, 'calculated that the Space-Time-Frame of reference could be "distorted", or affected, by objects travelling at near light-speed, I recall.'

'More than calculated,' said Michael Barlow, the brave physicist who had held the about-to-explode laboratories while Hooke and his team were charging up to Grantham in the old blue Volvo. 'It's been proven time and again.'

Professor Hooke groaned, almost, but not quite, inaudibly. He stopped himself pitching in with a sarcastic remark about wizards, warlocks and magicians. But his weary cynicism was not lost on the assembled company.

Barlow soldiered on. 'And recent experiments show that light, at light speed, can be channelled into a vortex – and retained inside that space. We can define and confine a space-time object. We can reduce the time dimension to zero – and stretch the distance.'

Hooke sniffed.

Mary Bullock, however, was not deterred by the distinguished professor Hooke. She was avidly following Michael Barlow. Her nimble fingers, her talent for arithmetic and her iPhone gave her the answer that the others were avoiding thinking about. 'That means…if we convert all the elapsed time, three hundred and fifty-two years, to miles. Get rid of time altogether… Archie and Isaac…'

Hooke snorted dismissively.

'…Are 2,069,291,331,131,900 miles away – about two thousand and sixty-nine trillion miles. That's one hell of a distance to track a mobile phone location…,' she trailed off, defeated by the mind-boggling astronomical distance.

'Plus, of course, the sixty-two miles between here and Woolsthorpe. If that is indeed where they have gone,' said Hooke with even heavier sarcasm, which challenged anyone to continue that ludicrous line of thought.

'The Hubble telescope is currently capable of capturing coherent signals from thirteen billion light years away,' put in a quiet voice. There were astrophysicists in the room; younger and less awed by the prestigious Professor Hooke than were his immediate team.

'That's approximately thirty-seven million times further than Sergeant Bullock's calculation…which is a reasonable margin to play with.'

The room fell silent as they waited for Professor Hooke's next withering remark. But he really was, as Archie would have it, quite bright, and knew when to button his lip and bide his time.

The young interloper continued. 'Though what is being proposed is scientifically completely impossible and utterly insane, it may be no more insane than what we all witnessed when they vanished. The Very Large Array telescope could detect the faint tracking signals from a mobile phone, even two thousand trillion miles away.'

'Makes sense to me,' said Commodore MacDonald. 'How do we give it a go?'

Mary Bullock recovered her poise and her stance.

Doctor Beamish had been pressing the buttons on his scientific calculator. Head bowed over the keys, peering at the tiny screen, he added absently, 'Yes. And the LIGO detector can pick up wavelengths one ten-thousandth times smaller than the width of a proton… We know the mobile phone's wavelength. We know the bearing. We can get the space-time-distance to within a few metres – refining Mary's work…,' he was almost talking to himself. 'We can probably adapt a receiver of some kind… But can we penetrate? Can we focus in on a signal from the past? Was Feynman right? In practical terms?'

The young astrophysicist breezed in again. 'All the signals we get from light-years away are coming from the past. That's how we calculate the age of the universe.'

'Let's recap,' said Beamish. 'Let's go back to the rogue energies, atomic energies, that yesterday we all feared might destroy this laboratory – and possibly the whole of Cambridge.'

'Did we?' countered Hooke. 'Did we ALL think, imagine that would happen? Did we get it on record? Was it witnessed? Could it have been a case of mass hysteria?'

'Yes, Professor. Yes. Our conversations are recorded on at least six mobile phones and we are recorded on several video phones. And, no, Professor, it was not a case of mass hysteria. Unless you personally want to be seen as the most hysterical leader of the day. It was you who called me and my armed team – and urged us to come a.s.a.p. by helicopter to find a fellow you described as using the name "Isaac Newton", – with, I recall, a ten-year-old boy. And to avert "an atomic incident or explosion", as I recall,' MacDonald stressed. He had no time or patience for political manoeuvring, or academic reputational finessing.

'It happened. We tracked the signals. We found Isaac. We brought him here. He disappeared. Let's stick to the facts.'

Hooke was silenced. Down for the moment. Down but not out.

Beamish tried again. 'Isaac and Archie were in Grantham. The radio waves flowed between them and this room. Between Isaac's study on the river bank and our cyclotron. We tracked them both ways. They were here in this room – and most of us saw them vanish. In an instant. What was happening to "conjure up" – I use the term deliberately – to conjure Isaac from the past? To start; to recover, to restore Archie Wilkins, we need to analyse why and how Isaac came into the present – and why and how he, with the boy, have gone back to the past. To his own time. Then we need to reverse the process.'

Hooke shifted his ground and became gracious. 'We have, Doctor Beamish, we only have, at present, your theory, your interesting and perhaps applicable theory, of entanglement – and of the conscious observer. You have proposed that Newton is entangled with the fabric of this room, with the whole college; and that Archie is entangled with Newton. Initially, it may be, through Archie using the ruined study as his "den" – and then after…ahem…Newton, shall we say, manifesting, by his study, now a ruin, the pair became more thoroughly entangled at a quantum level, as Archie became indispensable for Newton's continued presence in the present. And if I could extrapolate further' – Beamish gave Hooke a courteous nod – 'it might be that Newton carried documents and equipment to and from his riverside study and this laboratory, thus strengthening the entanglement between not only his person and these places – but also between the fabric of the buildings?'

Hooke and Beamish looked to each other for collegiate approval. Friends in common thought.

Hooke went further, coming down off his defensive fence. 'If we are able to track the in-built microwave mobile phone signal, despite its weakness, it could be tuned, perhaps – a very, very long shot – to be a carrier wave to guide radiation of energies such as created our emergency – only this time carefully controlled, of course – which might be those same energies that the boy and Newton experienced in their entanglement. It might give us access to a route to return the boy, Archie, to us here, might it not?'

Beamish and Hooke fell silent. The assembled scientists breathed quiet relief. They had something, albeit maddeningly ephemeral and intangible, to get to work on.

'Let's try and call his phone,' said Beamish.

'What transmitter and receiver should we attempt to focus on that merest whisper of a microwave tracker signal, three hundred and fifty light years away?' queried Robert Hooke. 'We'd better be quick. His battery will be running down.' Hooke did some rapid mental arithmetic at a speed few mathematicians could match; 352 years x 365 days x 24 hours x 60 minutes x 60 seconds x 186,000 miles (per second) and it came to 2,064,724,992,000,000 – or, as he said aloud – 'Over two trillion miles! Phew, that's one hell of a distance. Our boy is a very long way from home.'

17

AN INSOLENT BOY AND HIS MUSICAL BOX

DESPITE BEING three hundred and fifty years or so, or two thousand trillion miles, from his home, depending on your space-time frame of reference, Archie was enjoying the novelty of the Brave Old World of Newton's farm. The thick jacket stank of camphor, so he had thought to take it off, but it did confer warmth and a sense of rugged security so he kept it buttoned up over his own clothes, as Isaac had advised, and the smell slowly receded and ebbed away. In storage, the camphor had kept the fleas, moth-caterpillars, mice and lice at bay, so the material was clear of invaders.

Isaac had made his excuses and tucked himself away in a small room at the front of the house, buried in deep thought.

Archie wandered outside into the cool air and early spring sunshine. He thought to check his phone, saw that it had no signal, and meandered uphill on the off-chance that he might find one. The battery was down to seventy-five per cent power, so he delved into his back-pack and pulled out another gadget, wrapped by an elastic band in a small leaflet of operating instructions, emblazoned on the front page with '*Solar Charger Tollcuudda 10000mah Cell Phone Portable Power Bank Charger With 2 USB Port, 4 LED Indicator, 6 LED Flashlight External Battery Pack For iPhone Samsung HTC and Other Smartphone DYHK01 (green)*'.

His dad had sent him this neat piece of electronic wizardry from Manchester in time for Archie to go camping with the school last summer. And it actually worked. In anticipation of the trip to Skegness, three extraordinarily dramatic days ago, Archie had exposed the solar charger on his windowsill in the sunlight for an entire day. When he got home from school, its power meter indicated it was full, primed and ready to go. The sales blurb claimed that a fully charged Tollcuudda had the capacity to re-charge Archie's phone battery three times over. He would have power as long as the sun continued to rise.

He plugged the power-bank into his phone. It would take hours to transfer the charge, but he knew from his week of camping in the wilds of the Grantham hinterland that it would do the job. He decided that for the brief time he would be here at Woolsthorpe, before he went home, he would take photographs on his phone; and he had a comforting night-light, though he hoped to be home before dark.

He had walked a few hundred metres back up the grassy hill that he and Isaac had descended earlier to the farmhouse. He paused to stow the phone and charger in his backpack. As he did so, a horseman trotted over the brow, paused, then turned and rode towards him.

'You. You boy! I don't know you. Who are you? Where are you from? What are you about?'

The horse and rider loomed over him. The man was fiftyish, flourishing a crop banded with silver. He was shorter than Isaac, and broader, though dressed in the same style and, Archie guessed with his streetwise intuition, that he was a man of some authority. The animal was spirited. It rolled its eyes and it shifted its hooves as the rider hauled back on the reins. Archie skipped away to protect his feet. He had never ridden any animal, never mind a bloody big charger such as this, and he was not about to trust its temper or footwork. Neither horse nor man seemed welcoming. Archie set the blank, deadpan expression that he reserved for unidentified incoming alien adults. 'When in doubt – say nowt,' thought Archie.

His interrogator thought otherwise. He leaned down and prodded Archie quite sharply with the crop. 'Are you deaf, boy? I said, are you deaf? Who are you? What's your business here?'

Archie was cornered. 'I'm with Isaac,' he muttered. Then thought of a better, more proper and credible response. 'I'm here with Professor Newton. We just came from Cambridge. Me and the Professor.'

'Cambridge?' The horse and man backed off. 'Against the plague laws? You've come from Cambridge? In the travel ban. Do you have a Permit? Have you a Travel Permit? Have you permission? Have you a certificate of good health? – Boy?'

Archie hadn't left all his wits back in the twenty-first century. He had read with ghoulish fascination about the Black Death and he intuited this man's genuine fear of the terrible disease.

He adopted his backward-idiot-child impersonation. He scoffed, as if at himself. 'Cambridge. No! We wus just looking at pictures of Cambridge. Only *pictures*. His college in Cambridge. We've just come from lookin' at pictures of Cambridge. Only pictures. In his study. Just down by the river. Just over this hill. Me. I've never bin to Cambridge. But I 'ave bin to Grantham. Grantham market. I've bin there.'

The man was slightly mollified but kept his distance; not entirely convinced by Archie's impromptu performance. 'And your name, lad? What is your name?' Then, shrewdly: 'And how did you come here? I don't know you. Whence came you?'

'Me name is Archie. Master Archie Wilkins.' And he added as an afterthought, 'Sir.' And he bowed slightly, as he had seen in period plays on TV.

'I am Squire Thatcher. Sir Roland Thatcher,' still keeping his distance. 'From the neighbouring estate. The Manor.' He nodded towards the north. But the polite exchange didn't divert his dogged suspicions. 'And how came you here? Is Professor Newton a relative of yours? You have a strange appearance and an odd manner,' added the squire.

Archie had an inspiration. 'He's teaching me about, about… gravity. About weights falling, an' things. Everything about gravity.'

This was not a line the country squire cared to explore. 'And your home? I said, where is your home?'

Archie paused. Then found familiar ground. 'Grantham. I'm from Grantham. We live near the church by Clothfield…'

'Ahaa! The Church of Saint Peter and Saint Paul. Yes. That's Belton isn't it. The Clothfield is a few furlongs to the south.'

'Yeah. Yeah, that's it,' encouraged Archie, easily slipping into his natural, amiable, teaching mode.

The tension eased. But Squire Thatcher was not about to abandon his duties to his neighbours, particularly at this time of the shocking, appalling news from London, which he was minded to discuss with Professor Newton. Hence this morning visit. His Neighbourhood Watch responsibilities warned him to check out this stranger – this strange child – with the good professor. The boy might be local, but he also might be a displaced wanderer, a plague refugee from London and a thief.

He nudged his mount a few feet nearer. 'We'll go together and meet your tutor, Professor Newton. Walk ahead of me. Down to the house, Master Wilkins.'

Archie could see no option but to comply. He started back down the slope with the unpredictable great beast clomping and snorting a few feet behind. After twenty or so paces, as the horse didn't stomp or bite or push him, Archie surmised that it was content to follow him – if 'content' was the appropriate description for this fidgeting, agitated, nodding, mane-tossing, half-ton or so of animal flesh at his shoulder.

'C'mon lad. Walk on,' urged the squire, from his superior seat high up on the polished, decorated saddle, with dependent belts and buckles and stirrups, and a smart case – something like a briefcase with a colourful crest – over the horse's well-groomed left flank. The boy's cropped hair, his impeccably stitched backpack and trousers and his multi-coloured shoes – and his lack of respect or fear, as if he were of equal status to Sir Roland – intrigued him. 'Are your family Cromwell adherents, lad? Of the Commonwealth? Or are you loyal followers of the King?'

The question flummoxed Archie. He had little notion of Cromwell and he was only aware of the queen, Queen Elizabeth the Second, as a royal personage. From the squire's tone he knew this was an important and crucial matter. He recalled a line from a detective film, when a suspect was wriggling in the iron jaws of logical inquisition, not wanting to answer but needing to appear cooperative. The detective was eventually pushed to demand, 'Why do you always answer my questions with another question?'

Archie remembered the right phrase. 'What makes you ask?' he said.

Sir Roland spluttered at the boy's damned impertinence, which was even delivered in what sounded like a friendly and compliant manner. Should he have the boy horsewhipped by his tutor? But his curiosity overcame his annoyance. He really wanted to know more of this youngster.

'Your style of hair, is, I venture, that of the Roundheads... Or could it be a religious order? An acolyte in a monastery, perhaps? And your shoes and pack are of very high quality. Extraordinary quality and rich colours. The finest stitching I have seen. And the weave of your kitbag is the finest I have ever seen. Is your family wealthy?'

Archie had been through this before, with Isaac and his silver foil. He didn't want to go along the single-parent family route again, and he sensed that a sullen silence would not be welcome to this heavy-set man on his very heavy prancing steed, a few inches from his head. Best to show respect while giving him an answer. 'About me family, it's best if Professor Newton fills you in, er…Sir.'

They had arrived in the farmyard. The kitchen door was still wide open. Mrs Cartwright bustled out to meet them. 'Good morning Squire, and welcome. I see you've met our Master Wilkins. Can I offer you anything, Sir?'

'I need to speak with Professor Newton, if he's at home. Quite urgently. Yes – quite urgently indeed. Is he here Mrs Cartwright? I said, is he here?'

She looked up at him on his high horse; and took in Archie, looking a bit truculent and harassed. 'The master is in, Sir. Yes. I'll go and call him.'

'Thank you, Madam. Now, boy, take my horse,' he ordered as he made to dismount.

Archie started with fear and spun to face the huge beast. It stood taller than Archie at its shoulder and nearly three metres to the tips of its ears. 'Me? Take the 'orse? Where to? I don't do horses,' he added by way of excuse and explanation.

'Do as you are told, you disobedient brat. Or I'll take a whip to you,' threatened the squire. He called after the housekeeper, 'Mrs Cartwright. I said, Mrs Cartwright. What's wrong with this peculiar lad? What's wrong with him? What's he about, Mrs Cartwright?'

Mrs Cartwright hurried back. She wasn't at all sure what was wrong with Archie. He certainly was odd. Out of this world and frail for his age, she thought. And he clearly was afraid to take the horse to the drinking trough, then to the rail. But Isaac had told her he was indebted to the lad, and she had nothing against him. 'Don't you ride?' she asked, very puzzled. 'All boys can ride and stable and water an 'orse.'

'No. Never have. And I don't want to now,' said Archie, weighing up the spirited animal that loomed above him.

The squire and the housekeeper were astounded. It was a marvellous thoroughbred hunter; finely apparelled and equipped and brushed to a glossy, healthy sheen. All ten-year-olds would give their eye-teeth to handle such an expensive possession. It was as if Archie, in his own time, were being offered an Aston Martin to take to the car park, with the owner dangling the keys before his eyes. An offer that he was rejecting.

The squire had dismounted. 'Here. Take the reins, boy. I said, take the reins. Is he ill, Mrs Cartwright? Is he right in the head? Does he understand me, Mrs Cartwright?'

Archie backed off; his eyes wide with alarm. There was no way he was going to try to lead the frisky animal anywhere. And where was he supposed to lead it to? What do you do with a three-metre-high, head-tossing, clearly disturbed, deranged horse? A schoolboy definition sprang to mind: 'Dangerous at both ends and damned uncomfortable in the middle.' He backed off another few precautionary steps.

'Here. I'll take him, Squire. Give me the leading rein, Sir, and I'll tether him by the trough, across the yard,' said Mrs Cartwright. And so she did.

The squire glared at Archie, speechless.

Mrs Cartwright came back to the kitchen door. 'I'll tell the professor you are here, Sir. I think he's in his grandmother's sitting room,' and she hastened inside.

◆

Three hundred and fifty-two years away, in plague-free Cambridge, Commodore MacDonald was directing a fixed-Earth-orbit satellite, a mere three hundred miles overhead, out in space, via his mobile phone, through the agency of GCHQ, as the rest of the team held their breath. It had taken three hours to win the grudging cooperation of the spy facility and to recall, restore and fine-tune the frequency of the rogue runaway radiation that they had tracked the previous day, transmitted between Isaac and Trinity College, and which, they now surmised, had encompassed Archie.

'This place, the ruin by the river at Woolsthorpe, Professor Newton and the conscious observer, young Archie, are all, in Schrödinger's terms "entangled"', reasoned Doctor Beamish, while his mute colleagues kept their heads well below the parapet of peer-group disgrace and professional suicide.'And, if Feynman's theory is correct, the waves or particles, or wavicles, of those extraordinarily powerful transmissions, are time-independent. They are equally valid going forwards or backwards in time. In theory.'

Professor Hooke, mindful of his Nobel Prize-worthy paper, based on Beamish's outlandish theories, which Hooke was confident he could dress in more credible language and calculation, was following closely. 'And if we are to utilise such entanglement – assuming it is more than mere simile and metaphor with practical validity in our reality – another person who is presumably highly entangled with Archie Wilkins, is Mrs Wilkins. The boy's mother.'

Even the creative Doctor Beamish had not extrapolated that far. The room fell silent. But MacDonald had no investment in or reservations about protecting reputations. After the unbelievable events of yesterday, it made sense to him.

'Yes, of course. She must be entangled with her own son.

Sergeant Bullock, get Marjorie Wilkins in here. I saw her out in the courtyard a few minutes past.'

Now, joined by Archie's mother, with MacDonald's call on a speaker-phone, the group listened intently and stood by their diverse monitoring instruments as GCHQ technicians in Cheltenham minutely adjusted the orientation of a satellite and its radio settings, locked in orbit, three hundred miles above Cambridge. The electromagnetic frequency they had identified that had summoned Isaac from his study, connected him to Cambridge and brought him to Archie's side by the river, was located again. The radiation, now faded to almost nothing, was locked onto. Various screens flickered with activity and indistinct, chaotic images. Expert fingers teased the focus across a multitude of wavebands. The focus strengthened. The idea was to use it as a carrier-beam for Archie's telephone signal. Commodore MacDonald, with his phone plugged into mains power and on direct satellite up-link, dialled Archie's number.

Marjorie Wilkins closed her eyes – and prayed hard to her god, or her guardian angel, or her Lucky Cornish Pixie.

🍎

As Isaac strode out into the yard, annoyed at the intrusion and at being disturbed from his scientific contemplation, two bars of 'London Bridge is Falling Down' tinkled across the cobbles. Archie paled, as white as a sheet – and scrabbled to get into his backpack, frantically dragging out his mobile phone with the re-charger.

'Yes. Yes. Hullo. Hello. Hi. It's me. It's me. It's me, Archie! Say something. Speak. Hello!' But answer came there none. The screen was inactive, displaying the usual icons. The battery was slightly more charged.

'Here. What's that? What is it, boy? What have you here?'

demanded the squire.

Isaac stepped between them and blocked the squire's view of Archie. 'It is of little import, Sir Roland. A mere musical box. A child's toy. A damaged musical box that we hope to repair.' He put out an arm and shepherded the squire towards the kitchen. 'Am I forgetting my manners? Good morning to you, Sir. And welcome. What brings you here, Sir? Mrs Cartwright indicated your business is urgent.'

'Urgent indeed, Professor. They've sent messengers out from London.'

Isaac fell into his silent, expectant, tell-me-more mode.

'Last night, Professor. A relay rider arrived in Grantham last night.'

'I heard of it, Sir,' Mrs Cartwright said. 'Bad news of the plague. Very bad news.' She too waited expectantly.

'More than one hundred and fifty thousand dead. And that's just in London! The count was up to New Year's Day,' said Sir Roland. 'London is dying.

'I have just received word. They sent out riders, post-haste, relay-riders, along the Great North Road, before dawn. And to all points of the compass. Five hours only to Grantham. Fastest gallop ever over the distance. Bringing the news... And looking for aid and supplies.' He paused for breath.

'It is a cataclysm. All of London evacuated. Everyone fleeing.'

'We need more news, Sir Roland. We need to evaluate the consequences of such terrible news.' Isaac measured his words carefully.

'Certainly, Professor. Certainly. For us. For Grantham. We do. By hell, there might be columns of refugees. Ragged crowds looking for food and shelter. And the Plague, Professor. The Plague. All travel restrictions gone. They'll carry the Plague with them. We must build barriers. Protect the town. I said, protect the town...

And our estates and barns!'

Archie had slipped his 'musical box' into his knapsack and was listening intently. He had had lessons on The Great Plague and done a school project for homework. 'It stopped,' he stated with certainty. 'Bubonic plague – or was it Pneumonic? – stopped just after the Great Fire of London.'

And before Isaac could gag him, Archie continued, '…And that was in November 1666. Yes, November 1666. Two hundred thousand dead,' he concluded triumphantly. 'What's the date now? Where are we up to?' he added with an open smile.

Sir Roland gaped at the boy. Isaac moved to silence him.

Mrs Cartwright answered, 'Surely you know. It's March. Springtime. In the Year of Our Lord sixteen sixty-six,' she whispered, and backed away wide-eyed, staring at Archie.

Archie saw the shocked looks and felt the frozen silence. But he mistook the reason. 'Then you'll be all right,' he assured them brightly. 'Only a few died in Grantham. Just a handful. About thirty – I think. All by Christmas time.'

Isaac got to Archie's side and put a large hand on his forehead as he hissed in his ear, 'Be silent!' He turned to the other two. 'He's feverish again. A frail child. An attack of the delusions. We should have kept him indoors. In bed. I'll take him in.'

'Hold!' ordered Sir Roland. 'Hold a moment, please, Professor. What is the lad saying? What is he saying?' He crouched, and crept forward, staring into Archie's face. 'What is this Great Fire he speaks of? Is he a seer? Is he prophetic? Does he have precognition?'

Isaac's hand slipped down, as if accidentally, over Archie's mouth. He managed a little-practised wry smile and an equally rare quiet chortle. 'Ah, no, Sir. If only he could see. If only! Why, last year, in one of these delusional fevers, Master Archie forecast our best-ever crop of apples. But…,' and Isaac, uncharacteristically, sniggered again, 'it was our very worst harvest.'

Mrs Cartwright made as if to comment, maybe to protest. But a frown from Isaac gave her pause. She looked at Archie with mixed emotions. But she, too, knew when to be silent.

'But, though misguided, he is innocent and harmless, Sir. Just rambling. A dreamer. Quite harmless. If you'll excuse me…excuse us, Sir Roland… I'll take Master Archie indoors to rest.'

Muzzled, Archie let Isaac lead him by the head into the kitchen – and push him into the hall, closing the hall door. Isaac returned to the yard. 'An apt student but an overly sensitive youngster,' he explained dismissively.

'Now, Sir Roland. Please, tell me your plans to take measures for the protection of Grantham and our houses. Perhaps over a glass of porter.'

And he led the squire around the front of the house, to enter the main sitting room by the front door. Archie, at last getting the message, had made himself scarce.

18

FROM DEEP SPACE TO
A DEVILISH DEVICE

Although not officially admitted to as a SETI listening unit, which it certainly was, a large radio observatory in Zelenchukskaya, in southwestern Russia was where two young Russian astronomers first picked up the faint, confusing, wavering, whispering radio signal, using the RATAN-600 radio telescope.

"Ello, hello. Say something. It's me, Archie…'

But as it was very faint, brief, and in English, they did not attach any importance to it. When the wavelengths were analysed and the likely direction and source-area identified, it was clearly a freak case of interference, maybe reflected off a satellite in fixed-Earth orbit. No mobile phone signal could possibly be arriving from 352 light years away, from, it seemed, a nondescript, unmapped part of the Milky Way Galaxy. An initial flutter of hope that it could be an alien signal from Little Green Men, discovered by Russia, faded away as the signal faded – and as native English speakers interpreted what was being said. The Search for Extra Terrestial Intelligence settled back into alert, if bored, watchfulness. The observers' hopes for a Nobel Prize were shelved, for the time being. They later filed a technical note that was eventually buried in a huge data bank.

As the Earth turned, The Perkins Laboratory in Delaware, Ohio, detected the whisper from Archie's mobile phone, in the same hour as did duty-officers manning the Arecibo dish in Puerto Rico. Less constrained by cynical strait-laced managers than were the Russians, both observatories did report the odd signal, if only to alert other radio telescopes to rule it out as a SETI communication. A hum of amused chatter went from SETI unit to unit as Archie's voice echoed off the ionosphere and various satellites, while the scientists doodled on their calculators and figured out that Archie, if an alien, was over two thousand trillion miles away. This little green Englishman was unlikely to arrive before lunch. A few of the SETI searchers did however ponder on how a standard mobile phone signal could disguise itself so convincingly – as if coming from outer space. One or two played around with outlandish theories of space-time distortion, as they had no real alien signals to analyse.

So, Archie's phone did get noticed, and the amused SETI chatter came back to GCHQ in Cheltenham – and Commodore MacDonald was informed. He was breathless with suppressed excitement; took three deep calming breaths and passed the astonishing news onto the Cambridge team.

As a military man of action, it took him only a few seconds to react. 'We MUST try again. We must use the same wavelengths and phone the wee lad again.'

Archie's mother bit her knuckles. The assembled scientists froze in their tracks and stared silently at MacDonald; then they swapped glances around the room. Who would be the first brave academic to volunteer support for this mad Royal Marine, sending messages into the past?

'Yes,' said Robert Hooke, seizing the moment and speaking slowly, as if to himself, 'we must repeat the experiment. Perhaps with even greater power. We could boost our communication. I suspect... I imagine that perhaps, our, ahem, phone call, could have been channelled by the same signals; the same unstoppable flow that took over our instruments yesterday...and...conjured a representation of Isaac Newton.'

As Robert Hooke bravely took over leadership of the scientific logic, inching his way towards a prize-winning theory on the basis that Fortune Favours the Bold (and the boldest plagiarist), no one cared to contradict him. He continued, 'But, is there a way we can boost Archie's response?'

'I think NASA has developed a way to boost faint signals from distant regions,' chipped in a researcher. 'I've got a layman's summary on the TIME website news here...'

'Well, do read it out, please. Verbatim if you would,' Hooke requested.

'It says:

Researchers at NASA's Jet Propulsion Laboratory and the California Institute of Technology, both in Pasadena, have developed a new type of amplifier for boosting electrical signals.

An amplifier is a device that increases the strength of a weak signal. 'Amplifiers play a basic role in a wide range of scientific measurements and in electronics in general,' said Peter Day, a principal scientist at JPL and a visiting associate in physics at Caltech.

'For many tasks, current amplifiers are good enough. But for the most demanding applications, the shortcomings of the available technologies limit us.'

One of the key features of the new amplifier is that it incorporates superconductors—materials that allow an electric current to flow with zero resistance when lowered to certain temperatures.

For their amplifier, the researchers are using titanium nitride and niobium titanium nitride, which have just the right properties to allow the pump signal to amplify the weak signal.

Although the amplifier has a host of potential applications, the reason the researchers built the device was to help them study the universe. The team built the instrument to boost microwave signals, but the new design can be used to build amplifiers that help astronomers observe in a wide range of wavelengths, from radio waves to X-rays.

'I know Peter Day at Jet Propulsion,' said Dr Beamish. 'I'll call him. Maybe we can borrow time on the instrument they've built. And route Archie's incoming phone signals via Pasadena.' Within a minute he was walking away from the crowd, speaking into his cell phone, a hand to his other ear.

🍎

Back in Woolsthorpe, Archie avoided the sitting room, where he could hear Isaac and Squire Thatcher planning to divert plague-carrying London refugees from Grantham, and he went to the kitchen. Mrs Cartwright was there with a spry older woman, Isaac's grandmother, Margery Ayscough. Isaac's mother, Hannah Ayscough, was away visiting her sister in Lincoln. They offered Archie a piece of fruit cake, which he ate with gusto. Grandma Ayscough surveyed him with intelligent, fierce brown eyes, noting his garb, shoes, pallid complexion and alien mannerisms.

'Where did you meet Isaac?' she asked pointedly, clearly as a prelude to more queries.

Archie paused thoughtfully, rather as Isaac might; he swallowed a mouthful of fruit cake and replied, '…Er, I wus sitting, down on the river, near the workshop place. And Professor Newton came out of the building…' He omitted to mention that the studio was then a three-hundred-year-old ruin. 'And we got to talking. And I gave him a sandwich…'

'What's that? What's sandwich?' jumped in Grandma.

Archie just stopped himself from coming out with his stock scornful response: 'Hey! Everyone knows what a sandwich is. You gotta know what a sandwich is.' Instead, he paused again. 'Er, it was bread with peanut butter. And I gave him an orange…' He trailed off, as the two women stared at him – not with disbelief, but deeply puzzled. '…Er, yeah. I gave him a peanut butter sandwich – and an orange.'

'In early spring,' said Mrs Cartwright. 'You gave the professor an orange? An orange from Spain? In March?'

'And what's "peanut"?' queried Grandma, sharply.

Archie knew this from his TV watching. 'Peanuts grow in the desert in hot countries. On the ground,' he told them with utter certainty. 'Yeah; on the ground. They were first called groundnuts…'

He again ran out of words as his audience stared at him, mouths agape. They obviously didn't know about peanuts – or peanut butter. And, Archie guessed, Grandma was about to focus on Spanish oranges in March. She had a tenacious, inquiring mind, like her grandson, he decided. She would pin him down in the crushing jaws of Newtonian logic until she had fathomed the mysteries.

He pressed on, knowing no other tactic. 'Er, and they mash up the nuts to make butter. Butter you can put on your bread. Smooth or crunchy. It's dead nice, really. But it can stick to the top of your mouth. Some people don't like that.'

'Ahha!' Mrs Cartwright came to his aid. 'You mean like treacle. It sticks like treacle.'

'Er…yeah. I guess so. It sticks like treacle.' Archie had never eaten treacle, but he knew the phrase well, and he happily trotted it out now to break the log-jam.'Peanut butter sticks like treacle. But it ain't sweet. It's…nutty.'

The two ladies had closed their mouths and had moved closer to him, their faces intent and burning with curiosity.'And you gave my grandson an orange? A Spanish orange?'

Archie thought for a moment, his schooling re-asserting itself.

'No,' he said slowly. 'Not a Spanish orange. Not from Spain. I think it was an Outspan. Yeah. I'm sure it was an Outspan. They come from South Africa, don't they?'

He looked at the two adult faces for confirmation of his supermarket shopping-trolley knowledge. But both their mouths were agape once again.

The silence was interrupted by heavy footsteps down the hall. The kitchen door was thrown open. Sir Roland marched in. A few steps behind, Isaac filled the hallway.

Sir Roland, not usually the most sensitive of souls, stopped as the wall of Grandma's and Mrs Cartwright's concentrated silence hit him head-on. He followed their questioning eyes, and found Archie in the focus. Isaac stopped at the door, blocked by Sir Roland's stout back.

At that moment, Archie's phone rang – playing and repeating a few tinkling snatches of 'London Bridge is Falling Down'. He turned chalky white, snatched his bag off his back; dived into the front pocket and pressed the phone to his ear; trailing a wire to the pocket. In his panic he didn't see that he'd pushed the hands-free loudspeaker button.

'Hello. Hello. Hello! It's me, Archie. It's me. Can you hear me? It's me, Archie. Archie Wilkins. I'm here. With Isaac. Here at Woolsthorpe. At a farm. It's me!' he almost, but not quite, sobbed.

From trillions of kilometres away, Commodore MacDonald's

voice whispered across unbridgeable space-time and seeped into the dead silence of the kitchen. MacDonald wasted no words. He spoke slowly and clearly.

'Yes Archie. I hear you. How's the battery?' His Scottish brogue fell into the room, faint as the most distant cry of a wandering lost spirit – but audible. Isaac pushed past Sir Roland into the kitchen.

Archie knew the value of short, direct messages. He usually had to pay for them out of his limited pocket-money. 'It's OK. I've got a solar charger.'

'We are going to bring you home. Say hello to your mum.'

Marjorie Wilkin's voice – fainter and shaking – filtered through the speaker.

'Are they feeding you? Are you warm?'

'Yes Mum. I'm good! Isaac is taking care of me.'

The commodore came back on line. 'We will lose connection in a minute. Professor Newton, we will call this time tomorrow. Same time, exact same place. Archie MUST have his phone ready. We rely on you.'

Archie put the instrument to Isaac's mouth. Isaac had seen how he should speak, into the phone – briefly and economically. 'You have my pledge Commodore. We will be ready.'

The phone wheezed, crackled and buzzed into silence.

Archie looked at the screen. It showed the standard icons. It was silent. It was offline. The battery was down to ten per cent.

Archie was exhausted and exhilarated. He put the phone into the front pocket of his backpack. And then he noticed the dazed looks on all the adult's faces, including Isaac's. They stared at him in deep shock. Squire Thatcher was the first to move. His quivering hand reached out toward Archie, toward the backpack, toward the pocket where the phone was.

'Witchcraft,' he hissed, before drawing a deep breath that restored his normal voice. 'The boy is demonic. Demonic. I must take him and his devilish devices to the bishop. He must be questioned. There will have to be a trial. I knew. I said, I knew, on first meeting, that he came from the realms of evil and strangeness….'

'The lad is my apprentice. He is my guest. He is in my house. And he has my protection,' said Isaac, calmly, with heavy authority. 'I am a member of the Anglican Church at the University of Cambridge. I have religious knowledge and authority. I can quote the Bible from memory. I vouchsafe that the lad, Master Archie Wilkins, is no demon, nor sprite, nor witch, nor warlock, nor goblin, nor faerie. He is an ordinary youngster. A little frail. A little fanciful. But as holy and pleasant a child as any would wish to meet…'

'Be that as it may,' Sir Roland broke in, 'we all are witnesses that he was conversing with spirits – in this room, a few moments ago. And the spirits replied. I said, the spirits replied.' His voice rose in alarm at the memory. 'They spoke to the boy, and to you, Professor. Yes, they also spoke to you,' he accused Isaac. 'Mistress Ayscough and Mrs Cartwright are my witnesses who will swear to the events. We all recall the voices from nowhere. The demonic voices from the other side.'

Isaac had to move fast to counter the rising hysteria that could commit Archie and himself to prison, to torture and to execution for witchcraft. Archie sensed the seriousness of the charges; he anxiously watched the men's faces, first one, then the other, trying to gauge the state of the argument.

'I am above such suspicions, Sir Roland. As you know, I have been tested, questioned and appraised by the professors of my college – professing the holy faith – some of the highest, most learned and holiest men in the land, and I am accepted as an equal into their community. If you accuse me of witchcraft, you also accuse my whole collegiate community. Is that what you intend, Sir Roland? To take this matter to our patron, His Majesty, King Charles? Are you prepared to stand before that highest of all courts

145

and level your charges against me, even though I can offer perfectly rational, perfectly normal explanations for the events of today? Shall we go before the King, Sir?'

Sir Roland was stirred but not shaken. He did know that his neighbour was a sober and devout young man who led a blameless puritan life of study, contemplation and science. He would confidently take the case forward in the local community, where he held sway and rank and power. But he quailed at the thought of pressing his accusations against such an exemplary citizen in the King's Court, before Peers of the Realm. The professor might well apply his widely acknowledged intelligence to win the day, and even to turn the tables on him. The risk was high. But Sir Roland knew what he had seen and heard.

'We are old friends and neighbours of this village and township, Professor Newton. Though I trust my senses and my reason, I will gladly hear your explanation. Though I am minded that I should take this stranger, this strange boy, to the local magistrate's court for examination.'

Isaac opened his mouth to protest. Sir Roland hurried on. 'But I agree Professor, I said, I agree to hear you out. On the clear understanding and solemn promise that we take the boy's device to the church, this night, to be tested with prayers and holy water by the clergy. I may then be at peace.'

Getting the drift that the squire wanted to take away his phone and douse it in holy water, while ignorant medieval congregants mumbled prayers at it, Archie opened his mouth in panic – but a swift, terribly fierce frown from Isaac shut him up. At least for now.

'You are most accommodating, my good sir,' said Isaac. 'The explanation to the mysterious voices is quite simple.' He smiled, an act which did not come easily to his stern features.

'As I explained earlier, Sir, the small device he holds is a musical box. In good repair it plays the nursery tune, 'London Bridge is

146

Falling Down'. At present, it is faulty. When time allows, I intend to repair the delicate clockwork and restore the whole tune.' Isaac drew breath and held one of his long pauses, which he hoped would calm the disturbed squire and housekeeper...and his sharp-eyed grandmother. 'It is a precious, valued gift from Master Archie's own, dear mother. He would be quite bereft if parted from it, even for a few minutes.'

Sir Roland was not convinced. He knew what he had seen and heard. 'And the voices, Professor? The whispering voices that came from nowhere – out of the air? We all heard them, didn't we, ladies? I said, we all heard the voices. You heard them, did you not?' he accused, swivelling to glare at the women, daring them to disagree.

'And the lad spoke to them. I said, he spoke to them. He replied to the spirits...or demons,' he added darkly. 'And, Professor, so did thee. And so did thee, sir. Here,' he demanded, thrusting out his hand at Archie, 'Give me the musical box. I said give it to me.'

Isaac once again stepped between Sir Roland and Archie. 'Master Wilkins,' he commanded, with heavy authority, knowing that he was risking failure and being tortured, then hanged for witchcraft. 'Do play the musical box for us. If it will play at all. Play the short piece it is capable of...if you can,' he added uncertainly – more in hope than with knowledge. 'You can make it play, again, can you not?'

Isaac had no idea if Archie could summon up the tune, but his day and night sojourn in the future made him believe in the magical powers of Archie's alien, miraculous community.

Archie got the point and followed Isaac's lead. 'Uh! Oh! Yeah! Yes. I can play the tune. If the clockwork is wound up, that is.' And he winked conspiratorially at Isaac. A gesture spotted only by Grandma Ayscough, who wondered at it – but wisely stayed mum.

Archie took the shell phone, flipped the cover open, revealing the polished, gleaming black screen banded in silver. He almost covered

147

it with his hands and flicked it ON. In two seconds he summoned the 'Settings,' went to 'Ringtone,' and flipped it. Isaac determinedly shifted his shoulders and arms to block Squire Thatcher's view.

The ringtone tinkled out the same few bars as before, repeating it several times before Archie moved a finger and dismissed it.

'That's it, Professor. That's all it will play. The mechanism is stuck; just repeating. It repeats just that bit of the tune.'

'Here! I said, here! Let me see that box!' demanded the squire. Archie held out the inert phone in the palm of his hand. The others gawped at it in wonderment. Without trying to snatch the alien object, Sir Roland leaned over Archie's hand and studied it.

'It's very small. A very small box,' he murmured. 'And it is exceedingly well-polished. Its lacquer is polished to perfection. Almost like glass. Like a black mirror… It's…it's a jewel. I said, it is jewel-like. Where was it made, Professor? Where did the boy get it from?'

Isaac closed his mouth and put on his 'I'm thinking about it,' face, which Archie knew could mean a long silence.

'Switzerland,' said Archie. 'Me Mum got it in Switzerland. Ya know, where they make all them clocks and things. And watches,' he added for good measure.

Isaac confirmed this in his calm, measured and credible tones. 'Ah, yes, Sir Roland. Of course. Switzerland. The Old Swiss Confederacy. Famous for their clockwork and miniatures. Excellent fine-instrument makers. Yes, indeed. It is most likely by a craftsman of the Swiss Confederacy.' And not to let the advantage of this credible provenance slip, he added, 'We, at the college, have been discussing inviting a Swiss worker in glass and lenses to design and make a device for looking at the very, very small – for the university.'

'You mean a microscope?' butted in Archie. 'Can you see germs and things?'

'A good micro-scope, accurately assembled, can indeed see the smallest things, Master Archie. But we should not impose our tedious studies on the good squire. Let us discuss it in our next class.'

Sir Roland was slightly mollified. He had heard and seen the 'devilish' device, and now saw it as a musical box; albeit a suspiciously foreign instrument from the other side of Europe.

'But the voices, Professor. The voices in the air. We all heard the voices – and the lad conversed with them. There was a man – a "commodore" as I recall you addressed him – and a woman. The boy's mother, asking Master Archie to come home. Am I mistaken, ladies?' he asked of the two women.

Mrs Cartwright quickly nodded her agreement.

Mistress Ayscough took her time from Isaac, her genius grandson, watching silently and astutely for clues. Isaac's face gave no such clues. At least none that Archie or Sir Roland could detect, but his grandmother had learned to read his poker face and barely noticeable body language. Spurning science, Mistress Ayscough relied on her family intuition. She gave a small, sharing-secrets-with-friends smile. A 'we know the truth, don't we,' glance.

'Well Sir Roland, it most certainly seemed to be a man's voice. With a broad north-country brogue, I believe.' She gave a chuckle, looking hard at Archie. 'Just the sort of strong brogue that a boy playing pranks on us, might manufacture, I imagine. Can you make that voice, young man? A north-country burr?' She smiled knowingly at Archie. 'Disguised as a distant whisper…?'

'Och aye. Mistress Ayscough. You mean my commodore voice,' Archie whispered gruffly, rolling his 'r's and making his lips round like an 'o', as he'd learned to produce a Scottish accent for the school play. He thought he did it rather well. And, unprompted, he slipped into a whispered, distant imitation of his mother's voice: 'Come home Archie. Come home.'

Mistress Ayscough rounded triumphantly on the assembled

company: 'See? It is as I thought. The boy is a mimic. He's learned to cast his voice, as some performers do at the Grantham Fair.'

Isaac intervened, adopting his sternest demeanour. 'Master Archie. It is unamusing to be fooled. To be misled by such tricks. It is the height of bad manners to involve our very good neighbour, here' – and he actually placed a hand on the squire's shoulder – 'in such deceptions. I do not approve of my students indulging in practical jokes.'

Archie managed to look sheepish.

'But…,' Sir Roland spoke again, dogged in his pursuit of the truth. A lesser man than Isaac Newton would have sighed deeply. But Isaac could keep his counsel better than most, particularly when threatened, however remotely, with a trial for witchcraft. 'You, sir, you, Professor, replied to the "commodore". Yet surely you knew it was a trick?'

'I confess, Sir Roland, my mind was elsewhere. Far from Master Archie's antics. I was calculating the size of the Earth, based on the recently published observation of the horizon. They have been newly measured with far greater accuracy than our predecessors' work.'

'In your head, Professor? Calculating in your mind?' At last, Isaac had drawn Sir Roland off his single track and brought up a topic that captured the squire's imagination. He capitalised on the diversion.

'Yes, indeed, Sir. We believe we can now calculate the circumference of our world to within a hundred miles. It will greatly aid my calculations of the movement of planets through the heavens, and the distance to the sun and moon.' Isaac was drawn into his own exciting fields of research – and Sir Roland gladly and avidly followed. 'Will it assist our mariners?' he asked eagerly. Isaac's expertise was already legendary, and as well attested as his habitual customary silences. Sir Roland was being treated to a rare glimpse of Isaac's thoughts about The Universe.

Catching the new mood, Isaac invited the squire back to his sitting room to continue the conversation over a glass of port, and to get him away from Archie – and the devilish device.

As the two men left the kitchen, Grandma Ayscough turned her shrewd eyes on Archie. 'Now, Master Archie – tell me all about that musical box and your voices…'

19

SCIENTIFIC MIRACLES ON THE RUN

In Trinity College, Cambridge, huddled in the rooms that Professor Sir Isaac Newton had once occupied, the scientists and military personnel were analysing the data of transmissions passed on to them from the spy centre, GCHQ, and the amplified version from Dr Peter Day, visiting Associate in Physics at JPL, the Jet Propulsion Laboratory in Pasadena. Archie's voice, a distant whisper, had been boosted sufficiently to be put on loudspeakers and heard by the whole team.

> 'Hello. Hello. Hello! It's me, Archie. It's me. Can you hear me? It's me Archie. Archie Wilkins. I'm here. With Isaac. Here at Woolsthorpe. At a farm. It's me!'

Even Robert Hooke suspended his disbelief, as did all of them. The boy is at Woolsthorpe farm. He is in the farmhouse. With Newton.

This transmission is reaching us from...' Hooke couldn't bring himself to make the ludicrous announcement that Archie spoke to them from the past, from three hundred and fifty odd years ago – '...from, approximately two thousand trillion miles away.'

'Not a very great distance in astronomical terms,' murmured a female colleague cautiously.

Hooke needed to maintain his leadership, while avoiding professional heresy and suicide. It was a difficult and perilous high fence to run along without plummeting into risible, fatal obscurity. But the stakes, the rewards, could be very high. He gratefully grasped at this straw in the wind.

'Yes. Quite! We detect radio signals from nearby galaxies, say the Sagittarius Dwarf galaxy, which is many times more distant.'

The astrophysicist was tapping keys on her scientific calculator. 'Yes, indeed. That galaxy is 81,000 light years distant. About 231 times further away than...er...Archie. And we get very clear signals from it.'

Hooke was content to let astrophysics take the limelight, and the heat, for the time being.

Bruce MacDonald agreed the science. 'Our communications are following the same radio wavelengths as your channels yesterday – pouring into this kit here.' He patted the laboratory equipment – too hard and heavy-handed for the comfort of the scientists. 'Same wavelengths, same general direction? Towards Grantham, I'll warrant?'

Dr Beamish responded. 'Absolutely, Commodore. Our Isaac-Woolsthorpe-quantum-entanglement is, I think, acting as a carrier wave for the telephone signals.'

'Transmitted backwards and forwards through time?' ventured MacDonald.

'We prefer, at present,' said Beamish, 'to bring the time-dimension to zero, for the purpose of our calculations, that is; and to, ahem, modify – yes that's it, to modify the three other dimensions, umm, relatively, by the same factor – and so we express these communications, with Archie, as across a great distance rather than across time.'

MacDonald nodded impatiently. Beamish continued.

'We are currently relying on Einstein's Relativity and Special Relativity as being more, ahem, technically acceptable than Feynman's multi-direction of time – for quantum particles, or wavicles. For discussion purposes, that is.'

'Well, whatever makes you comfortable, Doctor. Whatever gets us there faster. But I'll stick with the simpler explanation – that Archie is in 1666, we are in the present, and we are phoning him,' MacDonald insisted. 'That seems to me a bloody miracle...'

'It's quantum entanglement, I think,' said Beamish. 'And, yes, something of a miracle.'

'But the burning question, Doctor, for all of us,' said MacDonald to the group, 'is how the hell do we get the lad home? What do we have to do to bring him back?'

'We are working on it, Commodore. That's what we are assembled here to figure out,' answered Professor Hooke.

'My guess,' said Beamish quietly, 'is that we will have to switch on the cyclotron and the electron-microscope, boost the power enormously and synchronise the wavelengths with the carrier-wave.'

'Won't that blow us all to smithereens? Isn't that risking re-creating the nuclear emergency we were called out for? Ordered to prevent at any price?' asked MacDonald.

'We found a way to stop that runaway reaction,' Hooke replied. 'Professor Newton switched it off. We might be able to repeat that.'

'The world-famous, venerable City of Cambridge, and several hundred-thousand lives, weighed against the highly improbable recovery of a local youth,' came a cold voice from one of the scientists.

Back in Woolsthorpe, as the fine morning wore on, Sir Roland Thatcher had ridden off on his spirited horse towards his estate, buzzing with excitement about the information that Isaac had filled his head with; the size of the Earth; the distance to the sun and the moon; the implications for seafarers and marine navigation. It wasn't until he reached his own manor that his paranoid suspicions crept back into consciousness. That was a damned strange boy, with his voice tricks and his extraordinary music box, made with the finest craftmanship Sir Roland had ever seen. Damned odd. And hadn't Professor Newton agreed that he could bring away the device to be examined by the clergy – perhaps even by Bishop Mollineux? Yes, he had damned well agreed. Leave the boy under Newton's protection – but take the device. They had agreed on that.

Sir Roland did not even dismount. He shouted orders to have two sturdy ostlers from the stable-yard to accompany him as constables, turned his horse around, and the three men set off at a fast trot back to Woolsthorpe.

On its steady and reliable course through the heavens, the sun was at eleven o'clock high. The sky was a clear and cool blue. A light breeze caressed the land. Spring was painting its fresh green blush on the fields, the trees and the hedgerows. His horse was skittish and still eager, full of energy. And Sir Roland, fuelled by curiosity and fearful superstition, was on a mission to winkle out the devil. It could indeed be witchcraft. What else would answer the weird events he had witnessed?

Isaac sat at a desk in an upper window with a view of the Downs that lay between his farm and Sir Roland's estate. Open before him was the book of the universe that Archie had given him, *The Junior Book of Wonders – Our Universe*. It was, in 1666, the most accurate, up-to-date, most informative and most valuable book on astronomy in the world. He had turned the pages one by one, absorbing as much information as he could cram into his mind; skipping pages that he could not possibly comprehend (yet). He stopped at the section on radio-astronomy, which featured giant dishes of giant telescopes, pictured against backdrops of inky black skies dotted with stars and satellites. Here were printed a few examples of the vast distances from our sun and planet, to the nearby stars and galaxies, some measured in b.l.y. – billions of light years.

Isaac penned calculations, translating the speed of light over a period of time into English miles. Each answer made him gasp with disbelief and check his arithmetic. His arithmetic was correct. He found 'local,' measurement units, expressed in AUs, Astronomical Units, the ninety-three million-miles distance between the sun and the Earth, and discovered that light took about eight minutes from leaving the sun to arriving on Earth. He recalled that Archie's era was 2018, and deducted his own date, giving 352 years. It took Isaac twenty-minutes to make his first calculation of the distance that 'radio-beams' and 'light-waves', which the scientists had spoken of, spanned or 'propagated' in 352 years. With quill and pen, with few corrections, he found the answer, checked it and, as young Archie had done with internet numbers, he rounded it down, to two thousand trillion miles.

'You are a long way from home, young man. A very long way from home.'

And he leaned back into his chair and rubbed his eyes, closing and opening them to clear his vision. Blinking, he almost missed the small figure at the top of the hill, waving his arms above his head. But he didn't miss it. The lookout he had posted, anticipating Sir Roland's return to fetch the musical box – and perhaps to arrest Archie – gave Isaac about five minutes warning; roughly the time that sunlight took to travel halfway to Earth.

Isaac grabbed his greatcoat and hat, bounded down the stairs, scooped up Archie – too surprised to protest – and snatched his knapsack from the kitchen table. He ran out into the yard, where a farmhand held his horse, saddled and provisioned for a journey. Mounting the horse, he hauled an alarmed Archie up behind him, then trotted around the house, away from Sir Roland's approach and towards the woods, disappearing under cover on a little-known track towards Grantham. After all, it was Isaac's territory.

As Archie clung desperately to Isaac's greatcoat, awkwardly straddling the big Shire horse and bouncing uncomfortably out of rhythm with its gait, Sir Roland and his two constables trotted down the grassy hill and into the Woolsthorpe stable yard. The kitchen door was closed. Nobody came to greet the trio. The squire waited only a moment before dispatching one of the men to go around to the front door, then jumping from his mount and banging on the back door with his fist.

It was opened, slowly, by Mistress Ayscough who no longer looked sharp and alert, but unfocused and vague. Sir Roland would have pushed his way in had not Grandma's foot been placed strategically on a cast-iron doorstop just behind the oak door. His strong arm moved the door not at all. But he hadn't lost his determination or commanding voice. He insisted on seeing Professor Newton and 'that boy'.

After some confusion from Mistress Ayscough – perhaps due to her great age or a sudden onset of hardness of hearing, she told the squire, while still holding the door two-thirds closed, that both Archie and Isaac had gone to check the fences and take the air. He was not deterred. He drew himself up to his full, authoritative, male height, demanded grandma move aside and strode into the kitchen. Mistress Ayscough closed the door behind him. Mrs Cartwright looked up from her stove and smiled blandly at him. At the table under the window, a farmhand was shovelling soup into his mouth – and didn't pause to look at the squire.

Sir Roland made for the hall door, wrenched it open and went into the hall, listening carefully before calling out for Professor Newton and Master Archie. Answer came there none. Even Sir Roland hesitated to search all the rooms. He listened again; and heard only sounds from the kitchen. He spun on his heels, went back into the kitchen and commandeered Mrs Cartwright. 'Madam. Please fetch Master Archie's haversack!'. This was not so much a request as an order.

Mrs Cartwright nodded amiably and left the room. Sir Roland turned to the farmhand. 'You, sir. Did Professor Newton take horses, or are they walking?'

The man laid down a hunk of bread, and instead sucked the end of his spoon thoughtfully, until he judged the squire might retaliate. Then he shook his head. 'You'd never get that lad on an 'orse, Squire, I don't think.' Then, seeing Sir Roland's blood pressure rising: 'The professor took an 'orse. But I reckon the lad must be walkin', Sir.'

'Mistress Ayscough. Which direction, Mistress? Which direction? Where are they heading to?'

This seemed to confuse grandma more than ever. She looked panicked and perplexed. But gamely she started to form some sort of answer, as Mrs Cartwright returned. 'I reckon, Sir Roland, that Master Archie would have taken his pack with him, Sir. He seems to put it on his back wherever he goes. Even just around the house.' She was about to offer to go looking in the stable and outhouses to help the squire, but he was not waiting any longer.

'We have fast horses. We will soon catch them. My men know this farm well. We will apprehend them. I said, we will apprehend them.'

'Yes, Sir,' said Mrs Cartwright. 'I'd look in the south wood, near the river. The professor usually likes to go over there.'

This decided Sir Roland to look there last, not first. He knew when he was being bamboozled. And he left the house, mounted his steed and, with the constables in train, he set off towards the north wood – where his quarry had gone half an hour earlier.

Isaac and Archie had ridden less than a hundred yards into the trees on a narrow track before low branches, trailing brambles and fallen trunks forced them to dismount and lead the horse. Isaac strode ahead with urgency, with the horse and Archie following a few yards behind. Their pace was steady, but Isaac's thoughts were racing. He knew that there was no other, wider route through the woods, so the squire would either have to dismount as they had, or take a long detour around the perimeter, adding several miles before he might try to intercept them from the western edge. Ahead, as they descended the shallow slope, was the river, and at a pinch-point, a long, slender wooden footbridge, not capable of carrying a herd but perhaps strong enough to support a single horse. If they had time, if they were far enough ahead, Isaac and Archie might cross the bridge, then sabotage it. But how?

Loaded on the large horse were a spade and other tools – as well as some carefully sealed twists of ground pepper to deter tracking hounds. But no saw, damn it! There was, though – and Isaac ran back to check – yes, there was a stout length of rope and a hand axe. Isaac stepped out more quickly. Thank heaven he had chosen the Shire horse. It was very strong, weighing half a ton or so. Not quite as big as a carthorse. It had more the physique of a cavalry horse, a charger. If Isaac chopped at the main supporting posts on the bank, roped the horse to them and pulled sideways… He was reasonably certain he could make the bridge impassable.

But would it stop the squire? Could he ford the river, wade across, or swim his horse across? If so, Isaac would have lost their lead and the squire would overtake them.

'Archie,' he called. Archie jogged past the horse and caught up. 'Do you know the footbridge ahead of us?' Despite the new forest

– or very old forest – obscuring Archie's usual view of the river, he knew where they were and where the path led.

"'S no bridge in my time,' he said. 'But I know where you mean. High banks, 'bout twenty metres across. 'S deep there.'

Isaac welcomed the confirmation of the greater depth. 'Too deep for the squire's horse, methinks.'

'It's a big horse,' Archie mused. 'But I wouldn't want to risk it. The current speeds up there as well. And if they went down the bank, they'd have trouble finding a place to get out again. Safer to go downstream to the marsh.'

After the steep gully, the river widened, became shallower and slower, and seeped into bog land with reeds and rushes on both banks.

Isaac considered that they would lose time and that the river was no real barrier to Squire Thatcher. He gave up that line of defence. 'What would you do, Master Archie? What would you do to throw the squire off the scent?'

Archie had the huge advantage of dozens of adventure films where heroes and heroines were either chased or did the chasing; tackling savages, soldiers, gangsters, police squads, Red Indians, trappers, trackers, psychopaths, pirates, cannibals, and frenzied lovers. Even discounting the innumerable screaming car chases, Archie knew all the tricks, from a dozen diverse cultures, of laying false trails and evading pursuing hordes. 'We should cross the bridge. Hide. Then double back,' he announced with certainty. 'Is the horse quiet – if we hide off the track?'

'Yes. He is very calm and will stand still and not whinny. There is dense cover if we go into the forest. But Sir Roland may easily spot our trail. It is a big horse.'

Archie knew what to do. 'You take 'im in. I'll follow and cover our tracks.'

Isaac sensed that to Archie this was a child's game. He knew however that their freedom, perhaps their lives, were at stake. They could not afford to make mistakes. 'No. You lead the horse. At least four furlongs east of the path…'

'Eh! What?'

'That's some two hundred yards, Master Archie. One hundred and eighty-three of your metres. Approximately. And I will come behind and repair the signs to cover our trail.'

They crossed the wooden bridge, high above the waters. It creaked and groaned in protest, but it held firm with no tendency to sway. A few yards beyond they turned left into the forest.

Against his natural instincts and fears of clumping hooves, lumbering half-ton horses and large yellowed teeth at his shoulder, Archie took the leading rein and went ahead, weaving between trees, shrubs and gullies, into the dark woods. The horse trod peacefully, if heavily, behind, shouldering through the undergrowth and manoeuvring surprisingly neatly around trees and boulders. Isaac scrubbed out hoof and foot marks with his boots, reset bent branches and pulled small fallen trunks across their trail. Within minutes they had disappeared silently into the trees. After a few hundred yards they stopped and listened.

🍎

Minutes later they heard three horses stomping over the bridge. They caught the odd word, louder than normal, as the squire gave orders and directions.

A few minutes later, Isaac and Archie felt certain that the three pursuers had continued on, walking east along the path. Isaac could anticipate the time it would take for the squire to get to the edge of the woods where they would be able to ride again. He also anticipated that three such locals would divide their search – straight ahead towards Grantham and south and north along the margins of the woods.

He was right. The squire rode on towards Grantham and the two constables went left and right at a fast canter, heading for high ground from where they might see their quarry. The squire, becoming more paranoid by the moment as he failed to overtake Isaac, started to ascribe the lack of a sighting to the lad's witchcraft and wizardry. He fulminated over his indecision when he could, and should, already have taken the musical box and be even now at the bishop's mansion, plumbing the depths of its devilish secrets. He regretted that in his haste to get back to Woolsthorpe he had not thought to bring one or more of his hunting dogs or foxhounds. But he could circle back, round the border of the forest, collect dogs, and within three hours be back on the hunt. Tracking a slow farm horse, carrying two riders, could have only one outcome. Before nightfall, the squire would have caught up with and apprehended the fugitives.

Except that Sir Roland had insufficient data to factor in Professor Isaac Newton's genius and Master Archie Wilkins' in-depth education of hunts and escapes, gleaned from several hundred hours of TV dramas. These combined talents, enabling them to avoid the squire's traps and nets, might well qualify as magical – or as witchcraft. Sir Roland, from his primitive rural background, could not conceive that information, intelligence and science is many times more powerful and effective than any seventeenth-century black arts. How might the poor man have reacted to learning that only two days ago, Isaac and Archie had boarded a machine with a windmill on its roof and flown half a mile high, fifty miles south, from Grantham to Trinity College in under thirty minutes? Broomsticks and spells and devil worship could not compete. But the squire and his contemporaries would instantly believe the magic and reject the incomprehensible science – rather than consider and think. Thinking is the most energetic and demanding activity that humans undertake. For an easy life, thinking is best avoided. 'Isms' – set beliefs, above and beyond any question – are by far the simplest choice.

As Isaac and Archie waited in the silent forest, before heading back to the bridge, Isaac was thinking.

20

DOUBT – CREEPING ACROSS TWO CENTURIES

ARCHIE, ISAAC AND GOLIATH – the horse was called Goliath – re-crossed the bridge and, in silence, under the cover of trees and bushes, followed the river up to Isaac's study – and Archie's den. Goliath was loosely tethered by the river, from which he drank heartily and into which he peed mightily.

Still in deep thought, Isaac went to the wattle fence around the plot. He turned over a large stone, dug down and unearthed an old pot, and shook out a handful of gold sovereigns. They went into the study, to a locked larder, from where Isaac took a fat pack of leathery leaves and a jar of hard-packed dried fruits. 'Pemmican,' he said, nodding at the old leather. As Archie looked blank, he added, 'Dried strips of venison, and dried fruit. For our journey. We are going back to Trinity College. It is there that the strongest waves were detected. So strong that Professor Hooke feared an explosion. And, if I heard aright, it is there that this intertwining –

this pairing – this…'

'Entanglement!' chipped in Archie.

'Yes. Entanglement…first occurred. At Trinity, the signals that carried me into the future – and I'll warrant, carried thee and me back here – are at their most powerful. Our friends in the future will perhaps make the most effective connection to your tele…phone, in my laboratory at the college.

'So, Master Archie. If you are ready, we will make our way south and east, skirting Grantham, keeping to the forest for the first five miles – and then strike out for Cambridge.'

Archie looked out of the door at Goliath, grazing by the river. What he would give for his mum's old, comfortable car to whisk them the fifty miles to Cambridge. He sighed, buttoned his farm jacket, hitched up his backpack, and led them out. Isaac used the stirrups to get into the saddle, then leaned down and helped Archie to clamber up Goliath, who barely seemed to notice he was being used like a climbing frame. Perched on the broad rump of the big horse, Archie felt very insecure. His feet barely reached down to Goliath's flanks, so he couldn't get a grip with his legs. Isaac told him to grab his greatcoat and hang on. Reluctantly, unenthusiastically, Archie grabbed handfuls of the rough material and hitched himself into position.

'How long's it gonna take?'

Geeing up the horse to walk on, Isaac considered his answer – slowly. 'Well…Goliath is a fit and strong horse. He is unlikely to tire, even walking all day. But his natural gait is not fast. He can travel thirty or forty miles in a long day – from dawn till dusk – say, ten hours. But Cambridge is nigh on eighty miles – twice that distance. My previous journeys to Trinity have been by coach from Grantham on main routes, where we change horses and refresh at coaching inns along the way. The usual time on the fast coach is about eight hours including stops…'

'Eight hours!' complained Archie. 'All day! For two flippin', days!'

'But it is already near midday, so we have six hours of light. We will need to rest up for the night – I hope to find an inn. Unless...' Isaac mused, '...we will be well on our way; on the main road to Cambridge. If we can find a night coach, or a party with soldiers, we could press on with them through the evening...'

'Soldiers? Why soldiers?'

Isaac seemed surprised. 'Thieves, rogues, outlaws, vagabonds. Highwaymen. We must have an escort at night; particularly now that families are fleeing London. These are very unsettled times. In daylight, on a busy road, it is reasonably safe. And I have a pistol, ready-loaded, ready to fire. But at night, we will need a secure shelter; either at an inn, abbey or hostelry; or, as we did this morning, hidden off the beaten track, where we won't be found...'

'Outlaws!' echoed Archie. You mean like Robin Hood? And his Merry Men?'

Isaac dragged his mind back from calculating the distance to a secure place to rest for the night. 'Robin Hood?' he murmured. 'Ah! Robin Hod. I believe there was a book with his name in the title, published as our present king took the throne. Hmm! Yes, I confiscated a copy, during one of my lectures, from a student early last year – *Robin Hood and his Crew of Soldiers* – I recall it was called. Robert, Earle of Huntingdon was its previous rendition – more than one hundred years ago, I think. A romantic tale of freemen in the greenwoods, acting with conscience and kindness.' Isaac smiled grimly to himself and said over his shoulder, 'The reality of such outlaws, Archie, of gangs of bandits living in the rough, outside of society – is very different to that merry tale. If they attacked, and if they left us alive – which would be rare, as they don't leave witnesses – then they would certainly leave us with nothing; nothing at all. No money, no horse, no food, no clothes – and no chastity.'

'Eh? What's that? What's chastity?'

An Isaac pause followed.

'It is, young Master Archie, a vital quality of an unbesmirched soul. Fit for Heaven. Now, let us concentrate on planning our journey and our rests. We must make decisions before the day wears on. After Grantham, we will join the road – and, I very much hope, join other travellers.'

Isaac didn't share with Archie his fear that Sir Roland could be continuing his pursuit. He had heard, in the far distance, the baying of one or more hounds. As a countryman, he knew how effective dogs could be in following their scent. It was a blessing that the breeze was at their backs, blowing their scent forwards, not back to the nostrils of any hunters. But the squire and his ostlers knew this territory as well as did Isaac. They might have anticipated his direction and be back on their trail; on far faster mounts than Goliath. He urged Goliath on at a heavy canter, and twenty yards before the bridge he steered them into the shallows of the river, edging deeper into the centre of the stream as they neared the arch of the stone bridge.

'Take care, Master Archie. We mayhap get our feet and legs wet.'

Goliath waded forwards and sideways, going deeper, stepping carefully; not at all impeded by the downstream flowing rapidly against them. Isaac thanked his choice of this calm, strong great-horse, and his hours and days of fishing this stretch of river. He had good knowledge of the pits and troughs in the river bed. Archie wasn't at all sure that going for a swim, in this cold water, on the grossly uncomfortable back of a horse, was either sensible or well-advised. But, aware of the tension and concentration emanating from Isaac, he kept silent.

They came under the shadow of the dark arch, with the rush of water echoing from the stones. At the threshold Goliath plunged deeper, up to his chest. Isaac, soaked above his boots up to his knees, slowed the animal and helped it pick its way over the rocks in the base of this section. Archie lifted his feet and clung on tighter. The roof was only a few feet above their heads. Archie realised they were between a rock and a wet place. He hitched his backpack – with the precious mobile phone – higher, and quickly checked his Casio watch's message, 'waterproof to 30m', which he had no wish to test.

Cautious step by cautious step, Goliath waded under the short bridge and emerged into the afternoon light. Isaac steered him to the bank opposite the side they had entered, held to the shallows and walked on quickly, keeping to a sandy beach, covered with a few inches of water.

Archie felt it was safe to breathe again.

'We wus throwing them off the scent. Weren't we?' he ventured.

'Yes. Just that, Archie. Sir Roland is a determined fellow and may be still out to intercept us. I imagine he has sent back to fetch a hound or two – and will be trying to find our trail. It will be very dangerous if he were to overtake us.'

'What's he up to? What's his game? What does he want?'

Isaac relaxed a little, confident that their manoeuvre would fox the squire – at least for an hour or so. 'We are his game, Master Archie. He is hunting us as he would hunt a deer or a boar. What he wants…is to save this parish, indeed this county, from witches, warlocks and demonic devices; devices like your tele...phone.'

'What's he got against phones?' asked Archie truculently.

'Your device is strange to him. Strange to all of us in this time. He and most folk fear strangeness. They fear the unknown. They have no ability, no talent to think. So instead they fall back on primitive fears and resort to simple violence. They would rather destroy than explore. Your very existence is a threat to their peace of mind. They panic and attack physically. It would go badly for us, I'm afraid, if he arrested us and took us to the bishop, or the gaol.

So we must press on. And reach Cambridge as soon as we can.'

Archie was again silenced by the fear in Isaac's voice. Then another anxiety struck him. 'If we don't go back... Commodore MacDonald said he'd call at the exact same time...and place, tomorrow. He said to be ready.'

'I have considered that,' said Isaac. 'I understand that the commodore wants you to be in precisely the same place at the same time, so he can direct their...er signals to you.'

'Yep! Back at Woolsthorpe,' said Archie.

'I have factored his imperative into our predicament,' murmured Isaac. Then louder, 'But he is wrong.'

Archie had come to believe in Isaac's superior abilities – not least because the professors and officers back in Cambridge obviously held him in high regard. And Archie knew that Isaac Newton, Sir Isaac Newton, was in fact 'quite bright', a genius. But this direct contradiction of the commodore and the scientists and distinguished academics from the twenty-first century about mobile phone transmissions threw him into confusion. After all, Archie reasoned, Isaac, possibly Care-in-the-Community Isaac, Farmer Newton, didn't even know how to make a phone call. He couldn't even dial up a number. He couldn't even access the phone's calculator – or the address list. And here he was, bold as brass, claiming that MacDonald was wrong – and, Archie supposed, he claimed that he, Isaac, was right, about making calls across from the future to the past (or vice-versa). Archie's loyalty and faith began to waver.

His uncertain and frightened silence communicated itself to his host.

'Let me reassure you, lad. I have thought about and formed the theory, from all that we heard and witnessed in your time, that my person, and your person, and the immensely powerful energies that so terrified Professor Hooke and his colleagues, are focused on my being. I am, to borrow Dr Beamish's logic, Schrödinger's fictitious cat. And you, lad, are my Conscious Observer. I have concluded, concerning the forthcoming communication from Commodore MacDonald, that his signals are following…no, that's the wrong word; they are "accompanying" the flow of energy, of our entangled…er…sub…atomic particles – or waves.'

'Oh!' said Archie.

Isaac continued unabashed in the teeth of Archie's tacit cynicism. 'When they send you a signal, it will be attuned to myself – and thus to yourself – and travel along the path of Schrödinger's cat, tracking my entangled essence.'

Isaac shook his head – hard. He could hardly keep faith with his own theoretical surmise. But he was certain enough of his concepts to avoid the risk of being an easy target for Sir Roland's deeply paranoid, deeply ignorant aggression. Fitting the facts and figures gleaned from his brief stay in 2018 into a constructive and logical jigsaw, though he would prefer to have twenty years to brood over the data, he knew that Archie's rescuers would as easily contact him at Trinity College, as they might at Woolsthorpe – providing that Isaac, the focus of waves of entangled-photons, was by his side.

What bothered him, what nagged away at his subconscious, was the chance that if…if…if the scientists could draw Archie home – three hundred and fifty-two years through Time, which was a very, very big IF, then would Isaac also be transmitted back to the future?

He dismissed the nagging worry even before it took conscious shape. Archie had unquestionably and generously shared his vittels with the stranger from the future – Isaac would in turn apply his genius to restore Archie to his time – and to his mother. To his single-parent family home.

The team in Trinity College, a mere 352 years away, were at that moment – if Past, Present and Future Time could logically be collapsed into No-Time, into an eternal 'Now' that was shared by Isaac, Archie and the 2018 group – addressing the very same problem.

'...But the Earth is turning at one thousand miles an hour,' murmured Beamish into the silence of intense thought and concentration. 'Do we have to factor the rotation into our equations for the transmission?'

Cautiously, Hooke responded. 'I think not, Doctor. I think not. Relatively speaking, all the navigational factors remain as they were when Newton manifested here, in this time-frame, two days ago. Even the wavelengths should be unchanged... We are merely reversing the process, I think. And I hope.'

'Except for Archie!' said MacDonald. 'Archie didn't travel from the past with Newton. His journey back to Woolsthorpe is a new factor. How can we get Archie back without Professor Newton?'

There was a long silence.

'I, I think,' volunteered a brave female post-graduate, in too loud a voice, 'I think that his mother could be the conduit. Mrs Wilkins is probably as "entangled" with Archie as Newton is with this college and his farm. If we crank up the transmissions, then focus the waves on her – and attach receiving aerials to her; the entanglement with her son will switch the beam and get him back!'

The silence was now a shocked silence that would have deterred a more self-doubting, sensitive soul. But this young scientist was not a sensitive soul. In fact, she outright rejected any concepts of soul, magic or gods, or hierarchy. Pure logic was her ruling criterion. She pressed on. '...And we should simultaneously block Newton's entry with electronic sinks and dampers on all the Newton hot-spots in these rooms that we saw yesterday!'

'Two days ago,' muttered Hooke. 'It was two days ago. But, but, if we direct that energy at Marjorie Wilkins…' – Archie's mum jumped slightly, with popping eyes – 'it could be highly dangerous. Think of the runaway build-up that caused us to summon the Atomic Energy unit. We feared an atomic event – and with good reason. It could fry Mrs Wilkins in seconds. It would be a very great risk!'

The post-graduate looked at the agitated professor and shrugged. She had a child. What mother would not take that risk, would not risk her life, to recover her only child, her lost son, from…God only knows where.

'Mrs Wilkins could wear an aluminium-foil helmet,' came a sarcastic comment from the back of the room. 'I hear they ward off all alien transmissions.' A few faces gave small, wry smiles; but Commodore MacDonald's was not among them. He was by the window, urgently texting to The Atomic Energy Unit, needing VIP permission to refresh the threat of imploding or exploding the whole of Cambridge to attempt to rescue one quite ordinary ten-year-old boy.

●

Three hundred and fifty-two years earlier, but, according to modern esoteric philosophers of physics, in all probability at the same past-present-future time, one of Squire Thatcher's ostlers had found Goliath's hoof prints on the banks of the River Withan, by the library, and was excitedly blowing a small hunter's bugle to summon the squire and the other huntsman.

The trio of Archie, Isaac and Goliath were several miles upstream, walking steadily south-west in the shallows of the stream, skirting Grantham. The river would take them to the fording place where the road from London crossed. Once on the main road, barring accidents and attacks, they could make faster time towards Trinity College. Blessed Trinity, a safe haven, as Isaac now thought of it.

21

LIVING HISTORY LESSONS

IT WAS PROVIDENTIAL. It was fate. It was obviously intended by The Almighty, thought Sir Roland, that the hound he had arbitrarily chosen was a sturdy, curly-coated Irish water spaniel, trained for duck shoots and otter hunting. Having picked up Goliath's scent by the library, the dog spent little time casting around the river bank where the big horse had obviously entered the water, and it set off upstream. The spaniel could pick up scents in running water as readily as a foxhound could sniff the air and locate the direction of a fox or a hare. The bridge delayed them for a few minutes, as the spaniel was too short to wade the depths and, despite its partially webbed feet, unable to swim against the strong flow. But Sir Roland rode around the bridge, called the dog to follow him, and set it to work in the shallows on the far side until it picked up Goliath's scent, bayed and led off upstream. Sir Roland blew hard and repeatedly on a small hunting horn, summoning his two constables.

Up-river, Isaac and Archie heard the faint echoes of the horn, judging it to be little more than a mile or so behind them. Isaac immediately left the river – they were still downwind, so if they deprived the dog of their trail in the water the tracker would have to find where they left the river and follow the scents and hoof prints on the ground. They were skirting the western edges of Grantham, which was on their left, with several small-holdings and muddied farm fields that announced the outer suburbs. Isaac urged Goliath onwards, with Archie bouncing on the horse's haunches and hanging onto Isaac's greatcoat, towards some flimsy-looking shelters surrounded by inches of churned muddy slurry. The structures were pig-sties. The mud was littered with gnawed ends of turnips and kitchen scraps that the pigs, more boar-like than Archie had ever seen, had abandoned as not even fit for pigs. They made for a slight rise of green grass and weeds and stopped at a gap in a low wall where a gate-post had been driven into the ground, without a gate. Isaac jumped down, rummaged through the saddle bags and pulled out a leather pouch, from which he carefully scattered a black powder into the grass across the gateway.

'Dragon's Breath chilli-pepper, the most fiery pepper in England; from Cornwall. If that doesn't stop the hound, nothing will.' Isaac almost allowed himself a grim smile. 'Now we need to cover the hoof-marks.'

He remounted Goliath, advised Archie to hold on, and urged the horse into a canter – heading uphill towards the town. Isaac needed a cobbled road, the busier the better, to obliterate Goliath's large hoof prints.

A quarter of an hour later, Sir Roland on his spirited hunter, and one of the mounted ostler-constables, followed the water spaniel up the same field, through the milling pigs and up to the green triangle by the gateway. The dog sniffed and snuffled, certain of the distinctive pheromones stamped into the ground by Goliath. The men could see the deep hoof marks in the thin, new spring growth; informing them that the shire horse carried two riders. The dog excitedly cast left and right, across the prints – clearly hot on the trail.

Suddenly it stopped. It froze. It raised its head. It shook its head frenziedly. It sneezed explosively. Its eyes went red and watered copiously. It shook its head more frantically. Then, eyes streaming, whining pitifully, sneezing and making sudden little jumps, the poor animal raced back through the pigs and hurled itself into the blessed cool waters of the River Withan. It would be some days before its burnt-out nostrils would recover their powers to track a quarry.

The two men watched it panic in distress across the mud and into the stream. They could see nothing that might have caused it. Neither was inclined to get down and start sniffing the grass. They rode back to the river bank and watched as the dog splashed about, burying its face in the water then sounding off more pitiful whining mixed with quick barks, as it pawed at its eyes and nose. The ostler dismounted, handed his reins to Squire Thatcher and waded into the water to try to help the dog.

'They've damned well peppered it,' growled Sir Roland. 'Stay with it, man – and get it back to the manor.' As he spoke, he could see the second constable riding hard along the riverbank. He waved the man on. 'We'll follow the hooves. I said, we'll follow the hooves. Distinctive tracks. We'll get on. Can't be more than half an hour behind them. You take the dog home! Here – your reins.'

The squire and his constable galloped up the field, through the gateway and made for the top of the rise. They had lost time. But, if they rode hard, they might still overtake Isaac and the demonic Archie.

The trio, Archie, Goliath and Isaac, had made it into town, onto busy cobbled streets where the large hooves made no distinguishable marks. Some sections were strewn with hay to soak up slops and sewage from the buildings. Other stretches had gullies of slowly moving stinking water that carried away the horrible mixture. Heavy rains would either clear the ditches, for a time, or would spill over and spread the pollution evenly over the streets and wooden pavements – little more than tethered planks across the deeper, more evil puddles.

Archie looked at the drainage facilities with disgust – and smelt the foetid air – a mixture of sewage gasses and wood smoke. He tugged Isaac's coat. 'No bloody wonder you all got the plague. It's 'orrible. It's stinking 'orrible. Why don't you clean it up?'

An Isaac pause, then, 'You know of the plague? Of bubonic plague? The Black Death? Of its causes?'

'Oh yeah. We learned it at school last year. It was rats. The fleas on rats. Black rats that came on the ships. Rats died from the plague. Dropped out of the thatched roofs – and the fleas bit the humans,' he added with relish. 'It was cured,' he continued, with some authority, 'by the Great Fire of London. It burned everything up and stopped the plague.'

'Do you recall the date of that great fire?'

'Yup! I do. Did it for my project. It was September 1666, I think.'

'My good lord! That's the end of this very summer. And I recall you said at the farm, that two hundred thousand people died. But only a few in Grantham?'

'Yeah. Of the plague. Not of the fire. They dumped all the bodies outside London – outside the wall of London.'

Isaac fell silent as he considered Archie's prophecies. Both were terrible catastrophes. But were Archie's memories of his lessons accurate? It was not inconceivable that London – mostly built of wood – might be destroyed in a conflagration. Yes, that was awful, but credible. And the plague was raging throughout the nation, killing indiscriminately. How many? Isaac did not have the information. But so many deaths that Cambridge University had closed to avoid contamination – and he, Isaac had come home to Woolsthorpe.

If we control the rats, we can control the plague, he thought.

They sought the centre of town, found the crossroads where the fingerpost showed five different directions, and headed out towards 'BOSTON 25 MILES'. Isaac figured that Squire Thatcher would assume they would take The Great North Road due south towards Cambridge and London. At a gallop, the squire could catch up with them in less than hour. Isaac hoped his diversion would protect them from arrest.

The road took them east, out of the town gate. A hundred metres on, the cobbles stopped, and the road became a rutted lane. The macerated surface was repaired with stones, ashes, timbers and tied bundles of rushes. Cart and coach tracks were obvious to Isaac and he pointed them out to Archie, explaining the differences. One of the sets of grooves was made by the coach to the coast, pulled by four horses, that had set off at five o'clock that morning.

They were not alone on the road. After Isaac's warnings of thieves and rogues lying in wait for unwary travellers, Archie welcomed the intermittent two-way traffic. A few travellers cantered by on horseback, rode in stagecoaches, trundled along on farm and industrial wagons, clipped and jolted along in lightweight chaises and landaus. As for the majority, the peasants; they walked. The road surface was abominable; even in this dry spring weather it was deeply rutted with residual puddles of mud which concealed innumerable traps for wheels, hooves and unwary ankles.

On Goliath, now getting into his stride, they were higher than most, and though carrying the pair of them, Goliath was faster than most, apart from young gallants and a few cavalrymen who hurried by at speed. Isaac urged the horse into a ponderous canter and left it to weave its own path through the obstacles, ruts and the slower travellers. Archie started to enjoy the experience – and settled into his seat, swaying with the rhythm of the horse. It was another adventure with which to regale his schoolfriends when, or if ever, he saw them again.

The sun shone onto their faces from their right. Isaac pointed out that it was in the west-south-west and that there was only three hours of good light remaining. 'We will find a post or hostelry – an inn,' he explained for Archie's benefit. 'We can probably make another twenty miles before dusk. Goliath feels as if he has the strength in him. He was well-fed just before we left the farm and we've only come some six miles so far.'

As they left Grantham behind, the numbers using the road dwindled. For long stretches there were few or no other travellers and Archie began to realise how isolated and alone they were – vulnerable to ill-intentioned thugs and thieves.

An hour later, they had travelled seven miles east, to a rural crossroads. There, they turned south, keeping parallel with the Great North Road. Their 'road,' was now little more than a farm track through fields and patches of trees. The sun was lower in the sky, and Isaac hurried Goliath into a faster gait, which the horse uncomplainingly maintained.

On the Great North Road, Sir Roland and his constable pounded along towards Cambridge and London. As the miles rolled by under the horses' hooves, the two men strained to sit higher, so as to see further ahead. The highway was arrow-straight; built and bequeathed to the nation by Roman legions, fourteen centuries earlier. With each hill they crested, they were convinced they would spy their quarry, the demonic lad and the grave professor, plodding down the next slope on the shire horse.

But of Isaac and Archie and their big horse there was no sign. The night was closing in and the squire's horses were tiring. They had had a long day, ridden fast, and needed rest, water and feed. Sir Roland reined in, and over the next hill, searched for sight of a post-house or any available shelter. They came to a shallow stream running across the road, where they dismounted to let the horses drink – and to splash cool water over their own faces. The men were also getting tired. They knew that the next inn was about four miles south – and the road back to Grantham was five or six miles. They opted to go south, leading their mounts, allowing them to graze on brown clumps of tall grasses that had survived the winter. There would be no more gallops this day. The chase was over. Until the morning.

Goliath however, kept up his steady pace, seven miles or so east of the squire, through pleasant countryside that Isaac knew. He felt at ease on this route – which footpads and outlaws were unlikely to frequent, as they would look for the richest pickings on the main highways. Isaac felt the seven miles diversion was well worth the extra time it took. Just as long as Sir Roland did not intuit where his quarry had got to.

Nearly two hours later, as Archie, now in rhythm with Goliath's gait, started to nod off, and the waning sun cast long shadows, they reached a quiet inn – a very quiet inn. In fact they were the only customers. A small wooden painted sign announced the place as The King's Head – a perhaps now unwise political comment from the reign of Charles the First, who had lost his head to Cromwell a few years earlier. But the chances of Charles the Second happening by, feeling affronted by this reminder of his father's fate and taking retaliatory action, were remote.

The inn was no more than a modest house with five stables. Isaac hauled the saddle and saddle-bags off Goliath and removed the tack before the horse was stabled, with plenty of water and hay and some vegetables from the previous harvest. The innkeeper, his wife and three dogs subjected the trio to careful scrutiny, then, despite Archie's oddities, decided they were healthy and peaceable guests and greeted them amiably enough.

Darkness fell. Isaac and Archie could relax; it was most unlikely that Sir Roland would be abroad in the night on uncertain back-roads. The food available was pot-luck; whatever the family had added to the stock-pot, simmering over the fire for the past few days. It had matured into a thick, meaty, heavy stew – served with bread made that day. It was surprisingly tasty and filling. Isaac had a tankard of ale, advising Archie not to drink the water, and persuading him to try a half pint of small beer, which Archie found was also surprisingly pleasant.

It may have been small beer, the third or fourth watered-down brew from the barely mash, but it was the first alcohol Archie had ever drunk. He barely had the energy to visit the dark-shed Water-Closet (which had no water) twenty metres from the yard, then wash his face and hands under the pump in the yard, before making for their room and slumping onto a straw-filled mattress, where he immediately fell asleep.

Isaac enjoyed another tankard of ale by the fire while exchanging news with the family, particularly news of the plague and of London refugees. He was careful to obscure his identity, even though if anyone enquired of them, it would be apparent in moments who Archie and Isaac were, and in which direction they were headed. The inn visitors, few at the best of times, had slowed to a trickle of local workers. None had seen any refugees from London or elsewhere, but many alarming rumours were circulating in frightened tones of the numbers of deaths and the mystery of how the almost certainly fatal disease was spreading so rapidly. People had remembered how to pray, and church attendances had greatly increased. Lawyers enjoyed a rush of clients updating their wills and copying and filing property deeds. God and Mammon walked in lock-step to serve the terrified community.

At what Isaac judged to be about nine o'clock, he checked on Goliath, visited the waterless-closet that took a shovelful of earth to prepare it for the next visitor, washed at the pump and went to his straw-filled mattress on the floor in the guest suite. He quickly fell asleep, promising himself to be away at first light.

🍎

Three hundred and fifty-two years later – or was it simultaneously – the team at Trinity College had dispersed to their various quarters, still puzzling over the questions of time, distance, entanglement, radio waves, Schrödinger's cat, and the mysteries of existence. They had eaten in their rooms, at restaurants in the town, or in the college dining hall, and retired for the night. Professor Hooke had invited Doctor Beamish to dinner in Hall and they were now comfortably ensconced in Hooke's private rooms, with a vintage bottle of port.

'That Italian chap Rovelli seems to be cornering the market in popular physics,' Hooke said drily. 'Selling tens of thousands of his books on Time, and trite simplistic summaries for the hoi-polloi of the whole of particle and astrophysics.'

'It probably helps all scientists to have wide popular support,' commented Beamish absently. 'After all, our funding mostly comes from general taxation. From The People. I haven't read his stuff. Anything new?'

'Nothing that goes anywhere,' said Hooke. 'He rehearses a vague idea about Time; that we humans might be in a special "particular" zone of the universe where the fabled arrow of time based on increasing entropy points us all to the future. So we have developed the concept of Past Present and Future, which only pertains in our zone. He surmises that the rest of the observable universe is not governed by thermodynamic entropy, so the past, present and future are all simultaneous. Except in these "particular" zones.'

Beamish sipped his port and considered. 'Hmm. Like the multiverse ideas. Untestable and undemonstrable in our galaxy. Is it science, would you say? I recently read an idea about gravity that would challenge the inevitable Second Law and the inevitable cold, dark soup end of everything. If it has any merit, it puts the Big Bang in question. But is it science?'

Hooke sharpened his gaze a little, mildly interested. He sat more upright. 'Is that quantum-gravity? That's one of Rovelli's themes?'

'No. Rather the reverse. The paper speculates that gravity is caused by an absence of energy, not by gravitons. It claims that light has slight mass or pressure, which of course it does. And talks of the "deep ocean" of light – electromagnetic radiation – rather than a "field" of light that presses in on all planets, stars, galaxies – on all objects. Then, following the proven experiments, which you might know, of a Dutch scientist, Casimir, about wavelengths excluded from between flat plates – "Casimir Glue" – claims that internal pressure is reduced. A similar force occurs between tall ships at sea; the exclusion of big waves between them and the ocean outside draws or pushes them together.'

Beamish sipped some more port. Hooke leaned forward slightly, not interrupting. So Beamish pressed on.

'That's it, really. The idea is that the exclusion of energy inside objects creates a partial vacuum or "shadow", while the waves or wavicles outside in the vast ocean of the whole observable universe – which as we know is 43.7 billion light years deep – compress mass. Ultimately, the pressure is irresistible, and big masses collapse into black holes. The external pressure and internal vacuum is gravity… Or so the theory goes.'

Hooke had become intrigued. 'Of course, Isaac Newton experimented for some years, in his earlier years, with light, and theorised about colour being caused by the differing size and strength of the corpuscular particles – implying mass, though he described them as weightless. The debate in his day was waves or corpuscles – particles or flux. Newton split separate colours and settled on particles, Einstein's photons… I think that was in fact in 1666! But how does Casimir Glue circumvent the cold dark soup of thermodynamics?' he asked.

'It's cyclical. A circular argument,' said Beamish wryly. 'The energy that goes into black holes is recycled. Maybe via Hawking Radiation or, my own thoughts, at a far faster rate – exploding from black hole to white hole. The energy pours out again as the deep ocean of light penetrates the black hole vacuum; the electromagnetic shadow is illuminated with light and the interior vacuum is balanced. Black holes compress mass, energy, and heat – in contradiction to the Second Law – and release it as pure energy. Everything cycles. The universe is not doomed to freeze to death. Perhaps.' Beamish downed his port and wiggled his empty glass at his host.

Hooke refrained from comment. He refilled their glasses and changed the subject. 'We will be attempting to call Archie Wilkins again at ten in the morning. Do you have any idea, Doctor, as to how our signals are getting through?'

'No deeper ideas than we have discussed, Professor. I rely on Feynman's time-neutral subatomic events. We must, I think, follow the radiation signals as before – and again use the new boosters via Peter Day at JPL – and unscientifically, pray! Who is the patron saint of temporarily displaced persons and telephone calls?'

Professor Hooke gave a small smile. But answer came there none.

22

THE DEEP SPACE-
NETWORKED PHONE

A THIN, GREY, COLD LIGHT crept in like a sneak-thief through the
gaps in the wooden shutters into the bedroom at the King's Head.
Isaac pulled his greatcoat tighter and his blanket over his head and
tried to snuggle down into the hay of his uncompromising mattress.
But there was no depth or comfort to be had. He reluctantly opened
his eyes, and more reluctantly struggled into a sitting position.
Archie was hidden, curled up under two heavy blankets.

A cock crowed close by the window, and crowed again, and then
again, and kept up its raucous challenge to the new dawn. Archie's
hand emerged and waved feebly to ward off the alarm. The crow
kept crowing belligerently. Archie sat up.

Without any words – they rose. Archie followed Isaac down
and into the barely lit yard, scattering chickens and ducks.
Isaac bravely stripped off his coat, jacket, waistcoat, shirt and
undervest; vigorously pumped water into the trough and washed

himself. Archie watched warily. As Isaac clothed himself, Archie approached the trough with fear and deep suspicion, dipped a hand into the freezing water and splashed a little onto his face. And thus embarked on the unwelcome second phase of wakefulness. He sniffed the air for breakfast.

He didn't have long to wait. Mistress Greenlees, the innkeeper's wife, cheerfully rounded a corner carrying a pail half-full of still-warm milk. She had been up for an hour or so. 'Good morning, gentlemen,' she beamed. 'This way, if you please.'

Archie needed no directions, as the smell of baking drifted from the kitchen and led him by the nose. Compared to the thin, sunless air of the yard, the candlelit kitchen was a haven of warmth and promise. Mister Greenlees was pushing faggots into the hot stove. They enjoyed platters of fried eggs, bread and pickle and goats' cheese, with milk for Archie and beer for Isaac.

'We must get on the road,' said Isaac, settling the bill of sixpence each and tuppence for Goliath. 'And thank you for your hospitality.'

As they mounted Goliath and rode out of the yard of the hostelry, the first sunbeam of the dawn breached the eastern horizon and pierced low-hanging foliage, bringing light and promising warmth.

Seven or eight miles, and several folds of hills and woodlands to the west, Sir Rowland and his constable, rested and fed, had also risen at cock-crow, and they now trotted out onto the Great North Road. Sir Roland had a sudden intuition.

'He's going to Cambridge, without a doubt, he's going to his college – but he's not using the main road. I'll warrant he's taken the route from Boston. He's east of us. I said he's to the east of us. I know he's on the Boston road.'

'Could be, Sir. It could be,' said the ostler cautiously.

'We'll intercept them. Cut them off. It'll be too late if they reach Cambridge. He'll have his protectors there. He'll have powerful colleagues. We need to cut across to the left at the next village. Go east at the next crossroads. Don't you agree, man?'

The ostler nodded slowly. 'I know that track. It's an easy path. We can make good time, Sir. If you're right, Sir.'

The squire was feeling bullish; he had the demonic lad and Isaac within his sights. 'I'm sure of it, Mister Smythe, I'm sure of it. That big charger is a slow horse. We can catch them by lunchtime. I think we can catch them by lunchtime.' And he urged his horse into a canter.

'Lunchtime' was not a precise enough time for Isaac. He was acutely aware that Commodore MacDonald had said they would contact Archie again 'at the same time' tomorrow. He was also quite sure that the flux, waves, aether or whatever energies carried the signals focused on his presence, and that moving some miles from Woolsthorpe would not disrupt them.

His cogitations had confirmed that he was indeed entangled and was a version of Schrödinger's cat, as defined by the science of 2018; though beyond those beliefs he could not qualify his thoughts. Did Archie, the Conscious Observer, confer these magical characteristics on Isaac? Was the lad a vital part of the mechanisms that transcended Time itself? Were Past, Present and Future intertwined, interpenetrating, interlinked – as the telephone transmissions evidenced?

'What is the time, Archie, on your Casio device?' he asked over his shoulder.

'Oh! Huh! It's early. Still very early,' Archie replied truculently. 'But it's seventeen minutes past seven – of the clock. Too early, really. And me "device" is a "watch". We just call it a watch.'

Isaac took the reproof and correction in his, or rather in Goliath's, stride.

'Then we have two hours and forty-three minutes before the commodore will call you. Is the tele-phone empowered to receive his voice?'

Archie wrestled out of his backpack, took out the phone and checked. 'Oh Yeah! It's fine. The charger has filled the battery to maximum. In fact, I can disconnect it and put it in the sun again – to recharge the charger. It really works,' he added in admiration of his dad's choice, and of modern technology.

'Will you advise me when your "watch" nears ten of the clock, Master Archie?'

'Uh ha! Sure. Certainly, Professor.'

Isaac fell back into silent thought. First, he rehearsed what he had heard and then what he understood of the information he had gleaned in his short stay in two thousand and eighteen, particularly pertaining to his own and Archie's miraculous time travel. Then he revisited the conversations on Archie's telephone yesterday, and he recalculated the immense distance implied by 352 light years, recalling data from Archie's book on the universe. Reaching an impasse, he shelved further scientific investigation and turned his thoughts to Sir Roland; the dogged Sir Roland, whom he was sure would pursue them until they reached the relative security of Cambridge. Relative because most of the university would be empty, closed by fear of the plague. However, there would be numbers of officials and guardians upon whom Isaac could call to turn away and debar the persistent, superstitious knight, who imagined he was doing God's work and was fighting the Devil in arresting Master Archie and investigating his demonic devices. But Isaac also calculated that the squire on his fast horse could overtake them before lunch and – fixed and limited as he was – Isaac respected his local geographical knowledge enough to know that he would quickly realise the road they had taken.

They had to be on the lookout for an ambush as the squire

tracked from the south-west. On a rise, Isaac studied the path ahead, noting the distant steeples marking roads and tracks, and the valleys ahead filled with trees and shrubs. Calculating Goliath's speed and the likely speed of Sir Roland's party, he left their direct path and veered to the west, anticipating they would pass unseen through woodland behind Sir Roland. He then planned to find the Great North Road and ride hard till nightfall, when they might reach Cambridge. He felt that Goliath had the strength to carry them all day, with minimum time for water and food. As Sir Roland went east, Professor Newton would go west. It was, surmised Isaac with grim satisfaction, a perfect double-cross.

It was slower going, using footpaths and faint animal tracks, probably deer runs, but they had tacked steadily westwards and southwards for about thirty minutes when they were brought up in alarm by what Isaac would describe as a hullabaloo from a patch of dense woodland to their left. Even Goliath shied at the sudden noise as men shouted, clearly in conflict. Isaac reined in, soothed the horse, and listened hard. He told Archie to dismount and wait at this spot. Against his better judgement he urged Goliath towards the racket. Less than fifty yards through the shrubs, Goliath burst into a clearing.

Three ruffians, one mounted, stood over Sir Roland and the constable, who were sprawled on the ground. The constable had been clubbed in his face and was bleeding copiously; the squire had a broken leg. The three attackers were moving in for the kill; their prize would be two very fine horses, saddles, and all the possessions of the victims.

Mounted on his large charger, Isaac charged. He rode at the attackers' horse, half Goliath's weight, barged into it, knocking it sideways, and slashed his riding crop across the villain's face, knocking him out of his saddle. The man fell heavily to the ground, where he landed awkwardly, twisting a leg, while the startled horse pranced sideways and stood on the man's other leg. He howled in pain. The other two ruffians snarled at Isaac and leapt at him. One swiped at him with a heavy wooden club bound with iron, while the other came at him with a lethally honed sword. The club thudded into Goliath's saddle as Isaac shied away from the two, drew his pistol and shot the swordsman in the throat. He whirled Goliath on a sixpence and, despite the great animal's weight, yanked him back so that he reared and flailed at the cudgel with his hooves. The clubman dodged, got alongside Isaac and swung again. As his arm came up to strike a deadly blow, a shot rang out and the man fell dead. Sir Roland had had the courage and wit, even from his prone position and wounded, to unholster his flintlock pistol, ready-loaded and primed – and shoot.

The glade fell silent. The birds stopped singing. The breeze paused. The horses stood stock-still. Isaac dismounted.

'Thank you, Sir Roland,' he said. 'I'll warrant that you just saved my life.'

'…And thank *you*, Professor Newton. I'll warrant *you* just saved *my* life.'

Silence calmed the men, the horses and the environment.

The squire winced and groaned, as he tried to rise. Isaac moved to assist him. Behind him, Archie parted a low-growing bush and peered into the clearing with a shocked look on his face.

Smythe, the ostler, Sir Rowland's recently appointed constable, rolled over and struggled to his feet. His face was a bloody mess, but he bravely mopped it with a large kerchief and staggered upright.

'Here, man, use this water,' offered Isaac, holding out a leather flask. The outlaw whom Isaac had knocked off his horse, badly bruised across his face, tried to rise and run, but his twisted leg was far too painful. He slumped back to the ground, whimpering in pain.

Half an hour later, both the squire and his ostler were on

their feet. The squire's broken leg was in splints; straightened and supported with lengths of hazel-wood, bound with rope; a most painful process that Isaac had performed, which the squire bore heroically. His face was pale, and he was clearly in pain. Smythe, having staunched the wounds on his face, looked the worse of the two, but was actually less damaged and more able than his employer. Both were in shock. Between them they had tightly tied the outlaw like a sack over the saddle of his horse. Isaac took charge. 'It may be most advisable, Sir, if you ride with us to the Great North Road, and then turn for home. I calculate you will reach Grantham before dark.'

'We are obliged to you, Professor. That is sound advice,' said the squire.

Archie, still shocked at the violence and injuries, said nothing. His watch read 9.30am. All four mounted their horses. The squire required a lot of help; literally a leg-up. But once in the saddle, he seemed more himself and recovered his colour. Smythe, still mopping at his nose and wounds with cloths from his saddlebag, knew the direction and led off, taking the leading rein of the outlaw. Half an hour later, they sighted the main road. Archie prodded Isaac's back.

'Four minutes,' he muttered urgently.

'Sir Roland! Gentlemen, I trust you will now be able to continue – and find escorts, perhaps on the way to Grantham. And I hope some medical aid. We must leave you here and revert to our original route. We have an appointment to keep. Fare ye well.' Without leaving any time for a response, Isaac promptly turned Goliath around and hurried back into the woodland. The shrubs and trees closed behind them.

'Get the telephone ready, Master Archie. Get it out of your sack!' ordered Isaac. Archie was ahead of him, the phone already in his hand. Isaac set Goliath into a gallop, to get as far away from Sir

Roland as they could. Archie's watch showed they had one minute to go. Deep in dense undergrowth they stopped, and Archie slid down Goliath's flank, clutching his phone.

It rang. Tinkling out its short snatch of 'London Bridge is Falling Down' in the sharp morning air.

In the laboratory in Cambridge, Commodore MacDonald, Hooke, Beamish and the communications specialists team had boosted the power to the cyclotron and electron microscope. Once again, it picked up the extraordinary 'Newton-Wilkins Entangled Radiation' that had three days earlier threatened a nuclear event. They then tuned that radiation, which connected Isaac and Archie at its focus, via a Time-Frame loop cycling through Feynman-Past-Present-Future particle interactions, between Cambridge and Woolsthorpe, to the university's powerful microwave satellite uplink transmitter dish. Into this they had fed Archie's Unique Phone Identifier, obtained from GCHQ, which Cheltenham in turn had illegally hacked from the phone maker's manufacturing data. Then they fed in the telephone's wavelength over the widest possible waveband it could handle – 824MGHz to 894MGHz – (incidentally monopolising all mobile phone-mast cells within a two-hundred-mile radius and disconnecting all the other fifty-six innocent, hapless customers who were using each of the masts to call their mums and chums or follow celebrity tweets).

As the radio waves swamped the masts and were automatically directed into BT's wired networks, as all UK mobile phone calls are, millions of callers were cut off – since Archie's phone signals demanded precedence. With the help of Dr Peter Day at the Jet Propulsion Laboratory in Pasadena, the radio signals were boosted by CALTECH's zero-temperature astronomical faint-signals amplifiers, and blasted out across the universe via the twenty-seven dishes of the Very Large Array in Albuquerque. Characterised with Einstein-Podolsky-Rosen quantum photon entanglement, the Cambridge signals simultaneously, faster than light, manifested at all points in the universe, thus occupying all space-time-frames. Transcending time, the radio signals recognised the cell phone's built-in unique-identity and, despite broadcasting back to the Earth at only a millionth of a billionth of a watt, they rang Archie's phone.

'There will be dozens of LGM reports from all the SETI units globally as they pick up this phone call from outer space,' grinned Beamish.

'LGM?' queried Hooke sharply.

'Little Green Men,' answered Beamish, causing a welcome moment of amusement in the excruciatingly tense team.

MacDonald spoke into the speaker phone. The team recorded everything, every word, every fluctuation, every shift of direction. 'Hello. Hello. Archie, time is short. This is Commodore MacDonald. Please put Professor Newton on the line to speak with Professor Hooke.'

'OK,' said Archie, and handed the device to Isaac, who had also dismounted. Archie wrestled with Isaac's fingers to align the earpiece and mouthpiece. 'They have no time. Don't press any buttons,' he instructed Isaac.

'We are travelling to Trinity College,' said Isaac. 'We will arrive in five hours. The entangled waves follow Master Archie and me.'

Professor Hooke responded, thinking fast on his feet, incorporating their journey and timing. 'We have a plan to link Archie to his mother. Eleven o'clock tonight. Put Archie into the ground-floor room, number 2a, below your laboratory. You go to the bedroom, the study room 3, Staircase E, that you fled to two nights ago. We need you separated from Archie. Ensure the phone is fully charged.'

'I understand,' answered Isaac.

'Now,' continued Hooke with urgency. 'We are transmitting coding to convert Archie's phone to operate on 8.4 gigahertz, the x-band, the wavebands reserved for communicating with our distant space instruments. Hold the phone at arm's length for a count of sixty seconds – then speak to me. Do it NOW! Please!'

Isaac did as he was told; his arm fully extended as he counted up to sixty at a rate he reckoned to be one second apart. He could detect no change, no energies, no heat affecting the device. Archie watched him, agog with interest. After one minute, Isaac put the phone to his ear and said 'Hello'.

Hooke breathed a deep sigh of relief – which was echoed by the whole Cambridge team. They had calculated that the chips and connections in Archie's phone could take the new software without breakdown. They had tested the upload on ten similar mobile phones, but the only test that mattered was from the Deep Space Network to the phone Isaac held. The updating did not explode the circuits and the phone continued to function as normal. They calculated, hoped and prayed that the surprisingly robust chips and circuits in Archie's second-hand, aging, shell phone would handle their hastily but scrupulously written new code. It seemed to be OK. Isaac heard a subdued group-cheer as he waited for Hooke's reply.

'Our changes have worked, Professor. Tell Archie that he has the most special cell phone in the world – connecting to the Deep Space Network.

'Tonight,' pressed on Hooke, 'we will use immense electrical energies. It is dangerous to us all and we doubt we will be able to repeat the exp...the process.'

The verbal slip from 'experiment,' to 'process,' did not escape Isaac. But glancing at Archie's hopeful and trusting face, he chose to let it go. An obvious case of need-to-know. Archie did not need to know the dangers he would be exposed to this very night.

With the next essential communication successfully scheduled, and the transmission still strong and clear, both professors relaxed a little; both aware of the tremendous effort and organisation – and probably holy miracle – underlying this unique phone call that transcended time.

In the few seconds' relief, Isaac rushed in. He had a burning desire and need to know so many things. His mind was overwhelmed with vital questions that these brilliant future scientists might answer. With tremendous self-control he narrowly focused on the research he was doing that springtime. 'Professor Hooke, I have a colleague at Oxford of the same name. He has published *Micrographia*, viewing the smallest creatures, along with his theory of colour.'

'I have read his seminal work, Professor Newton.'

'In your future world; to what do you subscribe colours in light rays? Waves, corpuscular or another cause?'

'Briefly, sir, the building-blocks of matter, atoms…'

'I know of atoms,' said Isaac. This surprised Hooke but he did not divert from their subject. Time had never been so precious.

'Atoms are made of several dozen diverse "subatomic" particles which are both rays and corpuscles – wavicles. Far too minuscule for your microscopes to discover. We know of them through calculations confirmed by experiment.'

Isaac's silence was so intense it communicated his fierce interest across two thousand trillion miles – across the Time-Barrier. Hooke pressed on rapidly. 'White light comprises all wavebands – all rays of all colours – in turn made of photons – corpuscles, of all wavelengths. A red surface, for example, absorbs all the photons, except the red photons or rays, which are reflected back to our eyes. Receptors in our eyes, cells, react to the red photons – inform our brain – and we "see" that colour. A black surface absorbs all the colours, and so heats up in sunlight more than white, which reflects most of the photons.'

This was, to Isaac, an information overload too far. It raised a thousand questions that he needed a lifetime to frame – and perhaps find comprehensive answers to. He gasped, 'I am indebted to you, sir.'

The modern Hooke intuited and empathised with Isaac's state of mental turmoil and felt he should affirm the man. 'You, Professor, Sir Isaac Newton, are regarded today as the first and finest real scientist. Your work on the mechanics of the solar system is still relied on today – for the navigation of our flying machines, rockets, between planets and moons. You coined the term "gravity" to describe the force that holds the universe together. And you measured that force very accurately.'

Isaac gasped again as the implications struck him. He was bursting with questions to which his interlocutor in 2018 might have the answers.

Archie's phone crackled and fizzed. 'We are losing the signal,' shouted Hooke. 'Losing the signal,' he repeated, his voice a faint whisper. 'Eleven o'clock tonight.' And Hooke, Professor Hooke of 2018, was gone.

The glade fell silent. Rays of sunlight struck through the canopy and illuminated patches of undergrowth. Isaac gazed meditatively at the colours reflected into his eyes. His mind was exhausted. Goliath munched noisily on a patch of spring grass. Archie looked questioningly at Isaac's passive face. Isaac glanced back at him and shook himself.

'Tonight, Master Archie, they will attempt to transport you home… We need to get to my college as quickly as we can. Here, stow your device carefully. Professor Hooke asked me to inform you that it is now the most special "cell phone" in the world; it is connected to the Deep Space Network.'

'How did they do that? What did they do?' asked Archie excitedly. He couldn't wait to tell his school pals.

Isaac gathered his thoughts in another of his contemplative silences. 'I recall,' he said gravely, as if speaking to himself, 'that the scholars in Professor Hooke's team have composed, or written, new, er, Coding, while I held the phone at arm's length.'

'That's to protect your 'ed from the microwaves, I'll bet,' butted in Archie. 'They can burn your brain if you get too many of them.'

'Mayhaps,' murmured Isaac, still piecing together his answer, 'they uplifted their new code...'

'No,' said Archie. 'They uploaded the code, new software. A software update. They've updated me old phone. Me Mum's old phone, actually. Gosh – what will it do now?'

Isaac persisted with his measured explanation, overriding Archie's impatience at his seventeenth-century ignorance of mobile-phone technology. 'They have wrought changes to your device, I believe, that enable it to communicate with The Deep Space Network.'

'Whats'at?' queried Archie.

Isaac paused again. A longer pause than usual.

'I haven't the faintest idea,' he said at last. 'I was hoping you would know what your countrymen and contemporaries mean by that phrase.'

There was a hint of criticism in his voice. Archie was his future-scape tutor. Isaac had the wonderful illustrated astronomy book Archie had gifted him. He had lived in 2018 for almost a whole twenty-four hours. Archie had explained many incomprehensible things to him, albeit that Isaac had to interpret and fit into his logical constructs. He had quizzed some of the military detachment. He had seen the cyclotron and electron-tunnelling microscope and learned of the marvellous and fantastical science they represented. He had heard extraordinary theories from particle physics. He was hungry for more...and more...and more. Isaac could not rely on further conversations with the scientists of 2018. His last link to that new universe of facts, figures and knowledge, to 'The Biggest Library Ever – The Internet. Everyone has It,' was Archie. Ten-year-old Archie.

Isaac stared at Archie with deep frustration. But then his logical mind surfaced. He had to use the time left to learn what Archie knew of technological advances. If Isaac could reliably pin down endpoints, they would guide his enquiries and research. He looked a little more kindly on the boy – and tried to intuit the contents of the lad's brain. The Lord Would Provide.

Archie folded his phone and made to stow it in his backpack.

'Please, lad, keep the tele-phone fully empowered. I suspect it will be essential to tonight's work.'

'I'll get the charger topped up,' said Archie. 'I'll hold it out in the sunshine.'

They mounted Goliath. Archie, now an experienced pillion rider, could relax and match Goliath's rolling gait without hanging on to Isaac's coat.

'Back to the main road. And southwards we go. It should be safe from outlaws and will be the fastest route for us!'

'Heigh-Ho Silver!' called out Archie – expressing his feelings, which lay somewhere between sarcasm about Goliath's grounded, heavy bulk, admiration for Goliath's patient strength and a strong wish for his mum's comfortable car.

23

RAINSTORM WITH BRAINSTORM

IN 2018, THE SCIENTISTS had assembled and were working fast to prepare for that night's journey – Archie's journey – Archie's most uncertain journey through Space-Time, which most probably could only be attempted once. To boost the waveforms of the entangled particles up to the critical levels that had conjured Isaac into being (and threatened a nuclear event), it would require, they calculated, surges of electricity for several seconds of 400 megawatts. This amount would, for example, power 100,000 homes, so drawing it from the National Grid across Cambridgeshire would certainly dim the lights, darken TVs and momentarily pause factory production. They had debated whether to forewarn the energy industry or the government, before deciding that the debates it would cause would be so protracted, and their case for recovering a small boy from 1666 would be so impossible to argue, that they should just do it – and explain later, if at all. The laboratories had their own sub-station linked by six-inch-diameter copper cables, which could call on the National Grid and handle the surge – briefly. Three physicists were despatched to check the strength of all the connections between the sub-station, the labs and the microwave up-links. There would be sparks flying when they boosted the Newton-Wilkins-Entangled flux between Woolsthorpe, Cambridge and two thousand trillion Space-Time miles.

If the connection was safely made, and the process begun, this immense energy would draw Archie, in the form of a stream of his trillions of subatomic particles, along the path or paths of the entangled particles. The greatest danger to his safe passage was that on the journey some disruption, any one of several million possible disruptions, could occur – with Archie being stranded between Space-Time frames. A lost soul outside time, wandering the universe. There wasn't enough time and there was too little knowledge to calculate all the permutations. This would be an unprecedented experiment.

What was known, unless the entire affair was a fiction, an illusion, a delusion, mass-hypnotism, was that Isaac had 'travelled' to Archie's time – and that Archie and Isaac had travelled back to the seventeenth century.

Back in 1666, Archie prepared for the experimental event by tying his solar charger to Goliath's halter on the animal's brow, in the full sunshine coming from the south. As dusk fell, he intended to plug his mobile phone into the charger and top up the battery.

The three companions reached the road. The morning was wearing on and the weather was fine and brisk. A few distant travellers could be seen in both directions. Isaac urged Goliath into a canter, passing a milestone that showed Grantham as being thirty miles northwards and London a hundred-and-eight miles to the south. The surface was far better than on yesterday's Boston road, incorporating stretches of cobbles, with hollows repaired with cinders from coke-iron furnaces. They pressed on in silence; Isaac rehearsing questions about the future that he could put in simple terms to Archie, and which Archie might be able to answer reliably.

From his precarious perch behind Isaac's saddle Archie marvelled at how few people were on this main road. He tugged Isaac's coat. 'Professor, Sir, how many people are there?'

Isaac set aside his list of questions and made his usual considered pause. 'I see eleven or twelve fellow travellers, Master Archie. Eleven or twelve,' he called over his shoulder.

'No. Not here. I mean in the whole country. In England. How many people are there altogether?'

Isaac gathered his thoughts. 'At the last count, there were some five million souls in England. In fact, rather more – there were five million two hundred and fifty thousand people registered.'

Archie tried to compare this to numbers he could visualise – and failed.

'How many persons live in your time, Master Archie? What does the Census record in 2018?'

'Oh that,' said Archie. 'It were in the papers a few weeks back. In the *Daily Mail* I saw it.'

Isaac waited.

'It was sixty-something million. It was 'million', I'm sure. Yeah that's right. More than sixty million.'

'Gracious Heavens! In England. Sixty-million souls?'

'In the United Kingdom,' Archie corrected him. 'In England and Scotland, and Wales and Ireland; sixty million. An' it's growing all the time.'

Isaac pondered the information. 'That means that the population has grown twelve times since my era. Twelve times in three-hundred-and-fifty years. Surely it cannot be maintained. There are too many folk. Far too many. How can you feed so many? Where are all the houses?' He paused as he did some mental arithmetic. 'Why don't they move – from England – from Britain – to lands where there are few or no people?' he mused.

This was a question way beyond Archie's capacity or remit. But on behalf of the twenty-first century he felt an obligation to chew it over and come up with some answer. He went into an Isaac pause. Then he recalled some recent TV news, featuring a jolly beer-drinking man called Nigel Farage. 'Nah. There isn't anywhere. Everywhere is full. They are all comin' here. More and more are coming here, on little boats. An' walking. From all over. And there aren't enough schools for them. And they don't speak English… Me mum says it's a really, really big problem.'

Stop wars. Cure disease. Provide energy. Clothe the populace. And the human race will grow. It will explode. Isaac mused. And if Archie is correct that all regions are crowded, space must be found. Or, perhaps sudden plagues will restore the balance. Or those terrible bombs I have been told of. The 'nuclear' blasts, matching millions of tons of gunpowder. Or we must go out from the Earth, to spread to other planets.

The road came to a short stone bridge across a shallow river. Isaac took Goliath down the bank to the water and he and Archie dismounted while Goliath refuelled. Archie went to drink from the stream, but Isaac stopped him, saying, 'It could make you ill.' He rummaged in the saddle bags and produced two fat, leathern flasks. 'Here – sustain yourself with this, lad. Small beer. The alcohol keeps it pure.'

Archie sipped some gingerly. It was bitter compared to Coca-Cola or Fanta Orange or his usual school-break Ribena, but it did slake his thirst.

'We will have a bite of pemmican to keep us going,' said Isaac, passing Archie a strip of dried meat that looked little different from the horse's reins. But after gnawing on it for a minute or two, Archie could appreciate that it was, indeed, real, cooked meat.

From the other flask, Isaac swigged a mouthful of ale and then stoppered it. He checked his pistol, which he had reloaded at breakfast, and holstered it under his coat, across his chest. Five minutes later, they were back on the road, Goliath now walking with a spring in his step.

'Why can't we drink the water?' asked Archie. 'It looks clean enough.'

'People defecate in streams and rivers, and wash their privy parts. As do sheep and cattle. Animals die and putrefy in streams and ponds. Some country folk – peasants – can tolerate such polluted water, as long as it is boiled first. But most sensible folk only drink from known and trusted springs, or from caches of fresh, recent rainwater,' lectured Isaac. 'So, we usually drink beverages that contain alcohol, which cleanses the water. Even then, all ales and beers use spring water. Or they all should.'

Archie pulled his face into a silent 'Ugh!' Isaac's fellow citizens would benefit from a bit of Health & Safety law, he thought.

As midday approached, the brisk wind had turned colder and dark clouds were piling up on the distant western horizon. But, heavily garbed, neither of the riders felt chilled. Isaac turned up the collar on his greatcoat and Archie buttoned up his sturdy farm jacket over his school clothes. Goliath was glad of the cooling breeze. Ten minutes later, the clouds blocked the sun and scudded rapidly towards them. In another ten minutes, they felt the first drops of rain. The few people they could see on the road – riders, coaches and walkers – sought shelter under trees. Goliath pressed on with urgency. The wind strengthened, the sky darkened, and the rain started to patter. Isaac pulled down the brim of his large hat and covered the saddle with his coat. Archie was partly sheltered by Isaac, but his hair was already wet and water gently dripped down his neck. He hunkered down behind Isaac's back and turned his face leeward. The clouds grew blacker; the rain started to batter at them; there was a distant rumble of thunder.

'What time does your Casio Watch give us, Master Archie?' Isaac called.

'Twelve o seven,' Archie said loudly. 'Just after midday.'

'We must carry on. It is still twenty-five miles or so to Trinity,' decided Isaac. 'I want to get there before dark if possible.'

A lightning flash lit the clouds. They both counted the seconds until the thunder boomed out and shook the leaves.

'Five miles away?' shouted Isaac.

'Yep,' agreed Archie, 'and getting nearer.'

A few minutes later, there was a sudden powerful gust of wind. Rain poured down in sheets. Lightning cracked overhead as nature displayed its infinite powers to the puny humans who were foolish enough to brave its awesome strength. They ducked instinctively. Goliath sheared sideways, but Isaac expertly guided him back onto the course, leaning over his neck with reassuring murmurs. As he patted the muscular neck, Isaac should have noticed the solar recharger tied onto the halter across Goliath's forehead – and Archie should have remembered he had put it there to soak up sunshine, but now it was facing the full fury of the rain, wind and lightning.

The storm lashed at them as they entered an avenue of tall ash trees which afforded them some shelter from the bullet-like rain. The lightning cracked again, even closer. They winced as the thunder roared. It seemed to be tracking along their tunnel of trees, whose tops whipped wildly in the winds. Isaac was at last persuaded to stop and find what shelter they could. He jumped down, leaving Archie on Goliath's haunches and he led them into the trees; until they reached a copse of tall, dense holly trees.

Ignoring the prickling leaves, Isaac forced their way into the centre of the group – and suddenly the wind was howling over their heads whipping through the high ash trees, no longer driving rain into their collars and cuffs. It was calm in the copse. Archie slid off the horse. The three of them stood still with their backs to the wind, protected by the holly. But still wet – and getting wetter. The next crack of lightning was a few hundred yards to the south. The thunder was less deafening, the wind less fierce. The storm was moving on, sparing them, this time.

'Master Archie,' asked Isaac levelly, 'how have your people captured and tamed the lightning, the elec-tric-ity that serves all your homes and buildings?'

Archie had been rattled by the tempest. He didn't follow Isaac's train of thought. 'Eh? Yer wot?'

'When we sat by the pond, before the soldier-commandos came, you told me of "power stations" that feed elec-tric-ity into those thick cables held by pylons, which march across your countryside. Did you not?'

'Oh yeah. Yep. That's right. We get electricity from power stations.'

'And you said that if the electricity escapes, it can kill us. Like lightning?'

'Oh yes, it can,' said Archie, his confidence and assurance returning.

'How then, lad, how do your power stations get the elec-tric-ity – how do they tame the lightning?'

Archie thought hard. 'I dunno. I don't know that, sir. I don't know how they make it.'

Isaac pursued his only source of future technology, patiently and persistently. 'Do they perhaps fly kites into storm-clouds?'

'Kites?' exclaimed Archie. 'I've never heard that. No, I don't think so.' But he was willing to speculate. 'They burn stuff. A lot of stuff. And make piles of steam. Huge clouds of steam and smoke.'

He paused, hoping Isaac would pick up a clue or two. But Isaac was stumped.

Archie felt he'd let his friend down. He searched his memory hard for sources of electricity. 'Me bike! I know. My bike makes electricity.' Isaac tensed and stayed silent. 'Yeah! I've got lights on me old bike…' He looked at Isaac's expectant, grave, questioning face. 'Bicycle. Two wheels. Pedal bike. We ride on bikes and pedal with our legs.' Isaac strove to understand.

'How big is a…bike?'

Archie demonstrated the dimensions with his arms outstretched – 'And it's got two wheels. And a chain. And cogs. I pedal the cogs, that moves the chain, that moves the wheels…'

'I see,' said Isaac. 'Clockwork'. And because he was 'quite bright,' he did see. 'And this bi-cycle makes electricity?'

'Just a bit of electricity. Only enough to light the lights. It's got a dynamo – about this big.' Archie demonstrated size again and stared at Isaac, urging him to catch on. Isaac gazed steadily back, demanding more. Archie took a deep breath. 'My dynamo's got a little wheel on top. The big wheel of the bike turns the little wheel and somehow, inside, it makes a bit of electricity, enough to light a white light for the front and a red light for the back. They're only little lights. Very small light bulbs.'

They both fell silent. Isaac hadn't got it. Archie had failed to explain. They stared at each other. The wind had dropped. The rain was now a mere sprinkle. Thunder rumbled in the distance.

Archie could also be persistent. He pressed on.

'Them big power stations have bloody huge, really huge dynamos. And so do dams. I've seen them on the telly. They turn them with water from the dams. Huge dams. And other ways, too.' He had a sudden Eureka moment: 'It's turning the dynamos that makes the electricity. Yeah, the dynamos make electricity!'

Isaac followed unswervingly. 'Your bi-cycle dynamo, Master Archie. What happens inside your little dynamo when it is turned?'

Archie had no idea. He had never seen inside his dynamo. But he would not be defeated.

'It turns. Something spins inside. Quite fast. And electricity comes out of the wire at the bottom.'

It was Isaac's turn to examine his memory and knowledge of lightning and mysterious forces, that could be very small amounts of lightning. Some tiny, tiny, tiny amount of lightning. Glow worms perhaps? But no, they did not spark, they winked, and lasted for hours. Lightning was lightning-fast. Where had he seen tiny flashes of lightning. In a flash, he suddenly knew.

At the farm they had some long-haired cats. He had often stroked them. On rare occasions he had felt a minute shock – and so had the cat, which had leapt away. Several times he repeated the exercise. In the dark, the tiny shock came with a tiny light. That was it.

'Archie. Have you ever stroked a cat and felt a shock?'

'Oh yeah. Yes, I have. That's static. You can get it by combing your hair. And rubbing a balloon on a sweater.'

'Static?' Isaac was nearly there.

'Static – static electricity! That's it. You rub your hair and it makes static electricity. It'll make bits of paper stick to a comb.'

Isaac smiled. Archie smiled with relief. 'I know of that phenomenon, Master Archie. I know it! I would warrant that inside your dynamo, two substances rub together and make electricity.'

Archie now remembered 'Oh yes. That's how it works. It rubs the electrons off the metal – copper or something – and they flow down the wire. That's electricity,' he said triumphantly.

Isaac resisted the urge to press Archie on 'electrons'. He couldn't wait to have the time and silence to contemplate the entire process and fit it into his studies of lightning, and those pylons he had seen in 2018. But for now, he would store away this new data.

'You are most knowledgeable and well-informed, Master Archie.

I must thank you for this important scientific insight.'

'Oh, that's OK, Professor. You are most welcome, sir,' Archie replied, unconsciously echoing the manners and politeness of 1666.

Under the wide grey skies and a sprinkling of rain, they rode on. Their coats, leggings and shoes were soaked. Archie's hair was soaked. Isaac's hat drooped. But, under their heavy garments, they remained surprisingly dry and warm. The horse was doing a lot of work that warmed its muscles and sinews. Riding was quite hard work, even for experienced horsemen, so Archie and Isaac were also exercising their muscles as they matched Goliath's gait and balanced on his broad back. Despite the cool March air, the trio gently steamed as they progressed towards Cambridge. The storm had passed.

24

UNCHARGED

As GOLIATH CARRIED Archie and Isaac on towards Cambridge, the rescue team of experts were elated at the success of their interstellar phone call, but they were also baffled. Like many new discoveries in science, experiment and observations were running well ahead of theory. Relying on the familiar adage *'if it works don't fix it,'* they had recorded every step, every setting, every detail of the procedure that had resulted in the two conversations through or across time – which was ludicrous and totally impossible – and were meticulously preparing to repeat the stages to trigger the next miraculous event, scheduled for eleven o'clock that night.

Without revealing his thought processes, Hooke assumed that Beamish and his team were on the right track – they had to be, to explain the phone connections – and so he assumed that the next attempt, at eleven o'clock would also be successful. He delved into his now distant memories of learning about Quantum Entanglement, brushed up on the subject via his I-Pad and Wikipedia, which took him into academic papers in *Nature* and into several university libraries, and he formed a theory. If, IF, they could draw any one of Archie's quantum particles or wavicles along the timeline, then it in turn would, through quantum-entanglement with all the particles in Archie's mass, channel all his particles to the receiver in the room below the labs, where Archie's mother, also entangled with Archie, would be waiting.

Hooke puzzled through the question of how he, or they ('he,' if it was successful, 'they,' if it failed) could induce the current of trillions of particles to flow. 'It needs a very powerful reinforcement; a very powerful boosted radio transmission,' he mused, 'along Isaac's link between present and past, between his study at the farm and his labs in Trinity, to tease the initial quantum-entanglement into the stream – into the invisible undetectable linkage – faster than light.' He felt a strong twitch of embarrassment at that scientific heresy.

'In fact, in a timeless instantaneous communication' (he glanced nervously over his shoulder to check that neither Einstein's ghost, nor his colleagues were monitoring his thoughts) '...and, if EPR entanglement could function,' (it had been demonstrated in experiments many times – but Hooke was very cautious) 'then, with a huge boost, the stream would become a river, the river a torrent, the torrent a tsunami, and Archie would be transmitted.'

Hurrah! If not, however, the boy might be lost, forever, in the immensity of the universe. 'But,' thought Hooke dismissively, 'he is only one quite ordinary child in a world of seven billion.'

🍏

Three hundred and fifty-two years earlier, the quite ordinary child, Archie, was drying nicely on the back of Goliath. The storm clouds had rolled away into the vast skies, pursued by the trade-winds, heralding bright, clear skies, now sporting a layer of fluffy white clouds. The clouds parted and a sunbeam pierced the cloud cover, striking Archie in the face. He turned to welcome the warmth and light. 'Hey,' he suddenly called urgently to Isaac. 'Hey! Professor. Is me charger OK? It must be soaking wet.'

Isaac was not at that moment tuned into Archie's world. His mind was elsewhere.

'Charger?' he repeated. 'You don't have a mount. You have not a horse, Master Archie,' he called over his shoulder. But Archie was not behind him. The boy had leapt down and was running past Goliath, to jump into his path, waving his arms in panic. Goliath stopped, looking down at Archie with calm perplexity, not at all alarmed by this small person jumping up and barring his way.

'The charger. The charger!' shouted Archie at the baffled tall horse and bewildered tall professor, pointing hard at Goliath's ears. 'Get it, Professor. Give it 'ere. It's wet. It's wet!'

Isaac got it. He took the solar charger from Goliath's headband, passing it carefully down to Archie before dismounting. They huddled over the device in Archie's trembling hands.

It was certainly wet. The small inset windows were fogged and held onto raindrops in their corners. The black plastic cover was spattered with drops of water and the wrist strap was sodden. Archie wiped it on his jacket, then opened the farm coat and wiped it on his zipper jacket, then opened that and wiped it on his shirt.

They examined it again. The water had gone but the windows were still fogged. Archie peered closely at the tiny slot of a screen below the windows. The horizontal FULL-EMPTY indicator was a red bar. It indicated FULL. Archie breathed a deep sigh of relief – and wiped it again. And peered at it again. The indicator showed EMPTY. Then it slid up to halfway. Then back again to EMPTY. Then it flickered and switched off.

'Oh bloomin' 'eck!' Archie said, casting a pleading look at Isaac.

Isaac didn't react. He silently rehearsed his instructions from Hooke. *'Make sure the phone is fully charged, Professor.'* Archie was holding what Isaac understood to be 'the charger', and judging from Archie's distress, it was clearly damaged.

'Master Archie,' he said, slowly and calmly, belying his own panic. 'Your tele-phone, the musical box, does it have Charge? Is it possible to check it?'

Wordlessly, Archie slipped off his backpack and extracted the shell phone. It was reassuringly dry. He flipped it open, pressed a button and peered at the screen.

'It's here. Look. That's the battery icon. It's less than half-full...'

Isaac stayed calm and studied the little screen and its icons. 'And... perhaps you know, Master Archie, how many hours a half-full charge in...the...battery will last? How long will it persist?'

'It was much fuller. Much fuller before they called at ten o'clock,' said Archie with a quaver in his voice. 'I'll bet that download used a lot of it. Yeah,' he repeated. 'It'd be the download. The new software. Took a lot of power...' he trailed off miserably.

Isaac waited a few moments. 'And a half-charge will last...how long, lad?'

'Depends. Depends on a lot of things. Some days, I don't have to charge it at all. If I don't make calls, a full battery can last four or five days. Depends on the weather a lot. And other things that I don't understand.' Isaac followed Archie's answer unswervingly. 'But other days, it only lasts half a day before it's empty.'

'And that little emblem shows how full it is?' prompted Isaac.

'Yup – it's showing about half.'

'So, on some days, half-full will last all day. Or it might only last part of a day?' urged Isaac. 'It's about one-o'clock now. Can it last until eleven o'clock tonight?'

'Dunno. How many hours is that?' mumbled Archie miserably.

Isaac did the counting for him. 'Ten hours, lad. Can it last ten hours?'

'It might,' said Archie, lifting his head. Then, with a gleam of hope in his eyes, his voice grew stronger. 'If I switch it off, it'll probably last…and there's no masts. No masts are there? No network. So nothing's draining it. Is it?'

'*Make sure the phone is fully charged, Professor!*' But there was no purpose in reminding Archie of that imperative.

Archie switched the phone off and flipped it shut.

'The charger, lad. The solar charger. Can we dry it? Could I open and dry it?'

Archie was unequivocal. 'No. No. You'd just break it. And we'd never get it back together again. It's too small. I think it's all glued up. No screws anywhere. You'd only break it. I'll never get home, will I?' he ended despondently.

Isaac was not fazed. 'How does it work, Master Archie? How does it create charge? What is the "charge"?'

Archie looked at Isaac with blank eyes. He took two deep breaths and delved back into his peer-group understanding of the electronic communication society – a closed book to his parents' generation, but an entirely open book to Archie's age-group. He sighed, but sighed patiently.

'Them little windows' – he flourished the rain-damaged machine at Isaac – 'they take in sunshine…' He checked to see Isaac was following. '…And they turn it into electricity.'

'Like your bi-cycle dynamo?' pressed Isaac.

Archie had a long think about that. 'No – not like that. It's a solar panel. It turns light into electricity.'

'How?' demanded Isaac, drawing closer; so close that Archie had to back off.

'Not like a dynamo!' And Archie went into another contemplation of all he knew about telecoms and the internet and chips and things. 'It's like a leaf!' he announced triumphantly. 'Like a leaf on a tree. Sucks in sunlight and makes it into energy!'

Isaac's curiosity was maximally excited, but he kept it under control. 'A leaf takes in light and turns it into your...electricity? And your damaged charger would do the same?'

'Yeah! Big solar panels make enough electricity for a whole house. If the sun shines. You stick them on your roof an' they make electricity...'

'How?' insisted Isaac.

But Archie didn't know. Isaac's eyes bored into Archie's unyielding skull and silently cursed the boy's limited knowledge of the science of his own era.

'Is it,' ventured Isaac, 'the same electricity that, if it escapes from your wires in your house, can kill you?'

Archie considered the question. 'Yes. Yes. It must be. Course it is. And it's the same as in lightning. Yep! It's all the same stuff. There's only one electricity.'

'But, it comes at different...er...strengths?'

'Oh yeah. There's only a tiny bit in a phone battery. It can't give you a shock. It's too small. Too weak.' Archie was sure of his ground.

'A shock?' queried Isaac.

Archie remained patient in the teeth of Isaac's lack of the most basic understanding of commonplace electricity. 'Yes. If you touch a live-wire...that's a wire full of electricity...in a house or school... or in those pylons, it gives you a big shock. It makes you jump. Like when I touched the broken light switch in our kitchen,' he recalled, and he twitched at the memory to illustrate what he meant.

Isaac did his silent insistence thing, pressuring Archie to continue. But Archie added no more – and stared back at him.

Isaac retreated a few logical steps. 'So, lad, the charger absorbs sunshine and makes some weak electricity – and then you connect that device to your telephone – to the...er...store of electricity in the telephone. And that process makes the telephone full of charge?'

Archie nodded in agreement. 'Yes. It recharges the battery. Which just now is half-empty. It needs more electricity to be good for eleven o'clock tonight.

'I've switched it off. So it should last, I hope,' said Archie, with little hope.

'We will succeed, Master Archie. Have faith. The Lord will provide. I will examine the problem. I will think about it. Now, we must make all speed. Keep your charger in a dry pocket.'

They remounted Goliath, who had been happily tearing up and munching last winter's and fresh spring grass at the roadside, and they headed south on the Great North Road. They rode in silence; Isaac was deep in thought and Archie was deeply worried. But the clouds cleared, the sun shone, the air was fresh, and the countryside was beautiful. Goliath trotted on at a good pace.

Archie's black clouds lifted, and his spirits rose. It would be OK. Without speaking, Isaac reached down into a saddlebag and passed Archie some pemmican. Archie took off his damp farm jacket, draped it between Isaac and himself, put on his backpack that held the precious phone, loosened his zipper and breathed deeply.

An hour later, they came to a coaching inn, The Dancing Bear, which was far busier than the empty road had led them to expect. It was also far larger than Archie imagined such way-stations might be. They entered through a high and wide arch into a cobbled yard that was noisy with three public coaches being loaded or unloaded, accompanied by many loud instructions and imprecations. The coaches were without horses, which Archie could see were milling around in an adjoining stable yard that had twenty or more stables, several water troughs, and mangers fastened to the walls. Isaac led Goliath through for water and feed, leaving the saddle and tack on the horse, while Archie followed his nose to the kitchens and tables in the main rooms on the ground floor. Isaac draped his coat over the back of a chair near the fire. He took Archie's wet farm jacket and hung it next to the mantelpiece. The coach passengers, men, women and children, mingled with individual travellers – some finely dressed gentlefolk, soldiers, farmers and two or three clergymen in monk's habits.

As Archie threaded his way past the tables towards the inviting smells of fresh bread and meaty stews, the room grew increasingly silent, and the customers and servants turned to look at him with astonishment, perplexed by this strangely garbed and oddly groomed boy – from the future. As most of the room stopped what they were doing to stare at him, Archie paused, stopped and stared back, slowly turning his head to take in the crowd.

"Ullo," he greeted them self-consciously, becoming pink with embarrassment. He gave a little wave in no particular direction and a half-smile. Those nearest to him took a step away, leaving him in a clear space – and most certainly the centre of attention. Now everyone was looking at him with deep curiosity. Archie turned pinker, shading into red.

One of the finely attired ladies, about the same age as his mother, moved forwards. 'We should apologise, young sir, for our bad manners and for staring at you so acutely,' she said, opening her hands to indicate them all. 'But…you are most different. Most different. I am moved to ask, if you will forgive the question; are you from a foreign land? Have you come far?'

'Further, Madam, my good lady, than you can possibly imagine,' said Isaac, walking from the door over to Archie. He doffed his hat and bowed slightly to the room. 'Professor Isaac Newton at your service. This lad, Master Archie Wilkins, is my pupil, my student. And yes; he has been in foreign lands. We are journeying to Trinity College at the University of Cambridge.'

The lady, an attractive, svelte woman, moved nearer to Archie and closely inspected his jacket, to Archie's increasing embarrassment. 'Where, pray tell me, just where, did you acquire this marvellous material, with such strong, fast colours? And the tailoring, the stitching is exquisite. So precise. So regular. I must know, young man, if you would be so kind as to say, who is the maker? Where can I find the maker of such a garment?'

'We got it at Marks and Spencer's,' blurted out Archie, nonplussed by the woman taking hold of the sleeve of his jacket and testing the material. 'Me and me mum. Bought it at Marks and Sparks – just before Christmas – I'd grown out of me old one.'

'Mrs Elizabeth Collinge-Smith,' she said, turning to Isaac and holding out a graceful gloved hand. 'And where, Professor Newton, if you'd be so kind as to tell me, is this remarkable tailoring establishment? Cambridge? Grantham? Or even London, perhaps?'

Most of the room was now focused on Archie's exceptional jacket and the lady's question. Where indeed did the most skilled and excellent tailors, or dressmakers, have their place of business? And that extraordinary backpack, made with the same fabulous materials and stitching; who had made that artefact? The lad's trousers were plainer, but plainly of the very highest quality. And his remarkable shoes – the company had never seen such shoes. What a very strange boy!

Isaac had to step warily through the landmines innocently and unconsciously embedded in the lady's queries. If he said London, they would be seen as plague-refugees and, at best, thrown out in terror. If he said Grantham, there were probably Grantham citizens in the bar-room who would contradict him. Similarly, saying Cambridge risked being quizzed by travellers from that city. If he said nothing, the lady would press Archie for an answer; Isaac had to circumvent that possibility. Archie might give such alien information that he could trigger another 'demonic child,' response. That had to be avoided at all costs.

He extended his hand and barely touched the lady's fingertips, again inclining his head politely. 'I am pleased to make your acquaintance, Mistress Collinge-Smith. Are you travelling to or from Grantham? As a Grantham land-owner, I may be of some small service…,'

'You are most civil, Professor; thank you. Our party has journeyed through Grantham, from the north, from Lincoln. It has been a very long day, starting at first light.'

'A long journey, indeed, Madam.' Isaac deleted Lincoln from his possible answers and invited her by his expression to volunteer more.

'We have much further to go before nightfall. We are soon turning west towards Althorp; but I doubt we will arrive there this day.' This gave Isaac more clues as to places to avoid as the likely 1666 home of Marks and Spencer. The lady looked at him expectantly, still determined to find the boy's most excellent clothiers. Archie took a breath and was about to speak. Isaac swept his large hat across Archie's face. 'Hey!' exclaimed Archie. Isaac smoothly stepped in front of him – suppressing the urge to gag him with his hand.

'This lad,' said Isaac, 'has recently returned from Holland, the Low Countries, and I'm reasonably assured that his clothes were obtained there, perhaps a tailor in Amsterdam?' He aimed his question at Archie but had no intention of allowing Archie to answer. Isaac moved swiftly on as Archie's mouth started to open. 'Yes, indeed. The establishment is almost certainly in Amsterdam – isn't that so, Master Archie?'

'Uh! Yeah. Yes! I suppose so,' mumbled Archie. 'I think that's where me mum bought these clothes…but I didn't see the shop. She must have taken in me measurements.' He started to embroider the story. Isaac had to cut him off.

'Well, next time you write to your dear mother, would you be so kind to ask her to furnish you with the address? And we will pass it on to Mrs Collinge-Smith.'

'And now,' continued Isaac, 'we, too, have miles to go before nightfall; so we must take our leave, dear Lady. I will just purchase some bread and meat for our journey – then we also must press on.' He stepped over to the fireplace to collect their gently steaming coats, which he then dumped on Archie.

The space around Archie, as the other customers had stepped back as a precaution, had opened up sight of the main table of provisions. Without pause or thought of queuing, Isaac strode to the table, selected several tasty-looking cuts of food and a leathern flagon of ale, pressed a silver coin into a barmaid's hand, waved away her offer of change, and made for the exit, hustling Archie before him. His pace did not slacken as they crossed to the stables. A copper coin sufficed for the ostler, and Isaac took Goliath's leading rein, summoned Archie with an urgent look and they passed out through the coaching arch. Still without pause, Isaac pushed the provisions into a saddle-bag, mounted, hauled Archie up behind him – and they trotted away – heading south on the main road.

Goliath was refuelled and refreshed. Isaac and Archie ate some provisions and drank some ale on horseback. In silence they hurried on towards Cambridge. Isaac checked his pistol. Archie put the still-damp solar charger under his vest to dry it, he hoped, and he kept checking the battery level on his phone, then decided to switch it off again to save charge. The rainstorm clouds had cleared, allowing a misty warm sunlight to filter through. Archie's watch told him it was two o'clock.

Their diversions through the woods to evade Squire Thatcher had bypassed the town of Peterborough. The Great North Road now brought them to the hamlet of Stilton, where they stopped briefly by the village pump and trough to drink and splash fresh water over their faces. A few local folk cast enquiring glances at these travellers, but no one approached or hailed them. The villagers were well-used to passing traffic.

As they left the cottages behind, a milestone announced it was still thirty miles to Cambridge. 'Goliath trots about eight-miles every hour,' said Isaac, 'which means we will take only four hours to reach Cambridge. I don't think he will tire. We should arrive before dark.'

Archie, half-asleep from the effects of the ale, mumbled a polite reply, clutched the greatcoat and comfortably swayed with the rhythm of the horse's haunches.

25

ELECTRICITY IN A 17TH-CENTURY KITCHEN

Hours later, the sun was setting, casting long gentle beams of light from their right, flooding across the flat wetlands of Cambridgeshire. As they caught their first distant view of the spires and towers of the university, Isaac urged Goliath to step out as he and Archie sat up straighter, energised by nearing their destination. By the time they entered the city streets the sun had gone, to be replaced by twilight, which was fading into night. It was eerily quiet and empty. Few windows showed a light as Goliath's hooves rang on the cobbles.

'Of course,' Isaac remarked, 'most people left when I did, fearing the plague.'

He drew his pistol and held it on the saddle. Archie got the message and snapped to attention, straining to see into the shadows, aware now that outlaws and highwaymen constituted dangerous thuggish threats rather than being gallant, romantic gentlemen.

Ten minutes later they came to Trinity College. Goliath stopped outside the Great Gate under the Clock Tower. The huge doors to the coaching arch were determinedly closed, denying entrance to Neville's Great Court. No lights showed and no sounds came from within.

Isaac and Archie dismounted, stretched their legs, shook out their coats, and approached the iron-studded, impenetrable oak doors. Isaac gazed up at them, and thoughtfully and silently pressed a hand to the oak. The smaller arched doorway to their right, no bigger than a house door, looked more promising. Isaac moved to stand before it and hammered on it with the butt of his pistol, then waited. Answer came there none. He hammered on the door again. He and Archie could hear it echo within, but no one came.

Archie stepped back to get a better look at the tower. 'Hey – there's a light in that window, way up the tower,' he called.

Isaac joined him and they both stared up the face of the tower. There was indeed a faint light, probably a single candle, glimmering in a high window above the doors.

Isaac tried hammering again, on first the small door then the double gates. The blows were loud enough to wake the dead. But no one answered, not even to protest at the assault on their very solid doors.

'Ain't there any more doors or windows?' suggested Archie.

'The college is particularly well-fortified,' said Isaac. 'All lower windows are barred; and the other few service doors are just as solid as these.'

'I could throw a stone at the window,' said Archie.

'Hmm! It's quite high, about fifty feet. Not an easy target for a stone. I have another idea.'

Stepping further back from the tower, Isaac took careful aim with his pistol – and fired.

The gunshot exploded and echoed from the surrounding stone,

shattering the silence. The lead ball smashed one of the triangular glass panes in the high window. The candlelight flickered. A voice roared in protest and shock. The window was thrown open and an arm, shoulder and finally, a large head with a shock of hair was thrust out, slightly illuminated by the candle.

Before the enraged protestor could protest, Isaac called up with measured and certain authority, 'Ah! Mister Blockson. Did we disturb your sleep, or some other lawful evening occupation? My deepest apologies, my good man. But it is imperative that I get to my rooms at once! Right away!'

'What? Who is that? I can't see you. Who are you?' David Blockson couldn't decide whether to comply, in case the visitor had rank, or to hurl insults and heap abuse from a great height upon this vandal who had shot out his window and frightened him near to death.

'I am the designate Lucasian Professor of Mathematics, Isaac Newton, of this college, my good fellow. Pray, descend from your eyrie and admit us to the college. I have urgent business here.'

Shocked as he was, Blockson had his job to do and his duties as gatekeeper to perform. Archie and Isaac could see him in the candlelight, leaning further out and bobbing his head from side to side attempting to see them in the dark shadows below.

'I must see you, er, Professor. I can't just let anybody in through the gates, now, can I, sir?'

Isaac didn't find the need to answer.

'I'll lower a lantern, and if you'll oblige me by showing your face, Professor, I'll come down and open the door.'

'Yes indeed,' called Isaac.

'It'll take me a few minutes to collect the rope. If you'll excuse me, sir!' Blockson backed inside. A slow and impatient ten minutes later, a commotion in the window proved to be a lit lantern being carefully extended outwards, and then let down the wall, with frequent pauses to avoid masonry, ledges and obstructions. Isaac steered it down the last few feet and held the light to his face. He summoned Archie – and shone the light on him. 'My student,' he explained. 'And we have a horse.'

'Ah yes, Professor. I know you, sir. I know you, it's young Professor Newton. I'll be down promptly, sir. Just stand in the doorway, hold onto the lantern, and I'll let the rope fall.'

A minute or so later, they heard the bolts being drawn on the main doors. Blockson emerged, huffing and puffing and jangling keys, to usher them inside.

'We'll take the saddlebags to my rooms, Mister Blockson. Could you ask the ostler to stable the horse? If you would be so kind.'

Blockson was busy securing the great doors. Goliath clattered around on the cobbles. Archie held the leading rein – now an experienced and confident horseman. Isaac unhitched the saddle bags and retied the travelling tools to the saddle.

'There's no ostlers, gentlemen. Just meself. I'll take your horse to the stables. There's plenty of room and feed.'

'And what of other members of the college? Are any of my colleagues here?' asked Isaac with some concern.

'There's ten or so professors in the college at present. And thirty or so staff, sir. Including kitchen staff.'

'And food?' asked Isaac.

'Oh, indeed, sir. We are not short of provisions. And good ale and hock. Perhaps you will need something from the kitchens, after you've settled in?'

Archie looked up hopefully at Isaac.

'My student, Master Archie Wilkins, and I will visit the kitchens – quite soon, methinks. Master Archie, this is Mister David Blockson, who keeps us all safe and in order.'

Archie and the large man nodded at one another. Mr Blockson lit another lantern and led Goliath away across the quadrangle.

'Bloomin' good horse, that,' said Archie appreciatively to Goliath's retreating rear. 'Really good.'

Then Isaac led the way up one floor to his apartment and laboratory, which, even in the feeble lamplight, Archie recognised from his previous – or was it his prior? – visit 352 years earlier – or was it later?

His Casio device, his digital watch, tested as waterproof down to thirty metres, showed it was now 7.30pm. Three and a half hours to go till the perilous, scientifically unprecedented rescue attempt. He pulled out the solar charger and lead from under his shirt. It was warm and seemed dry, but the power indicator showed it was exhausted. It had no charge.

Anxiously, Archie got his phone, flipped it open and switched it on. The battery was at ten per cent – nearly empty. Isaac was peering over his shoulder, trying to interpret the indicators on the small screen.

'It's just ten per cent,' said Archie hoarsely. 'Nearly done. Almost empty. I'm not sure it will last till eleven.'

'Switch it off, lad. Save what we have.' Isaac was mindful of Professor Hooke's and Commodore MacDonald's imperative warning to 'make sure it is fully charged'. But he said nothing and put on his most reassuring expression, patting Archie's shoulder. He had not the faintest idea as to how they might feed electricity into Archie's musical-box device – but he knew that they must try. He mustered all the calm and confidence he could summon into his voice. He even murmured a short, silent prayer. 'It could work, Master Archie. It could work. All the power, all the energy we require will be directed from those remarkable fellows in the future. We are not required to do more than be willing participants. Your tele-phone, and myself, simply guide their immense energies. I am sure of this.'

He looked steadily at Archie. Archie looked despairingly back at him, near to tears. Archie knew that the next time he switched the phone on, it would probably show *No Charge*, as had happened many times before at this stage of battery life. And always when he most needed to make a call. There were no classmates here who could lend him their phone.

Isaac comforted Archie again. 'Should we fail tonight we will use your solar charger tomorrow. I'm sure the sky will be clear, and we can capture the sunlight to charge up the battery – for another attempt tomorrow or the next day. Your friends will not give up in their efforts to bring you home.'

🍎

In the same place in 2018, in Sir Isaac Newton's study, with Professor Hooke standing well back out of the limelight, Dr Beamish was in a scrum of colleagues, all looking intently at the dials on the equipment as power started to build up in accumulators and batteries. In two hours' time, these would unleash radio waves, back and forth to and from the Jet Propulsion Laboratory in California. From there to be boosted into the Very-Large-Array, Deep-Space-Network signalling dishes, which would be locked onto the faintest of faint remnants of Isaac's entangled-particles fields. And, more acutely, locked (impossibly) across time onto the Identifier wavelengths broadcasting from Archie's outmoded, second-hand, once-his-mum's, just upgraded to use Deep-Space-Network wavelengths, now rapidly draining, mobile phone.

'Please, everyone, check and double-check all the settings. And keep checking. In my estimation, and I stress it can only be an estimate – a guesstimate, really. We will only get one chance to do this. The signals are changing; to what we cannot know. I think that tonight is our one and only chance to get this right. Or the boy will be lost.'

Archie and Isaac stood stock-still in the pale lantern light. Isaac needed to take action. 'Come Master Wilkins, let us visit the kitchens and fortify ourselves for the night's work'. Archie thought that was a very good idea.

Leaving their damp coats aside, armed with lanterns, Isaac led the way to the college kitchens, passing through the echoing, empty dining-hall. Archie could have found them by simply following his nose, but he dutifully tagged along a few steps behind the professor – who was deep in thought. Archie had pocketed his precious phone – his passport home – and he again switched it on and checked the power level. 'Nuthin' left. I've got no power. Nearly zero.'

Isaac stopped and turned, shining his lantern on Archie's hand and phone.

'I think,' said Archie matter-of-factly, 'the new update takes a lot of juice, just to turn it on and off. I don't think we'll have enough for tonight.'

'Juice?' murmured Isaac, his mind racing to review the smattering of knowledge he had absorbed about Archie's telecommunications and the strange ephemeral energy needed to make it function.

'Yeah! Juice. Battery power. Electricity,' said Archie despondently. 'It's all gone. Almost nothing left.'

Isaac would not succumb to despair – one of the Mortal Sins, known as The Unforgivable Sin, as it denied God's Grace; which, if he believed in such things, could consign the sinner to the burning fires of hell for all eternity. 'Master Archie. Do you have that solar charger on your person? The device that was wetted?'

'Uh! No. It's in your rooms, Professor. In me backpack.'

'Then run and get it, lad. Run and fetch it here. Fast as you can.'

Galvanised into action, Archie paused only to say 'OK,' and he raced back the way they had come, lantern waving alarmingly in the dark corridor. Isaac watched him disappear, then allowed himself to feel baffled and frustrated – his face drained of animation and determination as thoroughly as the phone-battery had drained.

Within minutes Archie returned. 'Here it is, Professor. Here it is. Seems dry but there's no power on the meter. Nothing at all.'

'We will proceed to the kitchens,' said Isaac.

The kitchens comprised one large room, a tall half-cellar, with several fireplaces and iron stoves. Two of the fires were ablaze and one of the stoves radiated heat. Throughout the room there were candles set in groups with polished reflectors. The room was bright and warm. Overhead, pots, pans and implements were suspended from thick wires that criss-crossed the work areas. At the far end was a wide stone sink with a number of water taps. Next to the sink were cleaning areas and drains – and, to Archie's fascination, a substantial shallow stone basin, or was it several basins, full of water, and fish. The fish splashed around in the shallows, seeking depth and hoping to escape the light.

Three kitchen staff had drawn up stools to be near the comfort of the fires: two tubby men, cooks in traditional kitchen white, and a thin, bony woman wearing a dark smock, with raw hands and rolled-up sleeves. One of the cooks jumped to attention.

'Why, it's Professor Newton, is it not, sir? Yes, yes, I'm sure it is. We thought you to be at home, sir. Many miles away. Welcome, Professor. Welcome back. But we thought you gone – gone from the plague.'

All three were silently appraising Archie; the alien Archie, now shorn of his farm jacket and displaying his strange garb.

Archie in his turn was openly appraising the food he could smell and see. He got as near as he could to a spitted chicken, or was it a duck? He looked hard at two fresh loaves cooling in tins by the stove. There was no mistaking that this was a hungry ten-year-old. The cooks knew without question that he needed feeding.

'Chicken and fresh bread, sirs?' said the first cook. 'And mayhap you will enjoy your usual jar of ale with your platter, Professor?'

'That would be most welcome,' said Isaac. 'We have had a long journey and a very long day, and we have much work to do this night.'

'And the boy? Master…ahem? What will you care to drink with your supper, lad?'

'Not ale, or beer for me, thanks,' Archie said quickly. Then felt he should explain. 'I don't drink alcohol, you see.'

The thin woman responded, 'Over by the sinks. There is fresh spring water. It's very good, sweet water from a very safe source, under the college.'

'Oh! Yeah. That'll be very nice, thanks. Just right. Just right for me. Thank you most kindly, Madam,' Archie turned on as much olde-worlde charm as he could muster.

'And if we may,' said Isaac, 'we will dine here, in the kitchen, if it will not inconvenience you. The rest of the college seems cold and dark.'

'No inconvenience at all, sir. None at all. I'll set up a table by the fire over there.'

With supper on its way, Isaac conferred with Archie and took the solar charger over to the brightest lantern. 'If it drinks sunlight, to make elec-tricity. It may consume candle light, may it not?'

'I don't think so,' said Archie. 'But it's worth a try, ain't it?'

The misty condensation had gone from the solar window. The device seemed to be completely dry. Archie held the small panel as close to the lantern as he dared – a few inches back from the heat. The flame was reflected in the tiny glass window. They both stopped breathing and willed the red LED charging light to switch on. The battery icon was at zero. It was at least stable (on zero), no longer fluctuating from high to low to medium. Maybe it was now mended, so would it work?

What they did not know, though Isaac could guess from his studies of light and prisms, was that normal daylight, falling on a square metre, is equivalent to about five thousand candles. It would be nearly impossible to set up thousands of candles and focus all their light onto the little solar panel of the charger. As Archie held the charger still, Isaac started to calculate the difference between daylight and sunlight and candlelight, working from his experience with pin-hole light and darkened laboratories.

He sighed. 'Master Archie, I don't think the lantern can deliver enough light-power to re-charge this device. Perhaps tomorrow in full sunlight it will do it.' Isaac's face was full of regret.

Archie heard the sense in his words, nodded and sadly put the charger and lead into his pocket. Isaac moved across the kitchen to see how long supper would be. Archie wandered round in the opposite direction, over to the sinks and fish tanks. The fish, not quite out of water and in separate shallow stone vessels, looked as gloomy and futile as Archie felt. He dangled his fingers in the water, reminded of fishing with his pals in the river which flowed by Isaac's study today – and by Archie's den three hundred years later. The same river.

He knew about 'tickling trout,' to render them somnolent, and flicking the fish up onto the bank – but he had never managed to catch one that way. He tried it now in a tank of about a dozen large trout or perch. He began to stealthily sneak up on a fat, healthy-looking fish – and almost got to stroke it into a hypnotic state before it flicked away. Archie moved on to a deeper, darker tank that at first seemed empty, but then, even in the dim candlelight he glimpsed a long and wide, unmoving shape below a foot or so of water; a big fish that would make a fine supper for a family. He quietly pulled up his sleeve, introduced his hand, and slid it along underwater on the stone, towards the fish. It wiggled a little but didn't move away. He very, very gently extended his fingers and made to encircle the fish's belly.

From across the kitchen Isaac saw Archie jerk into the air, bellow and fall to the floor, flat on his back in the shadows. Three strides took him to Archie's side as the boy gasped and struggled to make his limbs do as they were told.

'Bloody hell,' yelled Archie. 'Bloody, bloody hell! What the hell happened? What is it? What happened?'

Isaac yanked him to his feet and brushed him down with his hands as Archie trembled and shook, until Isaac calmed him down sufficiently to assure him that the boy would recover. The three cooks came running over. Isaac made to take the long, dark fish out of its tank.

'No! no, sir! No, don't touch it. Don't touch that devil fish, sir!'

The head cook grabbed Isaac's arm to stop him. 'It's one of Professor Longman's specimens, sir. From foreign parts. Just brought here only three weeks ago in a wooden bucket. We've all been stung by it, sir. Just like the boy. It knocked me over too. Bang! Flat on my back in a trice.'

Archie, still shaky but too fascinated to stand back, crept into the group; all staring into the stone tank. The dark fish sank onto the bottom and sulkily showed them its back.

'I've bin electrocuted,' breathed Archie with astonishment, addressing Isaac. 'Just like on the living-room switch. That knocked me over, just the same. Threw me right across the room. Crack! It's an electric eel, isn't it? A bloomin' electric eel. That's what it is!'

Archie moved to get a closer look. The fish twitched. Archie jumped back.

Isaac, equally fascinated, stared silently at Archie, at the fish and then at the cooks. His eyes bored into them. But he was not seeing the other people, he was looking into his own thoughts, with great but suppressed intellectual excitement.

He took hold of Archie's shoulders and held his gaze in the iron jaws of Newtonian logic at full strength. 'If you please, Master Wilkins, repeat what you have just said. Repeat exactly what you just said.'

Archie drew breath and tried to back off. But Isaac held him firm. 'You mean, when I said, it's an electric eel. Is that what you mean?'

'Before that, my lad. What did you say before that?' Isaac was unavoidable and inescapable.

'I…I said, I think I said, I've been electrocuted. Is that what you mean?' queried Archie.

Isaac nodded. 'Yes. And about the living-room, er, switch.'

'Oh yeah! It was the light switch. There was a bare wire. Just a bit of wire. A bit of electric wire,' he added, for Isaac's benefit.

Isaac hung on. There was nowhere for Archie's imagination to roam off the point. 'And this elec-tro-cuted-ness.'

Archie corrected his English 'No – ELECTROCUTION is the right word.'

Isaac was unswerving. 'This electrocution at your home was exactly the same as when you touched the fish, right now? Here and now?'

'Yeah!' Archie rejoined excitedly. 'Wham. Threw me on the floor. Just the same. An electric shock. Right up me arm – and made me twitch all over.'

Isaac, still holding Archie's gaze, spoke over his shoulder. 'Master cook. If you please, would one of you immediately go and fetch Professor Longman. Pray, tell him it is a most urgent matter. Time is of the essence.'

'Yes, sir. Right away, sir.' The head cook hurriedly bustled away.

'Catfish! I have heard of this stinging fish,' exclaimed Isaac. 'From classical times it has been reported in Greek and Egyptian medical texts. And this sting.'

'Shock,' said Archie. 'It's an electric shock, not a sting. See – no bite or sting.' He held out his hands and lower arms for examination. 'It's electricity.'

Isaac lapsed into one of his long, wholly concentrated, thoughtful pauses.

'Is this, do you suppose, Master Wilkins, the same electricity that is delivered to your home? That empowers your tele-vision talking and moving pictures? That brings you the biggest library the world has ever known, the internet?'

Archie considered these questions with careful deliberation. 'Yep! I reckon there's only one electricity. It must be all the same stuff. Just more or less power, that can give you a big shock or a little one.'

'Then,' pursued Isaac, 'is it the same electricity that powers your tele-phone and the charger?'

Archie got the picture. He'd known from their first meeting that Professor Isaac Newton was quite bright. Here was another demonstration that proved his teacher's opinion. His mouth opened in mute admiration at his friend's leap of logic. 'You're bloomin' right,' he gasped. 'That eel has got electricity – real strong electricity – just like I plug into at home – to charge the battery. Can you get it?' he asked excitedly. 'Can you get it from the eel to my phone?' He glanced at his watch. 'It's half past nine. We've only got an hour and a half.'

'It is not an eel, Master Archie. I am almost certain it is a catfish. Professor Longman will inform us of its true identity and how we can safely handle it.' Isaac changed tack. 'The wire in your home… which carried the electricity into your fingers, at the 'switch', that electro-cuted you…'

Archie nodded his understanding.

Isaac continued his chain of thought. '...What was that wire made of?'

'Probably copper,' answered Archie promptly. 'Most wire I've seen was copper wire.'

'We have copper wire,' murmured Isaac. 'It is used in ornamentation and jewellery. There must be some in the college, somewhere.' And without pause: 'My good woman! Please go and find any copper-wire – on a bracelet, or necklace, or lantern, or oil-lamp, or as part of copper pans. There is a cabinet of curiosities in the Dean's study – look in there. Please find some; as much as you can find – as fast as you are able!'

As the kitchen maid hurried out, middle-aged Professor Longman, who belied his name by being short and grey-whiskered, was ushered in by the cook. He wasted no time.

'Professor Newton, you wanted me, concerning my specimen catfish *Gymnarchus Niloticus*. It is a rare and valuable creature, brought at great expense from Egypt.' He hurried over and checked that the fish was undamaged. 'It is kept here because this sink has a constant flow of fresh spring water. Cooler than the catfish is used to, but I have diverted some of the flow through a warm pan set on that stove...' – he pointed at a stove further along the wall – 'so the water approximates the temperature of the River Nile, its natural habitat.'

Isaac listened with half an ear. Archie was holding up his wrist and tapping the Casio device, mouthing the time. Time was indeed of the very essence if they were to comply with the instructions from the future. Isaac had to decide how to convey the urgency to Professor Longman and win his full cooperation. Isaac needed expert colleagues. He needed the power of collegiate collective thinking. He jumped in with both feet.

'Professor! We have only one hour to direct a little of the flow of the mysterious energy in your catfish to a "device" brought to me by Master Archie Wilkins, here.' Archie nodded at Longman. 'If we fail to do this, Master Archie is likely to die!'

'Hey!' protested Archie.

But Isaac needed to convey the compelling urgency of the case. 'Your tele-phone please, Master Archie,' he demanded, as Professor Longman took in the strangeness of this odd lad. As Archie took the phone from his pocket and held it out, Isaac grasped his wrist and tugged him towards Longman. 'Please, Professor; note the device on the boy's wrist. It shows the precise time – of every second – of every hour – every day. The device in his hand, communicates voices across vast distances and across Time! These are not miracles – they are science.'

Longman gawped – but did not panic. He had seen many strange, inexplicable things in his research and on his travels. And Professor Newton's reputation was already of the highest order.

'And, Professor, please note the lad's clothing and his backpack. He belongs in another place and another time. I am pledged to return him to his home, this night. We need to transfer an iota of the catfish's power to the lad's devices – or I fear he will perish.'

Isaac stopped. Longman needed seconds or minutes to absorb it all. Archie stared at Isaac, feeling betrayed. He didn't much fancy perishing in Trinity College in 1666 – or anywhere, at any time.

'But…but you said if it doesn't work tonight we could do it tomorrow. We can recharge the solar charger in the sunlight, tomorrow, you said!'

Isaac ignored him and stared at Professor Longman.

Archie's obvious distress and his tacit acceptance of Isaac's extraordinary pronouncements did more to persuade Longman than any intellectual analyses could. He took some deep breaths. 'How, Professor, how can this transfer be brought about? From my fish to this "device"?'

'I do not know, Professor. But my instinctive guess is to place the catfish in a copper pot; stimulate it to produce its sting and conduct that power through copper wire to the device,' Isaac said, with a quiet confidence that he had no belief in.

Archie looked desperately from professor to professor, seeking reassurance. They failed to reassure him, so Archie put his brain in gear and asserted his future-knowledge.

'It's too strong. The current is too strong. That bloomin' fish knocked me over. It'll explode the battery – set it on fire. You can't put that much electricity into a little phone battery. It's daft!'

There were five separate words in Archie's exhortation that Longman could give no meaning to. He was baffled by the alien language and underlying concepts. Isaac, however, managed to translate Archie's expert opinion, and then to comprehend the message. Isaac had seen power-transmission cables as thick as his wrist, looped from pylon to pylon. He had seen cables and wires of every size in the 2018 laboratories he'd visited. He'd noted how delicate the telephone, the charger and the Casio watch were. Now the variations made sense. Conveying electricity required matching the sources to the devices. The transmission had to be finessed. It was at least as fine and delicate a process as grinding a curved lens for a telescope from pure rock crystal. Or, could they commit a scientific heresy, and take a chance? Isaac was no stranger to making dangerous experiments in pursuit of knowledge.

'Professor Longman, would you agree to attempting a trial – an experiment – with your rare specimen? I'm reasonably sure the creature will come to no harm.'

'But…but…it might blow up me phone!' yelped Archie. 'And I'll be stuck here forever. I'll never get home if the phone isn't working, will I?'

Isaac tried to reassure the anguished boy. 'We will take great care. I am of a mind to see if the fish, the energy of the fish…

'Electricity,' corrected Archie. ''S definitely electricity. It gave me a real shock!'

Longman was looking from one to the other, still bewildered but focusing hard, determined to follow and translate their incomprehensible dialogue into a semblance of sense – that a senior Cambridge professor might come to understand. He was also anxious to protect his expensive catfish, transported only a few weeks ago from the River Nile.

'My thinking,' continued Isaac, calmly and steadily, 'is to connect the energy – the electricity,' he added hastily, 'to your charger. To your solar charger, and to observe if it will signal that, er, electricity is moving from fish to device.'

Archie nodded in agreement. Professor Longman gaped.

'We have decided,' said Isaac, in a tone that brooked no contradiction; a very senior professor, philosopher, alchemist and scientist addressing a small, barely educated boy, 'that the charger cannot be arranged to convey charge…electricity, to your telephone.' His logic hit its mark.

'Yeah. Yeah, we did. It's completely empty since it got soaked. Totally useless, probably,' Archie acknowledged generously, though aware that when it came to mobile phones and the internet society, his friend was more than three centuries behind the times. 'We could try it. Probably won't do it any more harm… And we've only got till eleven!'

They fell silent.

'I gather, if I hear aright, and if the many assumptions I have to make concerning the terms you are using,' piped up Professor Longman, 'and I confess I have only the slightest idea of what you refer to – that Master Archie has an important device, an instrument, that is at this time not functioning. To function again, it requires new energy; a charge of new energy that my Nile Catfish might provide.' He was making a statement not putting a question.

'…And this device, the small box he is holding, if imbued with new energy, will inform him and us, of his way home.' The professor was still not asking but was stating his theory. 'And further, Professor Newton, this intelligence, this direction has to become known to you…at eleven o'clock this very night?'

Archie was impressed. 'Wow. You wus paying attention. Really paying attention. That's about it, sir, Professor. 'Cept, if we miss tonight, I can leave the charger out in the sun tomorrow and have another go. Can't we?' he asked Isaac.

There was barely any hesitation. 'Of course. Of course. Nil desperandum! Nil desperandum, Master Archie.' Isaac forced cheerfulness into his voice.

It slipped by Archie, who nodded happily, but it did not go unnoticed by Longman. After years of collegiate life, he could read an academic's face and body language – even the poker-face of one of the most secretive and uncommunicative professors. His heart sank, for a moment, and he cast a concerned glance at this peculiar lad – this alien boy – far, far from home. 'Tonight,' he thought, 'is probably their only and last chance to send the boy to his home.' He could not figure out why this was so but, linking his intellect with his social intuition, he knew it to be true. Action without delay was paramount.

'Cook. If you please, bring me your largest fish-kettle. A copper fish-kettle – and a pan of warmed water. Not hot, just very slightly warmed. And a large jug of cold water. I will hasten and fetch my net and wooden handlers.'

Longman hurried out, crossing paths with the kitchen-maid as she bustled in, holding a lantern in one hand and triumphantly flourishing a prize in the other. 'I found a bobbin, sir. Here, Professor Newton. Here it is, a bobbin, wound with fine copper wire!'

Isaac was genuinely enthused. 'The Lord will provide,' he murmured under his breath as he took the bobbin and examined it closely. 'Oh! This is marvellous, good lady. You have wrought a miracle. It is exactly what I had hoped for – but thought we would not find. Where did you find it? Is a researcher carrying on experiments with this fine wire? Well, Madam – how come you by this wonder? Which study or laboratory or library housed it?'

The maid was flushed with the success of her hunt and affirmed by Isaac's excitement. Archie pressed in to see. 'Well, sir. Well! I looked everywhere. All the places you said. Everywhere – and I found a piece of bracelet that had a little wire – copper wire – but it was very little. Then I had a thought. A really excellent thought, sir.'

Isaac allowed her to tell her happy tale in full. Apart from the celebration she well deserved, it would, he hoped, give him some facts about the source and purity of the wire. 'I recalled. While you – all the college residents – were absent, to escape the plague. (Very wise, sir. Of course, very sensible.)' Isaac still didn't hurry her. 'Well, with the dining hall empty, they called in the embroiderers to work on that huge tapestry. You know, the one on the north wall – kings and queens, ladies, knights and pennants and everything.' Isaac nodded agreeably. 'Well, sir, they've put in large looms to weave it on.' The good lady had to pause for breath, taking little pants to refill her sparse, chicken-like breast, 'and for the tapestry, they are weaving some parts of the pictures in gold, silver…and…COPPER wire! And here it is!' she finished with a flourish.

Her jubilation was short-lived, replaced by her customary fear and worry that she may have acted without permission from her betters. 'You will return it sir? Will you not, Professor?'

'I will vouch for its safety, Mistress. It will be safe with me. And I will return it to the loom – with the other bobbins. You might like to show me precisely where it belongs when the moment comes. Very well done. Very well done indeed.'

Delighted with his compliments, she inclined her head in a little bow and backed away.

'Master Archie, we need space. And light. Please clear that bench to take the fish tanks and jugs – and bring as many lanterns as you can find. Check in the other rooms along the corridor. The cooks will help you. If you please – hand me the charger.'

Geared up for positive action, Archie jumped to it. Professor Longman returned at speed, puffing and panting. He brought several large fish-nets on poles, and wooden callipers or tongs of the sort used in washing sheets and the like. 'Wood,' he pointed out. 'The creature's sting is dulled by wood. It can't transmit the pain through wood.'

'It's electricity, sir. Not a sting. Electricity. And mind the wood and your hands are dry. Water conducts electricity – straight to you. It can give you a big shock. Make you jump, sir,' said Archie.

Longman was so utterly fascinated by Archie's incredible knowledge of the catfish's magical, dangerous power – an energy he had intended to discover for himself, to be the subject of his next major treatise – that he forgot for a moment the aim of their teamwork. 'I must keep this boy by me,' he thought. 'Where on God's Earth does he get his knowledge?' And then he called to mind the Casio clock device Isaac had shown him – and the tele…something device that they were embarked on mending. He stopped, and his mouth again gaped involuntarily.

'Let us push on, Professor. Time is of the essence,' called Isaac sternly from across the bench.

'Yes, yes, of course,' said Professor Longman apologetically. He went to the sinks, caught the fish in a net, settled it safely with the wooden tongs and carried it reverently back to the fish-kettle, now half-full of water. He tipped the catfish, with even greater care, into the copper fish-kettle, under the light of many lanterns, into the long, narrow pan. It thrashed and wriggled in the shallow water, seeking a dark, muddy river bed, before settling and becoming as still as a stone. In the stronger light, Archie judged it to be about one foot long – a third of a metre – and somewhat menacing.

The two professors applied themselves to securing two copper wires, cut from the bobbin, to the copper pan handles. They took wooden kitchen tools and rigged them as smaller tongs, bringing the ends of the wires close together. Professor Longman held them in place. 'If you please, Professor Newton, stir the fish with the large tongs.'

'Don't get your hands wet – or them wooden things,' warned Archie.

'And would you be so brave, in the spirit of experimentation, Professor, to use your fingers to bring the wires together – please.'

Isaac looked, paused, thought, and pinched the wires in his thumbs and forefingers – and closed the gap.

Archie stepped back.

'Aaagh!' Isaac shouted as his arms and hands twitched – but instead of letting go he gripped the wires more tightly. Tufts of his hair stood on end. Archie and Longman watched open-mouthed. Isaac shook. Archie stepped further back. 'It's getting weaker. It is lessening in strength. It is varying… Master Archie! Stir the fish again, with the large tongs.'

Though he thought Isaac had taken leave of his senses and might be descending into madness, and though he feared the wooden tongs would not be good enough insulation – inspired by his tutor, Archie took them up and gave the fish a vigorous prod.

'Aah haaa Aaagh!' exclaimed Isaac. 'It is very strong…for about three seconds…and then…' – he gasped – 'it lessens, it dwindles – but it does not stop entirely.'

Isaac let go and slumped over the table. He stopped trembling and slowly returned to normal. He raised his head. His face was its usual still and stern self, giving little away. 'I will rest a moment… then repeat the experiment,' he announced.

His companions stared at him wide-eyed. 'Professor Newton. Do you think it wise? Should we not first consider and analyse the consequences? You trembled so violently,' pleaded Longman.

'We have no time, Professor Longman. And…I am greatly intrigued. Greatly curious. This,' he said to Archie,'is your electricity. It is your energy. The power that drives your tele-vision, your internet, your lights in your homes. I now have some comprehension of this little-lightning; of the storm tamed and fed along wires. It is astonishing. It will change the world – forever!'

'Well, it already has,' said Archie, matter-of-factly. It does all the things you saw when we was at my house, and at the university. All them machines and computers and stuff. Good, ain't it? But getting it from a fish – that's really, really amazing!'

Longman was frantically attempting to unravel the meaning of their exchange. 'But, but, young man, where on earth do you live? What is this place Professor Newton speaks of? Where is your home that utilises this power? What, in heaven's name, is a computer?'

Archie took a deep breath and prepared to find a starting point to educate Professor Longman, in words of one syllable that a truly ancient professor of fishy biology might be able to follow.

Isaac intervened. 'We haven't time now, Professor. Too little time. Later, afterwards, we will explain what we are referring to. After eleven of the clock. What time is it now, Master Archie?'

'It's four minutes past ten already,' said Archie, glancing at his wrist. 'Gosh – we haven't much time. And,' he added with serious concern,'we've not had any tea, yet.'

'Later,' replied Isaac, picking up the wires. 'Please stir the fish again.'

The fish writhed and Isaac shook for a few more seconds. He let go with a gasp of relief.

'Hand me the solar charger, Master Archie. Professor, and Archie, your cooperation please. I must attach these wires to this, ahem, device. Where might they be best fixed to channel the fish's energy into the machine?'

Archie pondered briefly. Time was running out. 'Well, that little window is where the sun gets in – and inside it's turned into electricity. But, there's no sockets or nothing to put wires in to the window.' He paused. 'But I can plug it in to charge it at home. Under here,' he flipped a rubber stopper aside, 'there's a terminal for the plug. I mean the lead.'

'Put both the wires into that hole?' asked Isaac.

'Yeah,' said Archie uncertainly. Then his education from his peers kicked in. 'No! Not just that. No. You've got to have a positive and a negative; a plus and a minus – like on a battery.' He peered into the tiny hole and took the charger right up to a lantern. 'I can see two very small terminals,' he reported with excitement. 'We need a wire on each of them…but the wires mustn't touch, or they'll short-circuit.' Archie was most positive about these facts of electrical engineering. All three were peering into the black cavity and shifting the lanterns to illuminate the problem.

'May I suggest, gentlemen, that we put the wires in place and hold them in position,' ventured Longman, 'with a small piece of dough?'

'It could work,' said Isaac.

'S' long as it's not wet,' said Archie. 'Good idea,' he added approvingly.

The cooks provided some well-worked dough, like plasticine, and, relying on Archie's nimble fingers and three pairs of eyes, the wires were placed and held in contact with the terminals. The rigged charger was placed on the table.

'I will stimulate the fish,' said Isaac. He picked up the large tongs and prodded the fish, which was skulking on the bottom of the pan.

There was a small flash, a bang and a wisp of acrid smoke from the charger, as it tried and failed to absorb the 220 volts an angry catfish generates to see off enemies and to stun its food.

26

NIL DESPARANDUM

ARCHIE PICKED UP the still-smoking solar charger. The solar-panel window was blacked out. The device was well and truly dead. It would never drink in sunshine and trickle out electricity ever again. His face fell into a frightened and mournful expression. So near, and yet so far.

Professors Longman and Newton regarded the boy ruefully and sympathetically. Longman, as yet, had not the faintest idea where Archie had come from or where 'home' might be, but he could sense that the other two were as sure as could be that Archie would never see his home again.

'Is it beyond repair?' he asked. 'We could not try again?'

Archie shook his head, not trusting his voice.

'I would warrant,' said Isaac, 'that the charger is damaged beyond hope of rescue. I see no point in attempting to transfer energy from your remarkable fish to this small machine.' Then, to lift them from sinking in suicidal despair, he added, 'but…Archie and I will comply with his friend's edicts, at eleven of the clock this night… and pray, in the hope that they are able to send a message – even in this, our darkest hour.'

'Please, do tell me,' said Longman, 'where is the boy's home? Where would you send him, if conditions allow his journey?'

'I come from another time,' said Archie sadly. Isaac made no move to divert him. 'I come from a long, long time away. In the future. From three hundred years in the future. The fish,' Archie nodded at the electric skate in its shallow pan, 'could've re-charged me phone. Me cell phone. That reaches my friends – in the future.' He held out the empty charger, pointing it forlornly in the direction of 2018. 'But it's out of charge. Got no energy,' he added, for Longman's benefit. 'Run out of power,' he reaffirmed, close to tears.

The cooks backed off across the kitchen away from this alien, clearly deranged, crazed child. But the professors moved even closer to afford him support and comfort. Longman gawped at Archie, unable to assimilate the information. Isaac put a hand on Archie's shoulder.

'We will go to the stations that Professor Hooke and Doctor Beamish and Commodore MacDonald advised – and we will be there at the appointed hour. They have intelligence and powers we cannot even guess at. They will try – and by God, they will succeed, Master Archie. They will succeed and bring you home!'

Archie turned a deadpan, hopeless face up at his mentor. Hopeless yet compliant. It wouldn't work. It couldn't work. But he'd give a try.

Archie and Isaac quickly ate the chicken and bread the cooks served to them. Isaac quaffed a tankard of ale. Archie drank water. Then they left the kitchens and the bemused and intrigued Professor Longman, and made for the locations specified by Hooke and Beamish.

Isaac installed Archie in the ground floor room below his study and laboratory, checked that Archie turned his now powerless phone 'ON', silently slipped three gold guineas into his backpack 'for the journey', shook Archie's hand and said a stiff, choked 'farewell' – and went alone to the rooms on the second floor that he and Archie had requisitioned in 2018.

It was three minutes to eleven o'clock, to twenty-three hundred hours, according to Archie's Casio watch.

🍎

Mrs Wilkins, Archie's mother, in a highly nervous state, was accompanied by the imperturbable Sergeant Bullock to the ground floor study beneath Newton's study. On the floor above, Beamish, watched intently by Hooke, MacDonald and the entire team, switched on the cyclotron, the electron-scanning microscope, the monitors and the computers. All the readings were normal. Coordinated via hardened mobile phones, six scientists stationed at vantage points in and around the college, tuned scanners to pick up the frequencies of the Cambridge-Newton-Woolsthorpe entangled-particles carrier waves, which had so threatened their equipment, and the whole city, with annihilation just two days ago.

As the wavelengths were detected – and focused – two distantly related phenomena occurred.

In 2018, the laboratory equipment monitors went haywire. Walls started to warm, radiation levels readings leapt, and perspiration beaded the foreheads of Hooke, MacDonald and their teams, as nuclear implosion or explosion once again seemed imminent. This time, they had no time-displaced Professor Isaac Newton to align with the microsecond out-of-sync machines, and to switch off the flow.

In 1666, Isaac, alone in his borrowed study, isolated from his own rooms, felt the strange, compelling connection between entangled particles flowing from (or to) him, to Woolsthorpe and, with a new twist, to Archie a few dozen yards away. Isaac, felt it, analysed it and knew what it was.

At a few seconds to the appointed hour, Beamish instructed Peter Day at the Jet Propulsion Laboratories in Pasadena, who in turn authorised the controllers of the huge radar dishes in the Deep Space Network to activate signals which they had pre-set for this moment. The DSN, thanks to Commodore MacDonald's unique authority as the UK's highest-ranking Nuclear Protection Officer, authorised to take emergency measures – was attuned to the (illicitly obtained) Electronic Serial Number (ESN) or updated MEID, Mobile Equipment Identifier of Archie's mobile phone. This vital identifier had been hacked with the help of the global reach of the Government Communications Headquarters, GCHQ, at Cheltenham, from the cell-phone's manufacturers, Framepool in Shanghai, who fitted components and motherboards made by HTC in Shanghai. Their motherboards incorporated chips designed by INTEL in Santa Clara California, who complied with US regulations to give every chip a unique identity ESN number. The Cambridge team had substituted the original software when they downloaded the Deep Space Network's transmission wavelengths to Archie and Isaac, giving Archie's phone the unique capability to communicate via the DSN (Deep Space Network) frequencies – doubling its specific identity.

At precisely eleven o'clock, they hijacked electricity from the national-grid, power blinked off and on again across Cambridgeshire, and the electromagnetic quantum wavelengths activated – and spread throughout the universe, seeking Archie's mobile phone.

In the parallel time, earlier that day, when Archie and Isaac were beginning to despair that the battery power was draining away, MacDonald was conversing on the same subject with two astrophysicists and a software writer in the labs. 'We've sent Archie a load of new coding, to his old phone,' fretted the commodore. 'It'll need to be processed. Will it drain the battery?'

'Yes – of course,' was the unanimous response.

'But,' said MacDonald anxiously, 'we stressed that the battery must be fully charged. What if it's too low for this communication?'

The three experts waited politely for one of them to step up and explain that they had considered this conundrum. A female astrophysicist, Elizabeth, spoke for them.

'Well, Commodore,' she said cautiously, trying to gauge and match his technological savvy. 'There are two power sources in the phone. The apps battery that everyone knows. The power that drives speech, screen data and normal transmission, which we recharge daily or so. But even if that's at full charge it is only about four volts, via an internal, pretty useless, omni-directional stub of an aerial. By the time we receive it on Earth our radar dishes detect only one ten billionth of a watt.' She looked at her colleagues for affirmation. They nodded in mutual agreement. MacDonald opened his mouth, but Elizabeth swept on.

'So…it matters little if it's that battery, full or almost spent, or the other embedded power cell that signals to us.'

'What other?' demanded MacDonald, rhetorically, as he suddenly realised that he already knew the answer.

'The motherboard-embedded power cell. The one in the background that keeps the basic functions going,' said Elizabeth. 'It is where the inbuilt tracker signal comes from – even if the battery is dead. They can find any cell phone in the world, just from the tracker signal.'

'Ah! Of course – I know that. But I didn't know it is independent,' said Macdonald.

'It's puny. Very weak. Very weak indeed. It's the power that keeps the time and date and back-up, even when the battery is drained. But by the time it has crossed interstellar space – and particularly now we've tuned it to the DSN, the difference between it and a voice signal via the battery, is so minuscule as to make no difference.'

Her companions quietly murmured their assent.

MacDonald looked worried and a tad saddened. Elizabeth felt she had to cheer the man. 'We read and decipher signals from far greater distances than a mere two thousand trillion miles – just three to four hundred light years away.' She didn't point out that many such signals originated from immensely powerful events such as colliding galaxies, supernovae and stars falling into black-holes.

The others nodded encouragingly again. MacDonald was reassured.

'Good,' he said. 'As I understand it, we are aiming to follow two carrier waves. The original dangerous radiation that manifested Isaac Newton in Woolsthorpe, and his return with the boy into the past; and Archie's mobile phone. And to enhance them with energy we pirate from the National Grid – and direct them via entanglement…?' He paused for the scientists to boost his confidence about this most esoteric quantum theory. But they diplomatically gazed silently at their feet. MacDonald ploughed on. 'And focus them into the boy's phone signal, to have him link with his mother in the room below – and come back to us!'

Spelled out in MacDonald's forthright manner, without academic 'maybe, theoretically, perhaps, it might possibly be,' and other necessary qualifications – this had the four looking up at the ceiling as if at distant stars and horizons, with their mouths determinedly closed.

'Er, yes. Something like that, I suppose,' said Elizabeth, after a few seconds.

In zones and realms and turbulent seas of electromagnetic fields ruled by the capricious gods of cyberspace; in the mysterious depths of oceans measureless to man; in limitless space-time where past, present and future merge to simultaneously reform and inform all points in the universe; below the levels where quantum particles are forged from pure energy; where incomprehensible subtle and violent universal forces are organised by chaos to ultimately give birth to patterns of persistent chains of the sugar, deoxyribonucleic-acid, which miraculously begets life-forms, which are sometimes intelligent lifeforms – that sometimes act with reason, but more often act like total lunkheads – the Deep Space Network signals surged alongside and at right angles to the carrier wave of the mobile phone's identity and location signal.

As they broadcast to the very horizons of the sphere of the visible universe, 43.7 billion light years out from any centre of gravity we may choose, these energetic signals, wrought and broadcast by a precociously evolved primate organism on a small planet, in a little-known and little-regarded average solar system, orbiting an average galaxy – one of billions – the waves, the signals, the pitiful, mournful human cries for like-minded aliens to make contact, intersected, recognised and conjoined the location-signal from Archie's phone – and vibrating with joyful excitement – headed back to Earth.

They had found Archie, who had the phone in his pocket. They had found the wavicles from which Archie had sprung. The wavicles were entangled with trillions of other wavicles which rhythmically fluctuated between infinity and finity; between ephemeral eternal spirit and incarnated animated clay. One particle, entangled with its twin residing in Archie's mother, Marjorie, explored the radiating eternal spiritual pathway between mother and son. Being a Feynman subatomic particle and wavicle, it laughed in the face of space-time limitations. It found its twin, jiggling frantically somewhere in Mrs Wilkins' worried neo-cortex as she waited – for mere microseconds – in a study room on the ground floor of Trinity College, Cambridge University, in the Year of Our Lord two thousand and eighteen. It noted a diversionary side-stream of similar particles, with which it was related; not as energetically as it was bonded to Archie's mother, but related all the same.

That stream, that ocean of organised fields, it knew, linked to Woolsthorpe and a body, a body of limited years, limited to a mere eighty years or so, named Isaac, in an earlier or different space-time frame. This single, pioneering, sub-subatomic Archie-particle, organised pure energy; organised in Archie Wilkins, summoned all the other Archie-particles with which it was entangled and, notwithstanding Einstein's abhorrence at the concept of 'spooky action-at-a-distance' (because it contradicted his fact, the incontrovertible fact, that nothing travels faster than light), all the Archie particles or wavicles instantaneously wilfully reformed themselves. Respecting the Pauli principle that no two particles can occupy the same space, they reformed very close to, but not 'in' Archie's mother.

'Uh! Oh! Hello Mum,' said Archie.

27

THE RESTORATION OF UNIVERSAL LAW

AT THIS POINT in the proceedings, Father Time, an infinite entity outside of time, decided enough was enough, that too many crimes and contradictions against the universal order had been committed, and intervened to correct matters.

🍎

Doctor Beamish awoke early in his home in Oxford, made coffee and went to his desk in his dressing gown. He felt compelled to write down an outlandish theory based in both Newtonian and modern physics. He set out his theory in short, sharp paragraphs. It involved Schrödinger's cat, Quantum Entanglement, Time Travel and The Conscious Observer.

He read through the notes. 'If this ever saw the light of day,' he thought, 'I would be completely ruined. Never rely on Charms,

Omens, Dreams and Such-Like Fooleries,' he recalled from his childhood catechism. He put the notes in the bottom drawer of the desk, under a pile of older papers, and firmly locked the drawer.

🍎

Professor Hooke, in Cambridge, had had a disturbed night, of fantastical dreams and fearful nuclear explosions, in, of all places, Trinity College. He roused himself and sat up. On the bedside table was *Never at Rest – A Biography of Isaac Newton*. Worryingly he didn't recall reading it, but he did have a strong visual image of Newton; a tall, lugubrious, uncompromising figure – and of a boy. Was that Newton as a child?

'Ah! he rationalised, 'I must have been studying his portrait in the library. And there is undoubtedly another painting, of a boy, there as well.' Had he, he tried to recall, had too many glasses of fine wine last evening? There were blanks in his memory. And when did he obtain the book? He shook himself, opened his laptop – and booked a week's holiday in a quiet hotel in southern France.

🍎

Archie had, he supposed, nodded off – just forty-winks. He felt suddenly weak-kneed and faint. He had plumped to the ground, bruising his backside on a gnarled willow root, by the River Withan. He had just missed the bus for the school trip and wondered what he should do.

He heard some movement behind him. His hair prickled, he swung round – but it was only the wind stirring the mass of brambles over the derelict stone building that sat a few yards back from the river. 'Huh! Nothing!' he assured himself. 'Nobody there.'

Archie looked at the time. His digital Casio watch showed it was

10.04am precisely.

He hunkered down into his zipper jacket. Something clinked in his backpack.

He paused, the hairs on his neck rising again. He decided to check it out.

What was that in his pack? In the left-hand pocket, he was sure. Archie swung the pack to the front, fished in the pocket and pulled out, first his solar charger that looked more battered and worn than it should, and then, from the bottom of the pocket, he pulled out three large gold coins. They were dated 1666.

Isaac woke irritably in his study by the river. It was morning and he was puzzled. He had obviously fallen asleep in his armchair, still wearing his greatcoat and large hat. The fire had died down to a bed of warm ashes. His papers and books were on his desk with several crystal prisms, quills, paper and a bottle of ink, now hardening because he had neglected to put the stopper back. This made him more irritated. It was so uncharacteristic.

He dimly recalled a fast-fading dream. The oddest dream of his life. He thought to note it before the dream was lost, but the ink was too limpid, and it would take time and effort to make more.

He decided to wake himself up fully by washing in the river. He set aside his heavy outer clothes, and his shirt, then went out and knelt by the river. As he splashed water over his head, closing his eyes, flashes of the strange dream returned. He felt and heard movement behind him. He spun round quickly, feeling paranoid, but it was only his charger, Goliath, his large and pacific horse from the farm that he had ridden to the river the previous evening.

Isaac went back to his study and dressed. He hung the greatcoat on a hook on the door. It swung oddly, differently. What additional

253

weight had he put in one of the pockets, he wondered.

He delved into the large outer pockets – the contents were normal, as expected. He explored the inner pockets. He felt a book. He had not put a book in that pocket – or any pocket. He drew it out cautiously. It was flimsy – no solid leather binding. It was highly coloured, far more vividly coloured than any book he had seen. The title was in a printer's typeface he hadn't seen before. It read: *The Junior Book of Wonders – Our Universe*.

Isaac carefully, cautiously, curiously turned the pages. On an inner leaf was printed, 'This book belongs to ....' and in blue ink, in a child's hand, 'Archie Wilkins, 17 Blueberry Avenue, Clothfield'.

Isaac stayed in his riverside study for a week – reading and writing copiously, eating nothing, drinking a little water, sleeping when he collapsed in exhaustion, and clutching *The Junior Book of Wonders* tightly, twenty-four hours a day.

His grandmother eventually came to fetch him home. 'What ails you Isaac? What ails you? You must come and eat and wash.'

'I have found a book, Mistress Ayscough. A book that will change the world. That will transform all knowledge. That will usher in real science! I have much to do!'

ACKNOWLEDGEMENTS

Without whom none of this would have been possible:

Knowledge and inspiration from *New Scientist* and *Scientific American* magazines 1958-2019 and from dozens of celebrated authors of physics textbooks. And tutoring from David Chapple, OUDCE Particle & Astrophysics lecturer, who persevered with correcting my mathematics for three years.

Thanks to:

Wikipedia for masses of data keeping me bang up to date; Emeritus Professor of Physics, Fred Taylor, for discussing the time-travel books he gave me; Emeritus Professor of English, John Batchelor, for reading the drafts and for his generous written encouragement; Pauline, for bravely fending off sleep and feigning interest when I read chapters aloud; Rebecca for the light-fantastic Crookes Radiometer that spins on my window-sill; Sarah for her valuable Pro-Bono IPR work and advice; Dan & Co for publishing and designing this book; Clio and team for their vital, critical editing; despite the confusion over helicopters. Thanks to my family and friends for all their support. And last but not least – thanks to the very great genius of Isaac Newton, "who was quite bright in his day."